Smoke Placed His Beer Mug on the Bar and Slowly Turned to Face Red.

"Your boss has made his boast that he'll run me off my land. He's said he'll take my wife. But he won't face me alone. He'll send his riders to do the job. So if any of you have a mind to open the dance, let's strike up the band, boys."

Red jerked out his pistol. Smoke let him clear leather before he drew his right-hand Colt. He drew, cocked, and fired in one blindingly fast motion. The .44 slug hit Red square between his eyes and blew out the back of his head, the force of the .44 slug slamming the TF rider backward to land in a sprawl of dead, cooling meat some distance away from the table.

Smoke holstered his .44 in a move almost as fast as his draw. "Anybody else want to dance?" he said, smiling.

TRAIL OF THE
MOUNTAIN
MAN

WILLIAM W. JOHNSTONE

ZEBRA BOOKS
KENSINGTON PUBLISHING CORP.

This book is Western fiction. Any resemblance to actual living persons is purely coincidental. To the best of my knowledge, there is no town in Colorado called Fontana.

ZEBRA BOOKS

are published by

Kensington Publishing Corp.
475 Park Avenue South
New York, NY 10016

Fourth printing: August, 1991

Printed in the United States of America

Dedicated to Caroline Gehman. Have a nice day — or night — whatever.

Book One

This will remain the land of the free only so long as it is the home of the brave.

— Elmer Davis

I seen my duty and I done it.
— Anonymous

1

As gold strikes go, this particular strike was nothing to really shout about. Oh, a lot of the precious metal was dug out, chipped free, and blasted from the earth and rock, but the mines would play out in just over a year. The town of Fontana would wither and fade from the Western scene a couple of years later.

But with the discovery of gold, a great many lives would be forever changed. Livelihoods and relationships were altered; fortunes were made and lost; lives were snuffed out and families split, with the only motive greed.

Thus Fontana was conceived only to die an unnatural death.

Dawn was breaking as the man stepped out of the cabin. He held a steaming cup of coffee in one large, callused hand. He was tall, with wide shoulders and the lean hips of the horseman. His hair was ash-blond, cropped short, and his eyes were a cold brown, rarely giving away any inner thought.

The cabin had been built well, of stone and logs. The floor was wood. The windows held real glass. The cabin had been built to last, with a hand pump in the kitchen to bring up the water. There were curtains on the windows. The table and chairs and benches were hand-made and carved; done with patience and love.

And all about the house, inside and out, were the signs of a woman's touch.

Flowers and blooming shrubs were in colored profusion. The area around the house was trimmed and swept. Neat.

It was a high-up and lonely place, many miles from the nearest town. Below the cabin lay a valley, five miles wide and as many miles long. The land was filed on and claimed and legal with the Government. It belonged to the man and his wife.

They had lived here for three years, hacking a home out of the high, lonesome wilderness. Building a future. In another year they planned on building a family. If all stayed according to plan, that is.

The man and wife had a couple hundred head of cattle, a respectable herd of horses. They worked a large garden, canning much of what they raised for the hard winters that lashed the high country.

The man and woman stayed to themselves, socializing very little. When they did visit, it was not to the home of the kingpin who claimed to run the entire area, Tilden Franklin. Rather it was to the small farmers and ranchers who dotted the country that lay beneath the high lonesome where the man and woman lived.

There was a no-name town that was exclusively owned by Tilden Franklin. The town held a large general store, two saloons, a livery stable, and a gunsmith.

But all that was about to change.

Abruptly.

This was a land of towering mountains and lush, green valleys, sparsely populated, and it took a special breed of men and women to endure.

Many could not cope with the harshness, and they either moved on or went back to where they came from.

Those that stayed were the hardy breed.

Like Matt and Sally.

Matt was not his real name. He had not been called by his real name for so many years he never thought of it. There were those who could look at him and tell what he had once been; but this was the West, and what a man had once been

10

did not matter. What mattered was what he was now. And all who knew Matt knew him to be a man you could ride the river with.

He had been a gunfighter. But now he rarely buckled on a short gun. Matt was not yet thirty years old and could not tell you how many men he had killed. Fifty, seventy-five, a hundred. He didn't know. And neither did anyone else.

He had been a gunfighter, and yet had never hired out his gun. Had never killed for pleasure. His reputation had come to him as naturally as his snake-like swiftness with a short gun.

He had come West with his father, and they had teamed up with an old Mountain Man named Preacher. And the Mountain Man had taken the boy in tow and begun teaching him the way of the mountains: how to survive, how to be a man, how to live where others would die.

Preacher had been present when the boy killed his first man during an Indian attack. The old Mountain Man had seen to the boy after the boy's dying father had left his son in his care. Preacher had seen to the boy's last formative years. And the old Mountain Man had known that he rode with a natural gun slick.*

It was Preacher who gave the boy the name that would become legend throughout the West; the name that would be whispered around ten thousand campfires and spoken of in a thousand saloons; the name that would be spoken with the same awe as that of Bat Masterson, Ben Thompson, the Earp boys, Curly Bill.

Smoke.

Smoke's first wife had been raped and murdered, their baby son killed. Smoke had killed them all, then ridden into the town owned by the men who had sent the outlaws out and killed those men and wiped the town from the face of Idaho history.**

*The Last Mountain Man
**Return of the Mountain Man

Smoke Jensen then did two things, one of them voluntarily. He became the most feared man in all the West, and he dropped out of sight. And then, shortly after dropping out of sight, he married Sally.

But his disappearance did nothing to slow the rumors about him; indeed, if anything, the rumors built in flavor and fever.

Smoke had been seen in Northern California. Smoke had gunned down five outlaws in Oregon. Smoke had cleaned up a town in Nevada. Since his disappearance, Smoke, so the rumors went, had done this and that and the other thing.

In reality, Smoke had not fired a gun in anger in three years.

But all that was about to change.

A dark-haired, hazel-eyed, shapely woman stepped out of the cabin to stand by her man's side. Something was troubling him, and she did not know what. But he would tell her in time.

This man and wife kept no secrets from each other. Their lives were shared in all things. No decisions were made by one without consulting the other.

"More coffee?" she asked.

"No, thank you. Trouble coming," he said abruptly. "I feel it in my gut."

A touch of panic washed over her. "Will we have to leave here?"

Smoke tossed the dregs of his coffee to the ground. "When hell freezes over. This is our land, our home. We built it, and we're staying."

"How do the others feel?"

"Haven't talked to them. Think I might do that today. You need anything from town?"

"No."

"You want to come along?"

She smiled and shook her head. "I have so much to do around the house. You go."

"It'll be noon tomorrow before I can get back," he reminded her.

"I'll be all right."

He was known as Matt in this part of Colorado, but at home Sally always called him Smoke. "I'll pack you some food, Smoke."

He nodded his head. "I'll saddle up."

He saddled an appaloosa, a tough mountain horse, sired by his old appaloosa, Seven, who now ran wild and free on the range in the valley Smoke and Sally claimed.

Back in the snug cabin, Smoke pulled a trunk out of a closet and opened the lid. He was conscious of Sally's eyes on him as he removed his matched 44's and laid them to one side. He removed the rubbed and oiled gun belts and laid them beside the deadly colts.

"It's come to that, Smoke?" she asked.

He sighed, squatting before the trunk. He removed several boxes of .44 ammo. "I don't know." His words were softly spoken. "But Franklin is throwing a big loop nowadays. And wants it bigger still. I was up on the Cimarron the other day—I didn't tell you 'cause I didn't want you to worry. I made sign with some Indians. Sally, it's gold."

She closed the trunk lid and sat down, facing her husband. "Here? In this area?"

"Yes. Hook Nose, the buck that spoke English, told me that many whites are coming. Like ants toward honey was his words. If it's true, Sally, it's trouble. You know Franklin claims more than a hundred and fifty thousand acres as his own. And he's always wanted this valley of ours. It's surprising to me that he hasn't made a move to take it."

Money did not impress Sally. She was a young, high-spirited woman with wealth of her own. Old money, from back in New Hampshire. In all probability, she could have bought out Tilden Franklin's holdings and still had money.

"You knew about the gold all along, didn't you, Smoke?"

"Yes," he told her. "But I don't think it's a big vein. I found part of the broken vein first year we were here. I don't want it."

"We certainly don't need the money," she reminded him.

Smoke gave her one of his rare smiles, the smile softening

13

his face and mellowing his eyes, taking years from the young man's face. "That's right. I keep forgetting I married me a rich lady."

Together, they laughed.

Her laughter sobered as he began filling the cartridge loops with .44 rounds.

"Does part of it run through our land, Smoke?"

"Yes."

"I'll pack you extra food. I think you're going to be gone longer than you think."

"I think you're probably right. Sally? You know you have nothing to fear from the Indians. They knew Preacher and know he helped raise me. It's the white men you have to be careful of. It would take a very foolish man to bother a woman out here, but it's happened. Stay close to the house. The horses will warn you if anyone's coming. Go armed at all times. Hear me?"

"Yes, Smoke."

He leaned forward and kissed her mouth. "I taught you to shoot, and know you can. Don't hesitate to do so. The pot is boiling, Sally. We're going to have gold-hunters coming up against Franklin's gunhands. When Franklin learns of the gold, he's going to want it all. Our little no-name town is going to boom. For a time. Trouble is riding our way on a horse out of Hell. You've never seen a boom town, Sally. I have. They're rough and mean and totally violent. They attract the good and the bad. Especially the bad. Gamblers and gunhawks and thieves and whores. We're all going to be in for a rough time of it for a while."

"We've been through some rough times before, Smoke," she said quietly.

"Not like this." He stood up, belted the familiar Colts around his lean waist, and began loading the .44's.

"Matt just died, didn't he?" she asked.

"Yes. I'm afraid so. When Smoke steps out of the shadows, Sally—and it's time, for I'm tired of being someone else—bounty-hunters and kids with dreams of being the man who killed Smoke Jensen will be coming in with the rest of the trash and troublemakers. Sally, I've never been

14

ashamed of what I was. I hunted down and destroyed those who ripped my life to shreds. I did what the law could not or would not do. I did what any real man would have done. I'm a Mountain Man, Sally. Perhaps the last of the breed. But that's what I am.

"I'm not running anymore, Sally. I want to live in peace. But if I have to fight to attain that peace . . . so be it. And," he said with a sigh, "I might as well level with you. Peyton told me last month that Franklin has made his boast about running us out of this valley."

"His wife told me, Smoke."

The young man with the hard eyes smiled. "I might have known."

She drew herself up on tiptoes and kissed him. "See you in two or three days, Smoke."

2

"Word is out, boss," Tilden's foreman said. "It's gold, all right. And lots of it."

Tilden leaned back in his chair and looked at his foreman. "Is it fact or rumor, Clint?"

"Fact, boss. The assay office says it's rich. Real rich."

"The Sugarloaf?"

Clint shrugged his heavy shoulders. "It's a broken vein, Boss. Juts out all over the place, so I was told. Spotty. But one thing's for sure: all them piss-ant nesters and small spreads around the Sugarloaf is gonna have some gold on the land."

The Sugarloaf was Smoke's valley.

Tilden nodded his handsome head. "Send some of the crew into town, start stakin' out lots. Folks gonna be foggin' in here pretty quick."

"What are you gonna call the town, boss?"

"I knew me a Mex gal years back, down along the Animas. Her last name was Fontana. I always did like that name. We'll call 'er Fontana."

Tilden Franklin sat alone in his office, making plans. Grand plans, for Tilden never thought small. A big bear of a man, Tilden stood well over six feet and weighed a good two hundred and forty pounds, little of it fat. He was forty years old and in the peak of health.

He had come into this part of Colorado when he was

16

twenty-five years old. He had carved his empire out of the wilderness. He had fought Indians and outlaws and the elements . . . and won.

And he thought of himself as king.

He had fifty hands on his spread, many of them hired as much for their ability with a gun as with a rope. And he paid his men well, both in greenbacks and in a comfortable style of living. His men rode for the brand, doing anything that Tilden asked of them, or they got out. It was that simple.

His brand was the Circle TF.

Tilden rose from his chair and paced the study of his fine home — the finest in all the area. When that Matt What's-His-Name had ridden into this part of the country — back three or four years ago — Tilden had taken an immediate dislike to the young man.

And he didn't believe Matt *was* the man's name. But Tilden didn't hold that against anyone. Man had a right to change his own name.

Still, Tilden had always had the ability to bully and intimidate other men. He had always bulled and bullied his way through any situation. Men respected and feared him.

All but that damned Matt.

Tilden remembered the first day he'd come face to face with Matt. The young man had looked at him through the coldest eyes Tilden had ever seen — a rattler's. And even though the young man had not been wearing a short gun, there had been no backup in him. None at all. He had looked right at Tilden, nodded his head, and walked on.

Tilden Franklin had had the uncomfortable and unaccustomed sensation that he had just been graded and found wanting. That, and the feeling that he had just been summarily dismissed.

By a goddamned saddle-bum, of all people!

No, Tilden corrected himself, not a saddle-bum. Matt might be many things, but he was no saddle-bum. He had to have access to money, for he had bought that whole damned valley free and clear. Bought most of it, filed on the rest of it.

And that woman of his, Sally. Just thinking of her caused Tilden to breathe short. He knew from the first day he'd seen her that he had to have her. One way or the other — and she was never far from his thoughts.

She was far and above any other woman in the area. She was a woman fit to be a king's queen. And since Tilden thought of himself as a king, it was only natural he possess a woman with queen-like qualities.

And possess her he would. It was just a matter of time.

Whether she liked it, or not. Her feelings were not important.

Three hours after leaving his cabin, Smoke rode up to the Colby spread. He hallooed the house from the gate and Colby stepped out, giving him a friendly wave to come on in.

Colby's spread was a combination cattle ranch and farm, something purists in the cattle business frowned on. Colby and his family were just more of them "goddamned nesters" as far as the bigger spreads in the area were concerned. Colby had moved into the area a couple of years before Smoke and Sally, with his wife Belle, and their three kids, a girl and two boys. From Missouri, Colby was a hard-working man in his early forties. A veteran of the War Between the States, he was no stranger to guns, but was not a gunhand.

"Matt," he greeted the rider. His eyes narrowed at the sight of the twin Colts belted around Smoke's waist and tied down. "First time I ever seen you wearin' a pistol, much less two of them."

"Times change, Colby. You heard the gold news?"

"Last week. People already movin' in. You wanna come in and talk?"

"Let's do it out here. You ever seen a boom town, Colby?"

"Can't say as I have, Matt." The man was having a difficult time keeping his eyes off the twin Colts. "Why do you ask?"

"There's gold running through this area. Not much of it —

a lot of it is iron and copper pyrites—but there's enough gold to bring out the worst in men."

"I ain't no miner, Matt. What's them pyrites you said?"

"Fool's gold. But that isn't the point, Colby. When Tilden Franklin learns of the gold—if he doesn't already know—he'll move against us."

"You can't know that for sure, Matt. 'Sides, this is our land. We filed on it right with the Government. He can't just come in and run us off."

The younger man looked at Colby through hard, wise eyes. "You want to risk your family's lives on that statement, Colby?"

"Who are you, Matt?" Colby asked, evading the question.

"A man who wants to be left alone. A man who has been over the mountain and across the river. And I won't be pushed off my land."

"That don't tell me what I asked, Matt. You really know how to use them guns?"

"What do you think?"

Colby's wife and kids had joined them. The two boys were well into manhood. Fifteen and sixteen years old. The girl was thirteen, but mature for her age, built up right well. Sticking out in all the right places. Adam, Bob, Velvet.

The three young people stared at the Colts. Even a fool could see that the pistols were used but well taken care of.

"I don't see no marks on the handles, Mister Matt," Adam said. "That must mean you ain't never killed no one."

"Adam!" his mother said.

"Tinhorn trick, Adam," Smoke said. "No one with any sand to them cuts their kills for everyone to see."

"I bet you wouldn't say that to none of Mister Franklin's men," Velvet said.

Smoke smiled at the girl. He lifted his eyes to Colby. "I've told you what I know, Colby. You know where to find me." He swung into the saddle.

"I didn't mean no offense, Matt," the farmer-rancher said.

"None taken." Smoke reined his horse around and headed west.

Colby watched Smoke until horse and rider had disappeared from view. "Thing is," he said, as much to himself as to his family, "Matt's right. I just don't know what to do about it."

Bob said, "Them guns look . . . well, *right* on Mister Matt, Dad. I wonder who he really is."

"I don't know. But I got me a hunch we're all gonna find out sooner than we want to," he said sourly.

"This is our land," Belle said. "And no one has the right to take it from us."

Colby put his arm around her waist. "Is it worth dyin' for, Ma?"

"Yes," she said quickly.

On his ride to Steve Matlock's spread, Smoke cut the trail of dozens of riders and others on foot, all heading for Franklin's town. He could tell from the hoofprints and footprints that horses and men were heavily loaded.

Gold-hunters.

Steve met him several miles from his modest cabin in the high-up country. "Matt," the man said. "What's going on around here?"

"Trouble, I'm thinking. I just left Colby's place. I couldn't get through to him."

"He's got to think on it a spell. But I don't have to be convinced. I come from the store yesterday. Heard the rumors. Tilden wants our land, and most of all, he wants the Sugarloaf."

"Among other things," Smoke said, a dry note to the statement.

"I figured you knew he had his eyes on Sally. Risky to leave her alone, Matt. Or whatever your name is," he added acknowledging the Colts in a roundabout manner.

"Tilden won't try to take Sally by force this early in the game, Steve. He'll have me out of the way first. There's some gold on your land, by the way."

"A little bit. Most of it's fool's gold. The big vein cuts north at Nolan's place, then heads straight into the mountains. Take a lot of machinery to get it out, and there ain't

20

no way to get the equipment up there."

"People aren't going to think about that, Steve. All they'll be thinking of is gold. And they'll stomp on anyone who gets in their way."

"I stocked up on ammo. Count on me, Matt."

"I knew I could."

Smoke rode on, slowly winding downward. On his way down to No-Name Town, he stopped and talked with Peyton and Nolan. Both of them ran small herds and farmed for extra money while their herds matured.

"Yeah," Peyton said. "I heard about the gold. Goddamnit, that's all we need."

Nolan said, "Franklin has made his boast that if he can run you out, the rest of us will be easy."

Smoke's smile was not pleasant, and both the men came close to backing up. "I don't run," Smoke said.

"First time I ever seen you armed with a short gun," Peyton said. "You look . . . well, don't take this the wrong way, Matt . . . *natural* with them."

"Matt," Nolan said. "I've known you for three years and some months. I've never seen you upset. But today, you've got a burr under your blanket."

"This vein of gold is narrow and shallow, boys," Smoke said, even though both men were older than he. "Best thing could happen is if it was just left alone. But that's not going to happen." He told them about boom towns. "There's going to be a war," he added, "and those of us who only wanted to live in peace are going to be caught up in the middle of it. And there is something else. If we don't band together, the only man who'll come out on top will be Tilden Franklin."

"He sure wants to tan your hide and tack it to his barn door, Matt," Peyton said.

"I was raised by an old Mountain Man, boys. He used to say I was born with the bark on. I reckon he was right. The last twelve-fifteen years of my life, I've only had three peaceful years, and those were spent right in this area. And if I want to continue my peaceful way of life, it looks like I'm

21

gonna have to fight for them. And fight I will, boys. Don't make no bets against me doing that."

Nolan looked uncomfortable. "I know it ain't none of my business, Matt, and you can tell me to go to hell if you want to. But I gotta ask. Who are you?"

"My Christian name is Jensen. An old Mountain Man named Preacher hung a nickname on me years back. Smoke."

Smoke wheeled his horse and trotted off without looking back.

Peyton grabbed his hat and flung it on the ground. "Holy Christ!" he yelled. "Smoke Jensen!"

Both men ran for their horses, to get home, tell their families that the most famous gun in the entire West had been their neighbor all this time. And more importantly, that Smoke Jensen was on *their* side.

3

When Smoke reached the main road, running east to west before being forced to cut due south at a place called Feather Falls, he ran into a rolling, riding, walking stream of humanity. Sitting astride his horse, whom he had named Horse, Smoke cursed softly. The line must have been five hundred strong. And he knew, in two weeks, there would probably be ten times that number converging on No-Name.

"Wonderful," he muttered. Horse cocked his ears and looked back at Smoke. "Yeah, Horse. I don't like it either."

With a gentle touch of his spurs, Smoke and Horse moved out, riding at an easy trot for town.

Before he reached the crest of the hill overlooking the town, the sounds of hammering reached his ears. Reining up on the crest, Smoke sat and watched the men below, racing about, driving stakes all over the place, marking out building locations. Lines of wagons were in a row, the wagons loaded with lumber. Canvas tents were already in place, and the whiskey peddlers were dipping their home-made concoction out of barrels. Smoke knew there would be everything in that whiskey from horse-droppings to snake-heads.

He rode slowly down the hill and tied up at the railing in front of the general store. He stood on the boardwalk for a moment, looking at the organized madness taking place all around him.

Smoke recognized several men from out of the shouting,

shoving, cursing crush.

There was Utah Slim, the gunhand from down Escalante way. The gambler Louis Longmont was busy setting up his big tent. Over there, by the big saloon tent, was Big Mamma O'Neil. Smoke knew her girls would not be far away. Big Mamma had a stable of whores and sold bad booze and ran crooked games. Smoke had seen other faces that he recognized but could not immediately put names to. They would come to him.

He turned and walked into the large general store. The owner, Beeker, was behind the counter, grinning like a cream-fed cat. No doubt he was doing a lot of business and no doubt he had jacked up his prices.

Beeker's smile changed to a frown when he noticed the low-slung Colts on Smoke. "Something, Matt?"

"Ten boxes of .44's, Beeker. That'll do for a start. I'll just look around a bit."

"I don't know if I can spare that many, Matt," Beeker said, his voice whiny.

"You can spare them." Smoke walked around the store, picking up several other items, including several pairs of britches that looked like they'd fit Sally. In all likelihood, she was going to have to do some hard riding before all this was said and done, and while it wasn't ladylike to wear men's britches and ride astride, it was something she was going to have to do.

He moved swiftly past the glass-enclosed showcase filled with women's underthings and completed his swing back to the main counter, laying his purchases on the counter. "That'll do it, Beeker."

The store owner added it up and Smoke paid the bill.

"Mighty fancy guns you wearin', Matt. Never seen you wear a short gun before. Something the matter?"

"You might say that."

"Don't let none of Tilden's boys see you with them things on. They might take 'em off you 'less you know how to use them."

Beeker did not like Smoke, and the feeling was shared. Beeker kowtowed to Tilden; Smoke did not. Beeker thought

Tilden was a mighty fine man; Smoke thought Tilden to be a very obnoxious SOB.

Smoke lifted his eyes and stared at Beeker. Beeker took a step backward, those emotionless, cold brown eyes chilling him, touching the coward's heart that beat in his chest.

Smoke picked up his purchases and walked out into the spring sunlight. He stowed the gear in his saddlebags and walked across the street to the better of the two saloons. In a week there would be fifty saloons, all working twenty-four hours a day.

As he walked across the wide dirt street, his spurs jingling and his heels kicking up little dust pockets, Smoke was conscious of eyes on him. Unfriendly eyes. He stepped up onto the boardwalk and pushed through the swinging doors. Stepping to one side, giving his eyes time to adjust to the murky interior of the saloon, Smoke sized up the crowd.

The place was filled with ranchers and punchers. Some of those present were friends and friendly with Smoke. Others were sworn to the side of Tilden Franklin. Smoke walked to the end of the bar.

Smoke was dressed in black pants, red and white checkered shirt, and a low crowned hat. Behind his left-hand Colt, he carried a long-bladed Bowie knife. He laid a coin on the bar and ordered a beer.

The place had grown very quiet.

Normally not a drinking man, Smoke did occasionally enjoy a drink of whiskey or a beer. On this day, he simply wanted to check out the mood of the people.

He nodded at a couple of ranchers. They returned the silent greeting. Smoke sipped his beer.

Across the room, seated around a poker table, were half a dozen of Tilden's men. They had ceased their game and now sat staring at Smoke. None of those present had ever seen the young man go armed before—other than carrying a rifle in his saddle boot.

The outside din was softened somewhat, but still managed to push through the walls of the saloon.

"Big doings around the area," Smoke said to no one in particular.

One of Tilden's men laughed.

Smoke looked at the man; he knew him only as Red. Red fancied himself a gunhand. Smoke knew the man had killed a drunken Mexican some years back, and had ridden the hoot-owl trail on more than one occasion. But Smoke doubted the man was as fast with a gun as he imagined.

"Private joke?" Smoke asked.

"Yeah," Red said. "And the joke is standin' at the bar, drinkin' a beer."

Smoke smiled and looked at a rancher. "Must be talking about you, Jackson."

Jackson flushed and shook his head. A Tilden man all the way, Jackson did all he could to stay out of the way of Tilden's ire.

"Oh?" Smoke said, lifting his beer mug with his left hand. "Well, then. Maybe Red's talking about you, Beaconfield."

Another Tilden man who shook in his boots at the mere mention of Tilden's name.

Beaconfield shook his head.

"I'm talkin' to you, Two-Gun!" Red shouted at Smoke.

Left and right of Smoke, the bar area quickly cleared of men.

"You'd better be real sure, Red," Smoke said softly, his words carrying through the silent saloon. "And very good."

"What the hell's that supposed to mean, nester?" Red almost yelled the question.

"It means, Red, that I didn't come in here hunting trouble. But if it comes my way, I'll handle it."

"You got a big mouth, nester."

"Back off, Matt!" a friendly rancher said hoarsely. "He'll kill you!"

Smoke's only reply was a small smile. It did not touch his eyes.

Smoke had slipped the hammer thong off his right-hand Colt before stepping into the saloon. He placed his beer mug on the bar and slowly turned to face Red.

Red stood up.

Smoke slipped the hammer thong off his left-hand gun. So confident were Red's friends that they did not move from the table.

"I'm saying it now," Smoke said. "And those of you still left alive when the smoke clears can take it back to Tilden. The Sugarloaf belongs to me. I'll kill any Circle TF rider I find on my land. Your boss has made his boast that he'll run me off my land. He's said he'll take my wife. Those words alone give me justification to kill him. But he won't face me alone. He'll send his riders to do the job. So if any of you have a mind to open the dance, let's strike up the band, boys."

Red jerked out his pistol. Smoke let him clear leather before he drew his right-hand Colt. He drew, cocked, and fired in one blindingly fast motion. The .44 slug hit Red Square between his eyes and blew out the back of his head, the force of the .44 slug slamming the TF rider backward to land in a sprawl of dead, cooling meat some distance away from the table.

The other TF riders sat very still at the table, being very careful not to move their hands.

Smoke holstered his .44 in a move almost as fast as his draw. "Anybody else want to dance?"

No one did.

"Then I'll finish my beer, and I'd appreciate it if I could do so in peace."

No one had moved in the saloon. The bartender was so scared he looked like he wanted to wet his long handles.

"Pass me that bowl of eggs down here, will you, Beaconfield?" Smoke asked.

The rancher scooted the bowl of hard-boiled eggs down the bar. Smoke looked at the bartender. "Crack it and peel it for me."

The bartender dropped one egg and made a mess out of the second before he got the third one right.

"A little salt and pepper on it, please," Smoke requested.

Gas escaped from Red's cooling body.

Smoke ate his egg and finished his beer. He wiped his mouth with the back of his hand and deliberately turned his back to the table of TF riders. "Any backshooters in the bunch?" he asked.

"First man reaches for a gun, I drop them," a rancher

friendly to Smoke said.

"Thanks, Mike," Smoke said.

He walked to the batwing doors, his spurs jingling. A TF rider named Singer spoke, his voice stopping Smoke. "You could have backed off, Matt."

"Not much backup in me, Singer." Smoke turned around to once more face the crowded saloon.

"I reckon not," Singer acknowledged. "But you got to know what this means."

"All it means is I killed a loud-mouthed tinhorn. Your boss wants to make something else out of it, that's his concern."

"Man ought to have it on his marker who killed him." Singer didn't let up. "Matt your first or last name?"

"Neither one. The name is Jensen. Smoke Jensen."

Singer's jaw dropped so far down Smoke thought it might hit the card table. He turned around and pushed open the doors, walking across the street to his horse. As he swung into the saddle, he was thinking. Should get real interesting around No-Name . . . real quick.

4

As Smoke was riding out of the town, one of Tilden's men, who had been in the bar around the card table, was fogging it toward the Circle TF, lathering a good horse to get the news to Tilden Franklin.

Tilden sat on his front porch and received the news of the gunfight, a look of pure disbelief on his face. "Matt killed Red? What'd he do, shoot him in the back?"

"Stand-up, face-to-face fight, boss," the puncher said. "But Matt ain't his real name. It's Smoke Jensen."

Tilden dropped his coffee cup, the cup shattering on the porch floor. "Smoke Jensen!" he finally managed to blurt out. "He's got to be lyin'!"

The puncher shook his head. "You'd have to have been there, boss. Smoke is everything his rep says he is. I ain't never seen nobody that fast in all my life."

"Did he let Red clear leather before he drew?" Tilden's voice was hoarse as he asked the question.

"Yessir."

"Jensen," Tilden whispered. "That's one of his trademarks. Okay, Donnie. Thanks. You better cool down that horse of yours."

The bowlegged cowboy swaggered off to see to his horse. Tilden leaned back in his porch chair, a sour sensation in his stomach and a bad taste in his mouth. Smoke Jensen . . . *here*! Crap!

What to do?

Tilden seemed to recall that there was a murder warrant

out for Smoke Jensen, from years back. But that was way to hell and gone over to Walsenburg; and the men Smoke had killed had murdered his brother and stolen some Confederate gold back during the war.*

Anyway, Tilden suddenly remembered, that warrant had been dropped.

No doubt about it, Tilden mused, with Smoke Jensen owner of the Sugarloaf, it sure as hell changed things around some. Smoke Jensen was pure hell with a gun. Probably the best gun west of the Mississippi.

And that rankled Tilden too. For Tilden had always fancied himself a gunslick. He had never been bested in a gunfight. He wondered, as he sat on the porch. Was he better than Smoke Jensen?

Well, there was sure one way to find out.

Tilden rejected that idea almost as soon as it popped into his mind.

He did not reject it because of fear. The big man had no fear of Smoke. It was just that there were easier ways to accomplish what he had in mind. Tilden had never lost a fight. Never. Not a fistfight, not a gunfight. He didn't believe any man could beat him with his fists, and damn few were better than Tilden with a short gun.

He called for his Mexican houseboy to come clean up the mess made by the broken cup and to bring him another cup of coffee.

The mess cleaned up, a fresh cup of steaming coffee at hand, Tilden looked out over just a part of his vast holdings. Some small voice, heretofore unheard or unnoticed, deep within him, told him that all this was enough. More than enough for one man. You're a rich man it said. Stop while you're ahead.

Tilden pushed that annoying and stupid thought from his mind. No way he would stop his advance. That was too foolish to even merit consideration.

No, there were other ways to deal with a gunhawk like Jensen. And a plan was forming in Tilden's mind.

*The Last Mountain Man

The news of the saloon shooting would soon be all over the area. And the small nester-ranchers like Nolan and Peyton and Matlock and Colby would throw in with Smoke Jensen. Maybe Ray and Mike as well. That was fine with Tilden.

He would just take them out one at a time, saving Jensen for last.

He smiled and sipped his coffee. A good plan, he thought. A very good plan. He had an idea that most of the gold lay beneath the Sugarloaf. And he'd have the Sugarloaf. And the mistress of Sugarloaf too.

Sally.

Sally had dressed in boys' jeans and a work shirt. Her friends and family back in New Hampshire would be horrified to see her dressed in male clothing but there came a time when practicality must take precedence over fashion. And she felt that time was here.

She looked out the window. Late afternoon. She did not expect Smoke to return for another day — perhaps two more days. She was not afraid. Whenever Smoke rode in for supplies it was a two- or three-day trek — sometimes longer. But those prior trips had been in easier times. Now, one did not know what to expect.

Or from which direction.

As soon as Smoke had gone, she had saddled her pony, a gentle, sure-footed mare, and ridden out into the valley. She had driven two of Smoke's stallions, Seven and Drifter, back to the house, putting them in the corral. The mountain horses were better than any watchdog she had ever seen. If anyone even came close to the house, they would let her know. And, if turned loose, the stallion Drifter would kill an intruder.

He had done so before.

The midnight-black, yellow-eyed Drifter had a look of Hell about him, and was totally loyal to Smoke and Sally.

31

Sally had belted a pistol around her waist, leaned a rifle against the wall, next to the door, and laid a double-barreled express gun on the table. She knew how to use all the weapons at hand, and would not hesitate to do so.

The horses and chickens fed, the cow milked, all the other chores done, Sally went back into the house and pulled the heavy shutters closed and secured them. The shutters had gun slits cut into them, which could be opened or closed. She stirred the stew bubbling in the blackened pot and checked her bread in the oven. She sat down on the couch, picked up a book, and began her lonely wait for her man.

Smoke put No-Name Town far behind him and began his long trip back to Sugarloaf. He would stop at the Ray ranch in the morning, talk to him. The fat was surely in the fire by now, and the grease would soon be flaming.

Some eight high-up and winding miles from the town, just as purple shadows were gathering in the mountain country, Smoke picked a spot for the night and began making his lonely camp. He did not have to picket Horse, for Horse would stay close, acting as watcher and guard.

Smoke built a small fire for coffee, and ate from what Sally had fixed for him. Some cold beef, some bread with a bit of homemade jam on it. He drank his coffee, put out the fire, and settled into his blankets, using his saddle for a pillow. In a very short time, he was deep in sleep.

In the still unnamed town, Utah Slim sat in a saloon and sipped a beer. Even though hours had passed since the shooting of Red, the saloon still hummed with conversation about Smoke Jensen. Utah Slim did not join in the conversations around the bar and the tables. So far, few knew who he was. And that was the way he liked it — for a time. When it was time for Utah Slim to announce his intentions, he'd do so.

He was under no illusions; he'd seen Smoke glance his way riding into town. Smoke recognized him. Now it was just a waiting game.

And waiting was something Utah was good at. Something any hired gun had better be good at, or he wouldn't last long in this business.

Louis Longmont stepped out of his canvas bar and game room and glanced up and down the street. A lean, hawk-faced man, with strong, slender hands and long fingers, the nails carefully manicured, the hands clean, Louis had jet-black hair and a black pencil-thin mustache. He was dressed in a black suit, with white shirt and dark ascot—the ascot something he'd picked up on a trip to England some years back. He wore low-heeled boots. A pistol hung in tied-down leather on his right side; it was not for show alone. For Louis was snake quick with a short gun. A feared, deadly gunhand when pushed.

Louis was not an evil man. He had never hired his gun out for money. And while he could make a deck of cards do almost anything except stand up and sing "God Save the Queen," Louis did not cheat at poker. He did not have to cheat. A man possessed of a phenomenal memory, Louis could tell you the odds of filling any type of poker hand; and he was also a card-counter. He did not consider that cheating, and most agreed with him that it was not.

Louis was just past forty years of age. He had come to the West as a mere slip of a boy, with his parents, arriving from Louisiana. His parents had died in a shanty-town fire, leaving the boy to cope the best he could.

Louis had coped quite well, thank you.

Louis had been in boom towns all over the West, seeing them come and go. He had a feeling in his guts that this town was going to be a raw bitch-kitty. He knew all about Tilden Franklin, and liked none of what he'd heard. The man was power-mad, and obviously lower class. White trash.

And now Smoke Jensen had made his presence known. Louis wondered why. Why this soon in the power-game? An unanswered question.

For a moment, Louis thought of packing up and pulling out. Just saying the hell with it! For he knew this was not going to be an ordinary gold-rush town. Powerful factions were at work here. Tilden Franklin wanted the entire region as his own. Smoke Jensen stood in his way.

Louis made up his mind. Should be a very interesting confrontation, he thought.

He'd stay.

Big Mamma O'Neil was an evil person. If one could find her heart, it would be as black as sin itself. Big Mamma stepped out in front of her gaming room and love-for-sale tent to look up and down the street. She nodded at Louis. He returned the nod and stepped back inside his tent.

Goddamned stuck-up card-slick! she fumed. Thought he was better than most everyone else. Dressed like a dandy. Talked like some highfalutin' professor—not that Big Mamma had ever known any professor; she just imagined that was how one would sound.

Big Mamma swung her big head around, once more looking over the town. A massive woman, she was strong as an ox and had killed more than one man with her huge, hard fists. And had killed for money as well as pleasure; one served her interests as much as the other.

Big Mamma was a crack shot with rifle or pistol, having grown up in the raw, wild West, fighting Indians and hooligans and her brothers. She had killed her father with an axe, then taken his guns and his horse and left for Texas. She had never been back.

She had brothers and sisters, but had no idea what had ever become of any of them. She really didn't care. The only thing she cared about was money and other women. She hated men.

She had seen Smoke Jensen ride in, looking like the arrogant bastard she had always thought he would be. So he had killed some puncher named Red—big deal! A nothing rider who fancied himself a gunhand. She'd heard all the stories about Jensen, and discounted most of them as pure road apples. The rumors were that he had been a Mountain Man. But he was far too young to have been a part of that wild breed.

As far as she was concerned, Smoke Jensen was just another overrated punk.

As the purple shadows melted into darkness over the no-name town that would soon become Fontana, Monte Carson stepped out of the best of the two permanent saloons and looked up and down the wide, dusty street. He hitched at the twin Colts belted around his waist and tied down low.

This town, he thought, was shaping up real nice for a hired gun. And that's what Monte was. He had hired his guns out in Montana, in the cattle wars out in California, and had fought the sheep farmers and nesters up in Wyoming. And, as he'd fought, his reputation had grown. Monte felt that Tilden Franklin would soon be contacting him. He could wait.

On the now-well-traveled road for beneath where Smoke slept peacefully, wagons continued to roll and rumble along, carrying their human cargo toward No-Name Town. The line of wagons and buggies and riders and walkers was now several miles long. Gamblers and would-be shopowners and whores and gunfighters and snake-oil salesmen and pimps and troublemakers and murderers and good solid family people . . . all of them heading for No-Name with but one thought in their minds. Gold.

At the end of the line of gold-seekers, not a part of them but yet with the same destination if not sharing the same motives, rattled a half a dozen wagons. Ed Jackson was new to the raw West—a shopkeeper from Illinois with his wife Peg. They were both young and very idealistic, and had no working knowledge of the real West. They were looking for a place to settle. This no-name town sounded good to them. Ed's brother Paul drove the heavily laden supply wagon, containing part of what they just knew would make them respected and secure citizens. Paul was as naive as his brother and sister-in-law concerning the West.

In the third wagon came Ralph Morrow and his wife Bountiful. They were missionaries, sent into the godless West by their Church, to save souls and soothe the sinful spirits of those who had not yet accepted Christ into their lives. They had been looking for a place to settle when they had hooked up with Ed and Peg and Paul. This was the first time Ralph and Bountiful had been west of Eastern Ohio. It was exciting. A challenge.

They thought.

In the fourth wagon rode another young couple, married only a few years, Hunt and Willow Brook. Hunt was a lawyer, looking for a place to practice all he'd just been taught back East. This new gold rush town seemed just the place to start.

In the fifth wagon rode Colton and Mona Spalding. A doctor and nurse, respectively. They had both graduated their schools only last year, mulled matters over, and decided to head West. They were young and handsome and pretty. And, like the others in their little caravan, they had absolutely no idea what they were riding into.

In the last wagon, a huge, solidly built vehicle with six mules pulling it, came Haywood and Dana Arden. Like the others, they were young and full of grand ideas. Haywood had inherited a failing newspaper from his father back in Pennsylvania and decided to pull out and head West to seek their fortunes.

"Oh Haywood!" Dana said, her eyes shining with excitement. "It's all so wonderful."

"Yes," Haywood agreed, just as the right rear wheel of their wagon fell off.

5

Smoke was up long before dawn spread her shimmering rays of light over the land. He slipped out of his blankets and put his hat on, then pulled on his boots and strapped on his guns. He checked to see how Horse was doing, then washed his face with water from his canteen. He built a small, hand-sized fire and boiled coffee. He munched on a thick piece of bread and sipped his coffee, sitting with his back to a tree, his eyes taking in the first silver streaks of a new day in the high-up country of Colorado.

He had spotted a fire far down below him, near the winding road. A very large fire. Much too large unless those who built it were roasting an entire deer—head, horns, and all. He finished the small, blackened pot of coffee, carefully doused his fire, and saddled Horse, stowing his gear in the saddle bags.

He swung into the saddle. "Steady now, Horse," he said in a low voice. "Let's see how quiet we can be backtracking."

Horse and rider made their way slowly and quietly down from the high terrain toward the road miles away using the twisting, winding trails. Smoke uncased U.S. Army binoculars he'd picked up years back, while traveling with his mentor, the old Mountain Man Preacher, and studied the situation.

Five, no—six wagons. One of them down with a busted back wheel. Six men, five women. All young, in their early twenties, Smoke guessed. The women were all very pretty, the men all handsome and apparently—at least to Smoke, at least at this distance—helpless.

37

He used his knees to signal Horse, and the animal moved out, taking its head, picking the route. Stopping after a few hundred twisting yards, Smoke once more surveyed the situation. His binoculars picked up movement coming from the direction of No-Name. Four riders. He studied the men, watching them approach the wagons. Drifters, from the look of them. Probably spent the night in No-Name gambling and whoring and were heading out to stake a gold claim. They looked like trouble.

Staying in the deep and lush timer, Smoke edged closer still. Several hundred yards from the wagon, Smoke halted and held back, wanting to see how these pilgrims would handle the approach of the riders.

He could not hear all that was said, but he could get most of it from his hidden location.

He had pegged the riders accurately. They were trouble. They reined up and sat their horses, grinning at the men and women. Especially the women.

"You folks look like you got a mite of trouble," one rider said.

"A bit," a friendly-looking man responded. "We're just getting ready to fulcrum the wagon."

"You're gonna do *what* to it?" another rider blurted.

"Raise it up," a pilgrim said.

"Oh. You folks headin' to Fontana?"

The wagon people looked at each other.

Fontana! Smoke thought. Where in the hell is Fontana?

"I'm sorry," one of the women said. "We're not familiar with that place."

"That's what they just named the town up yonder," a rider said, jerking his thumb in the direction of No-Name. "Stuck up a big sign last night."

So No-Name has a name, Smoke thought. Wonder whose idea that was.

But he thought he knew. Tilden Franklin.

Smoke looked at the women of the wagons. They were, to a woman, all very pretty and built-up nice. Very shapely. The men with them didn't look like much to Smoke; but then, he thought, they were Easterners. Probably good men

38

back there. But out there, they were out of their element.

And Smoke didn't like the look in the eyes of the riders. One kept glancing up and down the road. As yet, no traffic had appeared. But Smoke knew the stream of gold-hunters would soon appear. If the drifters were going to start something—the women being what they wanted, he was sure—they would make their move pretty quick.

At some unspoken signal, the riders dismounted.

"Oh, say!" the weakest-jawed pilgrim said. "It's good of you men to help."

"Huh?" a rider said, then he grinned. "Oh, yeah. We're regular do-gooders. You folks nesters?"

"I beg your pardon, sir?"

"Farmers." He ended that and summed up his feelings concerning farmers by spitting a stream of brown tabacco juice onto the ground, just missing the pilgrim's feet.

The pilgrim laughed and said, "Oh, no. My name is Ed Jackson, this is my wife Peg. We plan to open a store in the gold town."

"Ain't that nice," the rider mumbled.

Smoke kneed Horse a bit closer.

"My name is Ralph Morrow," another pilgrim said. "I'm a minister. This is my wife Bountiful. We plan to start a church in the gold town."

The rider looked at Bountiful and licked his lips.

Ralph said, "And this is Paul Jackson, Ed's brother. Over there is Hunt and Willow Brook. Hunt is a lawyer. That's Colton and Mona Spalding. Colton is a physician. And last, but certainly not least, is Haywood and Dana Arden. Haywood is planning to start a newspaper in the town. Now you know us."

"Not as much as I'd like to," a rider said speaking for the first time. He was looking at Bountiful.

To complicate matters, Bountiful was looking square at the rider.

The women is flirting with him, Smoke noticed. He silently cursed. This Bountiful might be a preacher's wife, but what she really was was a hot handful of trouble. The preacher was not taking care of business at home.

Bountiful was blonde with hot blue eyes. She stared at the rider.

All the newcomers to the West began to sense something was not as it should be. But none knew what, and if they did, Smoke thought, they wouldn't know how to handle it. For none of the men were armed.

One of the drifters, the one who had been staring at Bountiful, brushed past the preacher. He walked by Bountiful, his right arm brushing the woman's jutting breasts. She did not back up. The rider stopped and grinned at her.

The newspaperman's wife stepped in just in time, stepping between the rider and the woman. She glared at Bountiful. "Let's you and I start breakfast, Bountiful," she suggested. "While the men fix the wheel."

"What you got in your wagon, shopkeeper?" a drifter asked. "Anything in there we might like?"

Ed narrowed his eyes. "I'll set up shop very soon. Feel free to browse when we're open for business."

The rider laughed. "Talks real nice, don't he, boys?"

His friends laughed.

The riders were big men, tough-looking and seemingly very capable. Smoke had no doubts but what they were all that and more. The more being troublemakers.

Always something, Smoke thought with a silent sigh. People wander into an unknown territory without first checking out all the ramifications. He edged Horse forward.

A rider jerked at a tie-rope over the bed of one wagon. "I don't wanna wait to browse none. I wanna see what you got now."

"Now see here!" Ed protested, stepping toward the man.

Ed's head exploded in pain as the rider's big fist hit the shopkeeper's jaw. Ed's butt hit the ground. Still, Smoke waited.

None of the drifters had drawn a gun. No law, written or otherwise, had as yet been broken. These pilgrims were in the process of learning a hard lesson of the West: you broke your own horses and killed your own snakes. And Smoke recalled a sentiment from some book he had slowly and laboriously studied. When you are in Rome live in the

40

Roman style; when you are elsewhere live as they live elsewhere.

He couldn't remember who wrote it, but it was pretty fair advice.

The riders laughed at the ineptness of the newcomers to the West. One jerked Bountiful to him and began fondling her breasts.

Bountiful finally got it through her head that this was deadly serious, not a mild flirtation.

She began struggling just as the other pilgrims surged forward. Their butts hit the ground as quickly and as hard as Ed's had.

Smoke put the spurs to Horse and the big horse broke out of the timber. Smoke was out of the saddle before Horse was still. He dropped the reins to the ground and faced the group.

"That's it!" Smoke said quietly. He slipped the thongs from the hammers of his .44's.

Smoke glanced at Bountiful. Her bodice was torn, exposing the creamy skin of her breasts. "Cover yourself," Smoke told her.

She pulled away from the rider and ran, sobbing, to Dana.

A rider said, "I don't know who you are, boy. But I'm gonna teach you a hard lesson."

"Oh? And what might that be?"

"To keep your goddamned nose out of other folk's business."

"If the woman had been willing," Smoke said, "I would not have interfered. Even though it takes a low-life bastard to steal another man's woman."

"Why, you . . . *pup!*" the rider shouted. "You callin' me a bastard?"

"Are you deaf?"

"I'll kill you!"

"I doubt it."

Bountiful was crying. Her husband was holding a handkerchief to a bloody nose, his eyes staring in disbelief at what was taking place.

41

Hunt Brook was sitting on the ground, his mouth bloody. Colton's head was ringing and his ear hurt where he'd been struck. Haywood was wondering if his eye was going to turn black. Paul was holding a hurting stomach, the hurt caused by a hard fist. The preacher looked as if he wished his wife would cover herself.

One drifter shoved Dana and Bountiful out of the way, stepping over to join his friend, facing Smoke. The other two drifters hung back, being careful to keep their hands away from their guns. The two who hung back were older, and wiser to the ways of gunslicks. And they did not like the looks of this young man with the twin Colts. There was something very familiar about him. Something calm and cold and very deadly.

"Back off, Ford," one finally spoke. "Let's ride."

"Hell with you!" the rider named Ford said, not taking his eyes from Smoke. "I'm gonna kill this punk!"

"Something tells me you ain't neither," his friend said.

"Better listen to him," Smoke advised Ford.

"Now see here, gentlemen!" Hunt said.

"Shut your gawddamned mouth!" he was told.

Hunt closed his mouth. Heavens! he thought. This just simply was not done back in Boston.

"You gonna draw, punk?" Ford said.

"After you," Smoke said quietly.

"Jesus, Ford!" the rider who hung back said. "I know who that is."

"He's dead, that's who he is," Ford said, and reached for his gun.

His friend drew at the same time.

Smoke let them clear leather before he began his lightning draw. His Colts belched fire and smoke, the slugs taking them in the chest, flinging them backward. They had not gotten off a shot.

"Smoke Jensen!" the drifter said.

"Right," Smoke said. "Now ride!"

6

The two drifters who had wisely elected not to take part in facing Smoke leaped for their horses and were gone in a cloud of galloping dust. They had not given a second glance at their dead friends.

Smoke reloaded his Colts and holstered them. Then he looked at the wagon people. The Easterners were clearly in a mild state of shock. Bountiful still had not taken the few seconds needed to repair her torn bodice. Smoke summed her up quickly and needed only one word to do so: trouble.

"My word!" Colton Spalding finally said. "You are very quick with those guns, sir."

"I'm alive," Smoke said.

"You *killed* those men!" Hunt Brook said, getting up off the ground and brushing the dust from the seat of his britches.

"What did you want me to do?" Smoke asked, knowing where this was leading. "Kiss them?"

Hunt wiped his bloody mouth with a handkerchief. "You shall certainly need representation at the hearing. Consider me as your attorney."

Smoke looked at the man and smiled slowly. He shook his head in disbelief. "Lawyer, the nearest lawman is about three days ride from here. And I'm not even sure this area is in his jurisdiction. There won't be any hearing, Mister. It's all been settled and over and done with."

Haywood Arden was looking at Smoke through cool eyes. Smoke met the man's steady gaze.

This one will do, Smoke thought. This one doesn't have his head in the clouds. "So you're going to start up a newspaper, huh?" Smoke said.

"Yes. But how did you know that?"

"Me and Horse been sitting over there," Smoke said, jerking his head in the direction of the timber. "Listening."

"You move very quietly, sir," Mona Spalding said.

"I learned to do that. Helps in staying alive." Smoke wished Bountiful would cover up. It was mildly distracting.

"One of those ruffians called you Smoke, I believe," Hunt said. "I don't believe I ever met a man named Smoke."

Ruffians, Smoke thought. He hid his smile. Interesting choice of words to describe the drifters. "I was halfway raised by an old Mountain Man named Preacher. He hung that name on me."

The drifter called Ford broke wind in death. The shop-keeper's wife, Peg, thought as though she might faint any second. "Could someone please do something about those poor dead men?" she asked.

Dawn had given way to a bright clear mountain day. A stream of humanity had begun riding and walking toward Fontana. A tough-looking pair of miners riding mules reined up. Their eyes dismissed the Easterners and settled on Smoke. "Trouble?" one asked.

"Nothing I couldn't handle," Smoke told him.

" 'Pears that way," the second miner said drily. "Ford Beechan was a good hand with a short gun." He cut his eyes toward the sprawled body of Ford.

"He wasn't as good as he thought," Smoke replied.

" 'Pears that's the truth. We'll plant 'em for four bits a piece."

"Deal."

"And their pockets," the other miner spoke.

"Have at it," Smoke told them. "The pilgrims will pay."

"Now see here!" Ed said starting to protest.

"Shut up, Ed," Haywood told him. He looked at the miners. "You gentlemen may proceed with the digging."

"Talks funny," one miner remarked, getting down and tying his mule. He got a shovel from his pack animal and his

44

partner followed suit.

"You live and work in this area, Mister Smoke?" Mona asked.

"One miner dropped his shovel and his partner froze still as stone. The miner who dropped his shovel picked it up and slowly turned to face Smoke. "Smoke Jensen?"

"Yes."

"Lord God Almighty! Ford shore enuff bit off more than he could chew. Smoke Jensen. My brother was over to Uncompahgre, Smoke. Back when you cleaned it up. He said that shore was a sight to see."*

Smoke nodded his head and the miners walked off a short distance to begin their digging. "How deep?" one called.

"Respectable," Smoke told them.

They nodded and began spading the earth.

"Are you a gunfighter, Mister Smoke?" Willow asked.

"I'm a rancher and farmer, Ma'am. But I once had the reputation of being a gunhawk, yes."

"You seem so young," she observed. "Yet you talk as if it was years ago. How old were you when you became a . . . gunhawk?"

"Fourteen. Or thereabouts. I disremember at times." Smoke usually spoke acceptable English, thanks to Sally; but at times he reverted back to Preacher's dialect.

"He's kilt more'un a hundred men!" one of the miners called.

The wagon people fell silent at that news. They looked at Smoke with a mixture of horror, fascination, and revulsion in their eyes.

It was nothing new to Smoke. He had experienced that look many times in his young life. He kept his face as expressionless as his cold eyes.

Smoke cut his eyes to Bountiful. "Lady," he said, exasperation in his voice, his tone hard. "Will you please cover your tits!"

*The Last Mountain Man

Smoke had seen the remainder of the rancher-farmers in the mountain area and then headed for home. He almost never took the same trail back to his cabin. A habit he had picked up from Preacher. A habit that had saved his life on more than one occasion.

Even though he was less than five miles from his cabin when dark slipped into the mountains, he decided not to chance the ride in. He elected to make camp and head home at first light.

He caught several small fish from a mountain stream and broiled them over a small fire. That and the remainder of Sally's bread was his supper.

Twice during the night Smoke came fully awake, certain he had heard gunshots. He knew they were far away, but he wondered about it. The last shot he heard before he drifted back to sleep came from the south, far away from Sally and the cabin.

He was up and moving out before full dawn broke. Relief filled him when he caught a glimpse of the cabin, Sally in the front yard. Smoke broke into a grin when he saw how she was dressed . . . in men's britches. His eyes mirrored approval when he noted Seven and Drifter in the corral. As he rode closer, he saw the pistol belted around her waist, and the express gun leaning against the door frame, on the outside of the cabin.

Man and wife embraced, each loving the touch and feel of the other. With their mouths barely apart, she saw the darkness in his eyes and asked, "Trouble?"

"Some. A hell of a lot more coming, though. I'll tell you about it. You?"

"Didn't see a soul."

They kissed their love and she pushed him away, mischief in her hazel eyes. "I missed you."

"Oh? How much?"

"By the time you see to Horse and get in the house, I'll be ready to show you how much."

Fastest unsaddling and rub-down in the history of the West.

Passions cooled and sated, she lay with her head on Smoke's muscular shoulder. She listened as he told her all that had happened since he had ridden from the ranch. He left nothing out.

"See anyone that you knew in town? Any newcomers, I mean?"

"Some. Utah Slim. I'm sure it was him."

"I've heard you talk of him. He's good?"

"One of the best."

"Better than you?"

"No," Smoke said softly.

"Anyone else?"

"Monte Carson. He's a backshooter. Big Mamma O'Neil. Louis Longmont. Louis is all right. Just as long as no one pushes him."

"And now we have Fontana."

"For as long as it lasts, yes. The town will probably die out when the gold plays out. I hope it's soon."

"You're holding just a little something back from me, Smoke."

He hesitated. "Tilden Franklin wants you for his woman."

"I've known that for a long time. Has he made his desires public?"

"Apparently so. From now on, you're going to have to be very careful."

She lay still for a moment, silent. "We could always leave, honey."

He knew she did not wish to leave, but was only voicing their options. "I know. And we'd be running for the rest of our lives. Once you start, it's hard to stop."

In the corral, Seven nickered, the sound carrying to the house. Smoke was up and dressed in a moment, strapping on his guns and picking up a rifle. He and Sally could hear the sounds of hooves, coming hard.

"One horse," Sally noted.

"Stay inside."

Smoke stepped out the door, relaxing when he saw who it was. It was Colby's oldest boy, and he was fogging up the

47

trail, lathering his horse.

Bob slid his horse to stop amid the dust and leaped off. "Mister Smoke," he panted. So the news had spread very fast as to Smoke's real identity.

"Bob. What's the problem?"

"Pa sent me. It's started, Mister Smoke. Some of Tilden's riders done burned out Wilbur Mason's place, over on the western ridge. Burned him flat. There ain't nothing left no where."

"Anybody hurt over there?"

"No, sir. Not bad, leastways. Mister Wilbur got burned by a bullet, but it ain't bad."

"Where are they now?"

"Mister Matlock took the kids. Pa and Ma took in Mister Wilbur and his missus."

"Where's your brother?"

"Pa sent him off to warn the others."

"Go on in the house. Sally will fix you something to eat. I'll see to your horse."

Smoke looked toward the faraway Circle TF spread. "All right, Franklin," he muttered. "If that's how you want it, get ready for it."

7

Leaving Bob Colby with Sally, Smoke saddled Drifter, the midnight-black, wolf-eyed stallion. Sally fixed him a poke of food and he stashed that in the saddlebags. He stuffed extra cartridges into a pocket of his saddlebags, and made sure his belt loops were filled. He checked his Henry repeating rifle and returned it to the saddle boot.

He kissed Sally and swung up into the saddle, thinking that it had certainly been a short homecoming. He looked at Bob, standing tall and very young beside Sally.

"You stay with Sally, Bob. Don't leave her. I'll square that with your Pa."

"Yes, sir, Mister Smoke," the boy replied.

"Can you shoot a short gun, Bob?"

"Yes, sir. But I'm better with a rifle."

"Sally will loan you a spare pistol. Wear it at all times."

"Yes, sir. What are you gonna do, Mister Smoke?"

"Try to organize the small farmers and ranchers, Bob. If we don't band together, none of us will have a chance of coming out of this alive."

Smoke wheeled Drifter and rode into the timber without looking back.

He headed across the country, taking the shortest route to Colby's spread. During his ride, Smoke spotted men staking out claims on land that had been filed on by small farmers and ranchers.

Finally he had enough of that and reined up. He stared hard at a group of men. "You have permission to dig on this

49

land?"

"This is open land," a man challenged him.

"Wrong, mister. You're on Colby land. Filed on legally and worked. Don't be here when I get back."

But the miners and would-be miners were not going to be that easy to run off. "They told us in Fontana that this here land was open and ready for the takin.'"

"Who told you that?"

"The man at Beeker's store. Some others at a saloon. They said all you folks up here were squattin' illegal-like, that if we wanted to dig, we could; and that's what we're all aimin' to do."

So that was Tilden's plan. Or at least part of it, Smoke thought. He could not fault the men seeking gold. They were greedy, but not land-greedy. Dig the gold, and get out. And if a miner, usually unarmed, was hurt, shot in any attempt to run them off, marshals would probably be called in.

Or . . . Smoke pondered, gazing from Drifter at the miners, Tilden might try to name a marshal for Fontana, hold a mock election for a sheriff. Colorado had only been a state for a little over two years, and things were still a bit confused. This county had had a sheriff, Smoke recalled, but somebody had shot him and elections had not yet been held to replace the man. And even an illegally elected sheriff would still be the law until commissioners could be sent in and matters were straightened out.

Smoke felt that was the way Tilden was probably leaning. That's the way *he* would play it if Smoke was as amoral as Tilden Franklin.

"You men have been warned," he told the miners. "This is private property. And I don't give a damn what you were told in town. And don't think the men who own the land won't fight to keep it, for you'll be wrong if you do. You've been warned."

"We got the law on our side!" a miner said, considerable heat in his voice.

"What law?"

"Hell, man!" another miner said. "They's an election in

50

town comin' up tomorrow. Gonna be a sheriff for a brand-new town. You won't talk so goddamned tough with the law lookin' over your shoulder, I betcha."

Smoke gazed at the men. "You're all greedy fools," he said softly. "And a lot of you are going to get hurt if you continue with this trespassing. Like I said, you've been warned."

Smoke rode on, putting his back to the men, showing them his contempt.

An hour later, he was in Colby's front yard. Wilbur Mason had joined Colby by the corral at the sound of Drifter's hooves. A bloody bandage was tied around Wilbur's left arm, high up, close to the shoulder. But Smoke could tell by looking at the man that Wilbur was far from giving up. The man was angry and it showed.

"Boys," Smoke said. "You save anything, Wilbur?"

"Nothing, Matt . . . Smoke. You really the gunfighter?"

"Yes." He swung down and dropped Drifter's reins on the ground. "Do any of you know anything about an election coming up tomorrow in town?"

"No," they said together. Colby added. "What kind of election, Smoke?"

"Sheriff's election. Tilden may be a greedy bastard, but he's no fool. At the most, there is maybe twenty-five of us out here in the high country. There is probably two or three thousand men in Fontana by now. Our votes would be meaningless. And for sure, there will be Tilden men everywhere, ready to prod some of you into a fight if you show up by yourselves in town. So stay out until we can ride in in groups."

"Who's runnin' for sheriff?" Wilbur asked.

"I don't know. A TF man for sure, though. I'll check it out. Bob is staying with Sally, Colby. That all right with you?"

"Sure. He's a good boy, Smoke. And he'll stand fast facin' trouble. He's young, but he's solid."

"I know that. He said Adam was riding out to check the others . . . what's the word so far?"

"They're stayin', Smoke. Boy's asleep in the house now. He's wore out."

51

"I can imagine." His eyes caught movement near the house. Velvet. "Keep the women close by, Colby. This situation is shaping up to be a bad one."

"Velvet's just a kid, Smoke!" her father protested. "You don't think . . ." He refused to even speak the terrible words.

"She looks older than her years, Colby. And a lot of very rough people are moving into this area. Tilden Franklin will, I'm thinking, do anything to prod us all into something rash. He's made his intentions toward my wife public. So he's pulling out all the stops now."

Both Colby and Wilbur cursed Tilden Franklin.

Smoke waited until the men wound down. "How's your ammo situation?"

"Enough for a war," Colby said.

"Watch your backs." Smoke swung into the saddle and looked at the men. "A war? Well, that's what we've got, boys. And it's going to be a bad one. Some of us are not going to make it. I don't know about you boys, but I'm not running."

"We'll all stand," Wilbur said.

Smoke nodded. "The Indians have a saying." His eyes swept the land. "It's a good place to die."

8

Smoke touched base with as many small ranchers and farmers as he could that day, then slowly turned Drifter's head toward the town of Fontana. There was no bravado in what he was about to do, no sense of being a martyr. The area had to be checked out, and Smoke was the most likely candidate to do that.

But even he was not prepared for the sight that greeted him.

Long before he topped the crest overlooking the town of Fontana, he could see the lights. Long before the rip-roaring town came into view, he could hear the noise. Smoke topped the crest and sat, looking with amazement at the sight that lay beneath and before him.

Fontana had burst at the seams, growing in all directions within three days. From where he sat, Smoke could count fifty new saloons, most no more than hurriedly erected wooden frames covered with canvas. The town had spread a half mile out in any direction, and the streets were packed with shoulder-to-shoulder humanity.

Smoke spoke to Drifter softly and the big, mean-eyed stallion moved out. Smoke stabled Drifter in the oldest of the corrals—a dozen had suddenly burst forth around the area—and filled the trough with corn.

"Stay away from him," he warned the stable boy. "If anyone but me goes into that stall, he'll kill them."

"Yes, sir," the boy said. He gazed at Smoke with adoration-filled eyes. "You really the gunfighter Smoke Jensen?"

53

"Yes."

"I'm on your side, Mister Smoke. Name's Billy."

Smoke extended his hand and the boy gravely shook it. Smoke studied the boy in the dim lantern-light of the stable. Ragged clothes, shoes with the soles tied so that would not flop.

"How old are you, Billy?"

"Eleven, sir."

"Where are your folks?"

"Dead for more years than I can remember."

"I don't recall seeing you before. You been here long?"

"No, sir. I come in a couple weeks ago. I been stayin' down south of here, workin' in a stable. But the man who owned it married him a grass widow and her kids took over my job. I drifted. Ol' grump that owns this place gimme a job. I sleep here."

Smoke grinned at the "ol' grump" bit. He handed the boy a double eagle. "Come light, you get yourself some clothes and shoes."

Billy looked at the twenty-dollar gold piece. "Wow!" he said.

Smoke led the boy to Drifter's stall and opened the gate, stepping inside. He motioned the boy in after him. "Pet him, Billy."

Billy cautiously petted the midnight-black stallion. Drifter stopped eating for a moment and swung his big head, looking at him through those yellow, killer-cold, wolf-like eyes. Then he resumed munching at the corn.

"He likes you," Smoke told the boy. "You'll be all right with him. Anyone comes in here and tries to hurt you, just get in the stall with Drifter. You won't be harmed."

The boy nodded and stepped back out with Smoke. "You be careful, Mister Smoke," he warned. "I don't say much to people, but I listen real good. I hear things."

They walked to the wide doors at the front of the stable. "What do you hear, Billy?"

Several gunshots split the torch-and-lantern-lit night air of Fontana. A woman's shrill and artificial-sounding laughter drifted to man and boy. A dozen pianos, all playing different tunes, created a confusing, discordant cacophony in the soft air of summer in the high-up country.

"Some guy named of Monte Carson is gonna be elected the sheriff. Ain't no one runnin' agin him."

"I've heard of him. He's a good hand with a gun."

"Better than you?" There was doubt in Billy's voice at that.

"No," Smoke said.

"The boss of this area, that Mister Tilden Franklin, is supposed to have a bunch of gunhands comin' to be deputies."

"Who are they?"

"I ain't heard."

"What have you heard about me?"

"I heard two punchers talkin' yesterday afternoon, over by a tent saloon. Circle TF punchers. But I think they're more than just cowboys. They wore their guns low and tied down."

Very observant boy, Smoke thought.

"If they can angle you in for a backshoot, they'd do it. Talk is, though, this Mister Franklin is gonna let the law handle you. Legal-like, you know?"

"Yeah." Smoke patted the boy's shoulder. "You take good care of Drifter, Billy. And keep your ears clean and open. I'll check you later."

"Yes, sir, Mister Smoke."

Smoke stepped out of the stable and turned to his left. His right hand slipped the thong off the Colt's hammer. Smoke was dressed in black whipcord trousers, black shirt, and dark hat. His spurs jingled as he walked, his boots kicking up little pockets of dust as he headed for the short boardwalk that ran in front of Beeker's General Store, a saloon, and the gunsmith's shop. Smoke's eyes were in constant motion, noting and retaining everything he spotted. Night seemed to color into day as he approached the boom-town area.

A drunk lurched out from between two tents, almost colliding with Smoke.

"Watch where you're goin', boy," the miner mush-mouthed at him.

Smoke ignored him and walked on.

"A good time comes reasonable," a heavily rouged and slightly overweight woman said, offering her charms to Smoke.

"I'm sure," Smoke told her. "But I'm married."

"Ain't you the lucky one?" she said, and stepped back into the shadows of her darkened tent.

He grinned and walked on.

Smoke walked past Beeker's store and glanced in. The man had hired more help and was doing a land office business, a fixed smile on his greedy, weasel face. His hatchet-faced wife was in constant motion, moving around the brightly lighted store, her sharp eyes darting left and right, looking for thieving hands.

Other than her own, Smoke mentally noted.

He walked on, coming to the swinging doors of the saloon. Wild laughter and hammering piano music greeted his ears. It was not an altogether offensive sound. The miners, as a whole, were not bad people. They were here to dig and chip and blast and hammer the rock, looking for gold. In their free time, most would drink and gamble and whore the night away.

Smoke almost stepped inside the saloon, changing his mind just at the very last moment. He stepped back away from the doors and walked on.

He crossed the street and stepped into Louis Longmont's place. The faro and monte and draw and stud poker tables were filled; dice clicked and wheels spun, while those with money in their hands stared and waited for Lady Luck to smile on them.

Most of the time she did not.

Smoke walked to the bar, shoved his way through, and ordered a beer.

He took his beer and crossed the room, dodging drunks as they staggered past. He leaned against a bracing and watched the action.

"Smoke." The voice came from his left.

Smoke turned and looked into the face of Louis Longmont. "Louis," he acknowledged. "Another year, another boom town, hey?"

56

"They never change. I don't know why I stay with it. I certainly don't need the money."

Smoke knew that was no exaggeration on the gambler's part. The gambler owned a large ranch up in Wyoming Territory. He owed several businesses in San Francisco, and he owned a hefty chunk of a railroad. It was a mystery to many why Louis stayed with the hard life he had chosen.

"Then get out of it, Louis," Smoke suggested.

"But of course," Louis responded with a smile. His eyes drifted to Smoke's twin Colts. "Just as you got out of gunfighting."

Smoke smiled. "I put them away for several years, Louis. Had gold not been found, or had I chosen a different part of the country to settle, I probably would never have picked them up again."

"Lying to others is bad enough, my young friend. But lying to one's self is unconscionable. Can you look at me and tell me you never, during those stale years, missed the dry-mouthed moment before the draw? The challenge of facing and besting those miscreants who would kill you or others who seek a better and more peaceful way? The so-called loneliness of the hoot-owl trail? I think not, Mister Jensen. I think not."

There was nothing for Smoke to say, for Louis was right. He had missed those death-close moments. And Sally knew it too. Smoke had often caught her watching him, silently looking at him as he would stand and gaze toward the mountains, or as his eyes would follow the high flight of an eagle.

"Your silence tells all, my friend," Louis said. "I know only too well."

"Yeah," Smoke said, looking down into his beer mug. "I guess I'd better finish my beer and ride. I don't want to be the cause of any trouble in your place, Louis."

"Trouble, my friend, is something I have never shied away from. You're safer here than in any other place in this woebegotten town. If I can help it, you will be not backshot in my place."

And again, Smoke knew the gambler was telling the

truth. Smoke and Louis had crossed trails a dozen times over the years. The man had taken a liking to the boy when Smoke was riding with the Mountain Man Preacher. In the quieter moments of his profession, Louis had shown Smoke the tricks of his gambler's trade. Louis had realized that Smoke possessed a keen intelligence, and Louis liked those people who tried to better themselves, as Smoke had always done.

They had become friends.

Hard hoofbeats sounded on the dirt street outside the gambling tent. Smoke looked at Louis.

"About a dozen riders," Smoke said.

"Probably the 'deputies' Tilden Franklin called in from down Durango way. They'll be hardcases, Smoke."

"Is this election legal?"

"Of course not. But it will be months before the state can send anyone in to verify it or void it. By then, Franklin will have gotten his way. Initial reports show the gold, what there is of it, assays high. But the lode is a narrow one. I suspect you already knew that."

"I've know about the vein for a long time, Louis. I never wanted gold."

A quick flash of irritation crossed Louis's face. "It is well and good to shun wealth while one is young, Smoke. But one had best not grow old without some wealth."

"One can have wealth without riches, Louis," Smoke countered.

The gambler smiled. "I believe Preacher's influence was strong on you, young man."

"There could have been no finer teacher in all the world, Louis."

"Is he alive, Smoke?"

"I don't know. If so, he'd be in his eighties. I like to think he's still alive. But I just don't know."

Louis knew, but he elected to remain silent on the subject. At least for the time being.

Boots and jangling spurs sounded on the raw boards in front of Louis's place. And both Louis and Smoke knew the time for idle conversation had passed.

They knew before either man sighted the wearers of those boots and spurs.

The first rider burst into the large tent.

"I don't know him," Louis said. "You?"

"Unfortunately. He's one of Tilden's gunhands. Calls himself Tay. I ran into him when I was riding with Preacher. Back then he was known as Carter. I heard he was wanted for murder back in Arkansas."

"Sounds like a delightful fellow," Louis said drily.

"He's a bully. But don't sell him short. He's hell with a short gun."

Louis smiled. "Better than you, Smoke?" he asked, a touch of humor in the question.

"No one is better than me, Louis," Smoke said, in one of his rare moments of what some would call arrogance; others would call it merely stating a proven fact.

Louis's chuckle held no mirth. "I believe I am better, my friend."

"I hope we never have to test that out of anger, Louis."

"We won't," Louis replied. "But let's do set up some cans and make a small wager someday."

"You're on."

The gunfighter Tay turned slowly, his eyes drifting first to Louis, then to Smoke.

"Hello, punk!" Tay said, his voice silencing the piano player and hushing the hubbub of voices in the gaming tent.

"Are you speaking to me, you unshaven lout?" Louis asked.

"Naw," Tay said. The leather thongs that secured his guns were off, left and right. "Pretty boy there."

"You're a fool," Smoke said softly, his voice carrying to Tay, overheard by all in the gaming room.

"I'm gonna kill you for that!" Tay said.

Those men and women seated between Tay and Smoke cleared out, moving left and right.

"I hope you have enough in your pockets to bury you," Smoke said.

Tay's face flushed. both hands hovering over the butt of his guns.

He snarled at Smoke.

Smoke laughed at him.

"A hundred dollars on the Circle TF rider," a man seated at a table said.

"You're on," Louis said taking the wager. "Gentlemen," he said to Smoke and Tay. "Bets are down."

Tay's eyes were shiny, but his hands were steady over his guns.

Smoke held his beer mug in his left hand.

"Draw, goddamn you!" Tay shouted.

"After you," Smoke replied. "I always give a sucker a break whenever possible."

Tay grabbed for his guns.

9

"Your behavior the other day was disgusting!" Ralph Morrow would not let up on his wife. "Those men are dead because of you. You do realize that, don't you?"

Bountiful tossed her head, her blond curls bouncing around her beautiful face. Her lips were set in a pout. "I did nothing," she said defending her actions.

"My god, I married an animal!" Ralph said, disgust in his voice. "Can't you see you're a minister's wife?"

"I'm beginning to see a lot of things, Ralph. One of which is I made a mistake."

"In coming out West? Did we have a choice, Bountiful? After your disgraceful behavior in Ohio, I'm very lucky the Church even gave me another chance."

She waved that off. "No, Ralph, not that. In my marrying such a pompous wee-wee!"

Ralph flushed and balled his fists. "You take that back!" he yelled at her.

"You take that back!" she repeated mimicking him scornfully. "My God, Ralph! You're such a flummox!"

Man and wife were several miles from the town of Fontana. They were on the banks of a small creek. Ralph sat down on the bank and refused to look at her. A short distance away at their camp, the others tried without much success not to listen to their friends quarrel.

"They certainly are engaged in a plethora of flapdoodle," Haywood observed.

"I feel sorry for him," Dana said.

61

"I don't," Ed said. "It's his own fault he's such a sissy-pants."

All present looked at Ed in the dancing flames of the fire. If there was a wimp among them, it was Ed. Ed had found a June bug in his blankets on the way West and, from his behavior one might have thought he'd discovered a nest of rattlers. It had taken his wife a full fifteen minutes to calm him down.

Haywood sat on a log and puffed his Meerschaum. Of them all, Haywood was the only person who knew the true story about Ralph Morrow. And if the others wanted to think him a sissy-pants . . . well, that was their mistake. But Haywood had to admit that, from all indications, when Ralph had fully accepted Christ into his life, he had gone a tad overboard.

If anyone had taken the time to just look at Ralph, they would have noticed the rippling boxer's muscles; the broad, hard, flat-knuckled fists; the slightly crooked nose. It had always amazed Haywood how so many people could look at something, but never see it.

Haywood suppressed a giggle. Come to think of it, he mused, Ralph *did* sort of act a big milquetoast.

But it should be interesting when Ralph finally got a belly full of it.

Smoke cleared leather before Tay got his pistols free of their holsters. Smoke drew with such blinding speed, drawing cocking, firing, not one human eye in the huge tent could follow the motion.

The single slug struck Tay in the center of the chest and knocked him backward. He struggled up on one elbow and looked at Smoke through eyes that were already glazing over. He tried to lift his free empty hand; the hand was so heavy he thought his gun was in it. He began squeezing his trigger finger. He was curious about the lack of noise and recoil.

Then he fell back onto the raw, rough-hewn board floor and was curious no more.

"Maybe we won't set up those tin cans," Louis muttered, just loud enough for Smoke to hear it.

"Tie him across a saddle and take him back to Tilden Franklin," Smoke said, his voice husky due to the low-hanging cigarette and cigar smoke in the crowded gaming tent. "Unless some of you boys want to pick up where Tay left off."

The riders appeared to be in a mild state of shock. They were all, to a man, used to violence; that was their chosen way of life. They had all, to a man, been either witnesses to or participants in stand-up gunfights, backshoots, and ambushes. And they had all heard of the young gunslick Smoke Jensen. But since none had ever seen the man in action, they had tended to dismiss much of what they had heard as so much pumped-up hoopla.

Until this early evening in the boom town of Fontana, in Louis Longmont's gaming tent.

"Yes, sir, Mister Jensen," one young TF rider said. "I mean," he quickly corrected himself, "I'll sure tie him across his saddle."

Until this evening, the young TF rider had fancied himself a gunhawk. Now he just wanted to get on his pony and ride clear out of the area. But he was afraid the others would laugh at him if he did that.

Smoke eased the hammer down with his thumb. A very audible sigh went up inside the tent with that action. There was visible relaxing of stomach muscles when Smoke holstered the deadly Colt.

Smoke looked at the young puncher who had spoken. "Come here," he said.

The young man, perhaps twenty at the most, quickly crossed the room to face Smoke. He was scared, and looked it.

"What's your name?" Smoke asked.

"Pearlie."

"You're on the wrong side, Pearlie. You know that?"

"Mister Smoke," Pearlie said in a low tone, so only Smoke and Louis could hear. "The TF brand can throw two hundred or more men at you. And I ain't kiddin'. Now, you're tough as hell and snake-quick, but even you can't fight that many men."

"You want to bet your life, Pearlie?" Louis asked him. The man's voice was low-pitched and his lips appeared not to move at all.

Pearlie cut his eyes at the gambler. "I ain't got no choice, Mister Longmont."

"Yes, you do," Smoke said.

"I'm listenin'."

"I need a hand I can trust. I think that's you, Pearlie."

The young man's jaw dropped open. "But I been ridin' for the TF brand!"

"How much is he paying you?"

"Sixty a month."

"I'll give you thirty and found."

Pearlie smiled. "You're serious!"

"Yes, I am. Have you the sand in you to make a turn-around in your life?"

"Give me a chance, Mister Smoke."

"You've got it. Are you quick with that Colt?"

"Yes, sir. But I ain't nearabouts as quick as you."

"Have you ever used it before?"

"Yes, sir."

"Would you stand by me and my wife and friends, Pearlie?"

"Til I soak up so much lead I can't stand, Mister Smoke."

Smoke cut his eyes at Louis. The man smiled and nodded his head slightly.

"You're hired, Pearlie."

"Pearlie did *what*?" Tilden screamed.

Clint repeated his statement, standing firm in front of the boss. Clint was no gunhawk. He was as good as or better with a short gun than most men, but had never fancied himself a gunfighter. He knew horses, he knew cattle, and he could work and manage men. There was no backup in Clint. He had fought Indians, outlaws, nesters, and other ranchers during his years with Tilden Franklin, and while he didn't always approve of everything Tilden did, Clint rode for the brand. And that was that.

"Goddamned, no-good little pup!" Tilden spat out the words. He lifted his eyes and stared into his foreman's eyes. "This can't be tolerated, Clint."

Clint felt a slight sick feeling in his stomach. He knew what was coming next. "No, sir. You're right."

"Drag him!" Tilden spat the horrible words.

"Yes, sir." Clint turned away and walked out of the room. He stood on the porch for a long moment, breathing deeply. He appeared to be deep in thought.

Louis shut the gaming room down early that evening. And with Louis Longmont, no one uttered any words of protest. They simply got up and left. And neither did anyone take any undue umbrage, for all knew Louis's games were straight-arrow honest.

He closed the wooden door to his gaming-room tent, extinquished most of the front lights, and set a bottle of fine scotch on the table.

"I know you're not normally a hard-drinking man, my young friend," Louis said, as he poured two tumblers full of the liquid. "But savor the taste of the Glenlivet. It's the finest made."

Smoke picked up the bottle and read the label. "Was this stuff made in 1824?"

Louis smiled. "Oh, no. That's when the distillery was founded. Old George Smith knew his business, all right."

"Knew?"

"Yes. He died six—no, seven years ago. I was on the Continent at the time."

Smoke sipped the light scotch. It was delicate, yet mellow. It had a lightness that was quite pleasing.

"I had been to a rather obscure place called Monte Carlo." Louis sniffed his tumbler before sipping.

"I never heard of that place."

"I own part of the casino," Louis said softly.

"Make lots of money?"

Louis's reply was a smile.

It silently spoke volumes.

"Prior to that, I was enjoying the theater in Warsaw. It was there I was introduced to Madame Modjeska. It was quite the honor. She is one of the truly fine actresses in the world today."

"You're talking over my head, Louis."

"Madame Mudrzejeweski."

"Did you just swallow a bug, Louis?"

Louis laughed. "No. She shortened her name to Modjeska. She is here in America now. Performing Shakespeare in New York, I believe. She also tours."

Smoke sipped his scotch and kept his mouth shut.

"When I finally retire, I believe I shall move to New York City. It's quite a place, Smoke. Do you have any desires at all to see it?"

"No," Smoke said gently.

"Pity," the gambler said. "It is really a fascinating place. Smoke?"

The young rancher-farmer-gunfighter lifted his eyes to meet Louis's.

"You should travel, Smoke. Educate yourself. Your wife is, I believe, an educated woman. Is she not?"

"School teacher."

"Ah . . . yes. I thought your grammar, most of the time, had improved since last we spoke. Smoke . . . get out while you have the time and opportunity to do so."

"No."

"Pearlie was right, Smoke. There are too many against you."

Smoke took a small sip of his scotch. "I am not alone in this, Louis. There are others."

"Many of whom will not stand beside you when it gets bad. But I think you know that."

"But some of them will, Louis. And bear this in mind: we control the high country."

"Yes, there is that. Tell me, your wife has money, correct?"

"Yes. I think she's wealthy."

"You *think*?"

"I told you, Louis. I'm not that interested in great wealth. My father is lying atop thousands and thousands of dollars of gold."

Louis smiled. "And there are those who would desecrate his grave for a tenth of it," he reminded the young man.

"I'm not one of them."

Louis sighed and drained his tumbler, refilling it from the bottle of scotch. "Smoke, it's 1878. The West is changing. The day of the gunfighter, men like you and me, is coming to a close. There is still a great rowdy element moving Westward, but by and large, the people who are now coming here are demanding peace. Soon there will be no place for men like us."

"And? So?"

"What are you going to do then?"

"I'll be right out there on the Sugarloaf, Louis, ranching and farming and raising horses. And," he said with a smile, "probably raising a family of my own."

"Not if you're dead, Smoke." The gambler's words were softly offered.

Smoke drained his tumbler and stood up, tall and straight and heavily muscled. "The Sugarloaf is my home, Louis. Sally's and mine. And here is where we'll stay. Peacefully working the land, or buried in it."

He walked out the door.

10

Smoke made his spartan camp some five miles outside of Fontana. With Drifter acting as guard, Smoke slept soundly. He had sent Pearlie to his ranch earlier that night, carrying a hand-written note introducing him to Sally. One of the older ranchers in the area, a man who was aligned on neither side, had told Smoke that Pearlie was a good boy who had just fallen in with the wrong crowd, that Pearlie had spoken with him a couple of times about leaving the Circle TF.

Smoke did not worry about Pearlie making any ungentle-manly advances toward Sally, for she would shoot him stone dead if he tried.

Across the yard from the cabin, Smoke and Sally had built a small bunkhouse, thinking of the day when they would need extra hands. Pearlie would sleep there.

Smoke bathed—very quickly—in a small, rushing creek and changed clothes: a gray shirt, dark trousers. He drank the last of his pot of coffee, extinguished the small fire, and saddled Drifter.

He turned Drifter's head toward Fontana, but angling slightly north of the town, planning on coming in from a different direction.

It would give those people he knew would be watching him something to think about.

About half a mile from Fontana, Smoke came up on a small series of just-begun buildings; tents lay behind the construction site. He sat his horse and looked at Preacher

Morrow swinging an axe. The preacher had removed his shirt and was clad only in his short-sleeve undershirt. Smoke's eyes took in the man's heavy musculature and the fluid way he handled the axe.

A lot more to him than meets the eyes, Smoke thought. A whole lot more.

Then Smoke's eyes began to inspect the building site. Not bad, he thought. Jackson's big store across the road, and the offices of the others in one long building on the opposite side of the road. The cabin's would be behind the offices, while Jackson and his wife and brother would live in quarters behind but connected to the store.

Smoke's eyes caught movement to his left.

"Everything meet with your approval, Mister Jensen?"

Smoke turned Drifter toward the voice. Ed Jackson. "Looks good. The preacher's a pretty good hand with an axe, wouldn't you say?"

"Oh . . . him? 'Bout the only thing he's good at. He's a sissy."

Smoke smiled, thinking: Shopkeeper, I hope you never push that preacher too hard, 'cause he'll damn sure break you like a match stick.

Hunt, Colton, Haywood, and their wives walked out to where Smoke sat Drifter. He greeted the men and took his hat off to the ladies. Bountiful was not with the group and Smoke was grateful for that. The woman was trouble.

Then he wondered where the shopkeeper's brother was. He wondered if Bountiful and Paul might be . . .

He sighed and put his hat back on, pushing those thoughts from him. He dismounted and ground-reined Drifter.

"Going into town to vote, Mister Jensen?" Hunt asked.

"No point in it. One-sided race from what I hear."

"Oh, no!" Colton told him. "We have several running for mayor, half a dozen running for sheriff, and two running for city judge."

"Tilden Franklin's men will win, believe me."

"Mister Franklin seems like a very nice person to me," Ed said, adding, "not that I've ever met the gentleman, of course. Just from what I've heard about him."

"Yeah, he's a real prince of a fellow," Smoke said, with enough sarcasm in his voice to cover hotcakes thicker than molasses. "Why just a few days ago he was nice enough to send his boys up into the high country to burn out a small rancher-farmer named Wilbur Mason. Shot Wilbur and scattered his wife and kids. He's made his boast that he'll either run me out or kill me, and then he'll have my wife. Yeah, Tilden is a sweet fellow, all right."

"I don't believe that!" Ed said, puffing up.

Smoke's eyes narrowed and his face hardened. Haywood looked at the young man and both saw and felt danger emanating from him. He instinctively put an arm around his wife's shoulders and drew her to him.

Smoke said, his eyes boring into Ed's eyes, "Shopkeeper, I'll let that slide this one time. But let me give you a friendly piece of advice." He cut his eyes, taking in, one at a time, all the newcomers to the West. "You folks came her from the East. You do things differently back East. I didn't say better, just different. Out here, you call a man a liar, you'd better be ready to do one of two things: either stand and slug it out with him or go strap on iron.

"Now you all think about that, and you'll see both the right and wrong in it. I live here. Me and my wife been here for better than three years. We hacked a home out of the wilderness and made it nice. We fought the hard winters, Indians a few times, and we know the folks in this area. You people, on the other hand, just come in here. You don't know nobody, yet you're going to call me a liar. See what I mean, Shopkeeper?

"Now the wrong of it is this: there are bullies who take advantage of the code, so to speak. Those types of trash will prod a fellow into a fight, just because they think that to fight is manly, or some such crap as that. Excuse my language, ladies. But the point is, you got to watch your mouth out here. The graveyards are full of people ignorant of the ways of the West."

Ed Jackson blustered and sweated, but he did not offer to apologize.

He won't make it, Smoke thought. Someone will either run him out or kill him. And mankind will have lost nothing by his passing.

"Why is Franklin doing these things, Mister Jensen?" Haywood asked.

"Smoke. Call me Smoke. Why? Because he wants to be king. Perhaps he's a bit mad. I don't know. I do know he hates farmers and small ranchers. As for me, well, I have the Sugarloaf and he wants it."

"The Sugarloaf?" Hunt asked.

"My valley. Part of it, that is."

"Are you suggesting the election is rigged?" Haywood inquired.

"No. I'm just saying that Tilden's people will win, that's all."

"Has Mister Franklin offered to buy any of the farmers' or ranchers' holdings?" Hunt asked.

Smoke laughed. "Buy? Lawyer, men like Tilden don't offer to buy. They just run people out. Did cruel kings offer to buy lands they desired? No, they just took it, by force."

Preacher Morrow had ceased his work with the axe and had joined the group. His eyes searched for his wife and, not finding her present, glowered at Ed Jackson.

Maybe I was right, Smoke thought.

"Are you a Christian, Mister Jensen?" he asked, finally taking his eyes from the shopkeeper.

Bad blood between those two, Smoke thought. "I been to church a few times over the years. Sally and me was married in a proper church."

"Have you been baptized, sir?"

"In a little crick back in Missouri, yes, sir, I was."

"Ah, wonderful! Perhaps you and your wife will attend services just as soon as I get my church completed?"

"I knew a lay preacher back in Missouri preached on a stump, Preacher Morrow. Look around you, sir. You ever in all your life seen a more beautiful cathedral? Look at them mountains yonder. Got snow on 'em year-round. See them flowers scattered around, those blue and purple ones? Those are columbines. Some folks call them Dove Flowers.

71

See the trees? Pine and fir and aspen and spruce and red cedar. What's wrong with preaching right in the middle of what God created?"

"You're right, of course, sir. I'm humbled. You're a strange man, Mister Jensen. And I don't mean that in any ugly way."

"I didn't take it in such a way. I know what you mean. The West is a melting pot of people, Preacher. Right there in that town of Fontana, there's a man named Louis Longmont. He's got degrees from places over in Europe, I think. He owns ranches, pieces of railroads, and lots of other businesses. But he follows the boom towns as a gambler. He's been decorated by kings and queens. But he's a gambler, and a gunfighter. My wife lives in a cabin up in the mountains. But she's worth as much money as Tilden Franklin, probably more. She's got two or three degrees from fancy colleges back East, and she's traveled in Europe and other places. Yet she married me.

"I know scouts for the Army who used to be college professors. I know cowboys who work for thirty and found who can stand and quote William Shakespeare for hours. And them that listen, most of them, can't even read or write. I know Negroes who fought for the North and white men who wore the Gray who now work side by side and who would die for each other. Believe it."

"And you, Smoke?" Hunt asked. "What about you?"

"What about me? I raise cattle and horses and farm. I mind my own business, if people will let me. And I'll harm no man who isn't set on hurting me or mine. We need people like you folks out here. We need some stability. Me and Sally are gonna have kids one day, and I'd like for them to grow up around folks like you." He cut his eyes to Ed Jackson. "Most of you, that is." The store-owner caught the verbal cut broadside and flushed. "But for a while yet, it's gonna be rough and rowdy out here." Smoke pointed. "Ya'll see that hill yonder? That's Boot Hill. The graveyard. See that fancy black wagon with them people walking along behind it, going up that hill? That wagon is totin' a gunhawk name of Tay. He braced me last night in Louis's place. He

72

was a mite slow."

"You killed yet *another* man?" Ed blurted out.

"I've killed about a hundred men," Smoke said. "Not counting Indians. I killed twenty, I think, one day up on the Uncompahgre. That was back in '74, I think. A year later I put lead into another twenty or so over in Idaho, town name of Bury. Bury don't exist no more. I burned it down.*

"People, listen to me. Don't leave this area. We got to have some people like you to put down roots, to stay when the gold plays out. And it will, a lot sooner than most folks realize. And," Smoke said with a sigh, "we're gonna need a doctor and nurse and preacher around here . . . the preacher for them that the doc can't patch up."

The newcomers were looking at Smoke, a mixture of emotions in their eyes. They all wanted for him to speak again.

"Now I'm heading into town, people," Smoke said. "And I'm not going in looking for trouble. But I assure you all, it will come to me. If you doubt that, come with me for an hour. Put aside your axes and saws and ride in with me. See for yourself."

"I'll go with you," Preacher Morrow said. "Just let me bathe in the creek first."

All the men agreed to go.

Should be interesting, Smoke thought. For he planned to take Preacher Morrow into Louis's place. Not that Smoke thought the man would see anything he hadn't already seen . . . several times before, in his past.

*Return of the Mountain Man

11

Ralph Morrow was the first one back to where Smoke stood beside Drifter. "Where is your wife, Preacher?"

The man cut his eyes at Smoke. Smoke could see the faded scars above the man's eyes.

A boxer, Smoke thought. He's fought many times in the ring.

"Walking along the creek over there," he said, pointing. "I suppose she's safe. From hostiles," he added, a touch of bitterness in his voice.

"I'd think so. This close to town. Preacher? Anytime you want to talk, I'm available."

The man looked away, stubbornness setting his chin.

Smoke said no more. The others soon joined them and they made their way into Fontana. The newspaper man carried a note pad and had a breastpocket full of pencils. Smoke stabled Drifter with Billy and smiled at the boy. Billy was dressed in new britches and shirt, boots on his feet. "Give him some corn, Billy."

"Yes, sir. I heared that was some show last night over to Longmont's place."

Smoke nodded. "He was a tad slow."

Billy grinned and led Drifter into his stall, the big outlaw stallion allowing the boy to lead him docilely.

"What a magnificent animal," Colton remarked, looking at Drifter.

"Killed the last man who owned him," Smoke said.

The doctor muttered something under his breath that

Smoke could not quite make out. But he had a pretty good idea what it was. He grinned.

The town was jammed with people, bursting at its newly sewn seams. American flags were hung and draped all over the place. Notices that Tilden Franklin was going to speak were stuck up, it seemed, almost everywhere one looked.

"Your fine man is going to make a speech, Jackson," Smoke said to the shopkeeper, keeping his face bland. "You sure won't want to miss that."

"I shall make every attempt to attend that event," Ed announced, a bit stiffly.

Several of the miners who had been in Louis's place when Tay was shot walked past Smoke, greeting him with a smile. Smoke acknowledged the greetings.

"You seem to have made yourself well known in a short time, Smoke," Hunt said.

"I imagine them that spoke was some that made money betting on the outcome of the shooting," the lawyer was informed.

"Barbaric!"

"Not much else to do out here, Lawyer. Besides, you should see the crowds that gather for a hanging. Folks will come from fifty miles out for that. Bring picnic lunches and make a real pleasurable day out of it."

The lawyer refused to respond to that. He simply shook his head and looked away.

The town was growing by the hour. Where once no more than fifty people lived, there now roamed some five thousand. Tents of all sizes and descriptions were going up every few minutes.

Smoke looked at Ed Jackson. "I'm not trying to pry into your business, Shopkeeper, so don't take it that way. But do you have any spare money for workmen?"

"I might. Why do you ask?"

"You could get your store up and running in a few days if you were to hire some people to help you. A lot of those men out there would do for a grubstake."

"A what?"

"A grubstake. You give them equipment and food, and

75

they'll help you put up your building and offer you a percentage of what they take out of the ground. I'd think about it—all of you."

"I thought you didn't care for me, Mister Jensen," the shopkeeper said.

"I don't, very much. But maybe it's just because we got off on the wrong foot. I'm willing to start over."

Ed did not reply. He pursed his perch-mouthed lips in silence. "I thank you for your suggestion," he said, a moment later. "I shall . . . give you a discount on your first purchases in my store for it."

"Why, thank you very much," Smoke replied, a smile on his lips. "That's right generous of you, Ed."

"Yes," Ed said smugly. "It is, isn't it?"

The other men turned their heads to hide their smiles.

"How do I go about doing that?" Ed questioned.

"Just ask somebody," Smoke told him. "Find a man who is afoot rather than riding. Find one carrying everything on his back or pushing a cart. You'll probably get some refusals, but eventually you'll find your people."

Ed, Colton, Hunt, and Haywood walked off into the pushing, shoving hubbub of humanity, leaving Smoke and Preacher Morrow standing alone.

"You have no spare money, Preacher?" Smoke asked.

Ralph's smile was genuine. "Find me one who does have spare money. But that isn't it. I want to build as much of my church as possible myself. It's . . . a personal thing."

"I understand. I'm a pretty good hand with an axe myself. I'll give you a hand later on."

Ralph looked at the gunfighter. "I do not understand you, Mister Jensen."

Before Smoke could reply, the hard sounds of drumming hooves filled the air. "Tilden Franklin," Smoke said. "The king has arrived."

"Pearlie!" Sally called. "Come take a break and have some coffee. And I made doughnuts."

"Bearsign!" the young puncher shouted. "Yes, ma'am. I'm

76

on my way."

Sally smiled at that. She had learned that cowboys would ride a hundred miles for home-cooked doughnuts . . . something they called bearsign. It had taken Sally a time to learn why they were called bearsign. When she finally learned the why of it, she thought it positively disgusting.

"You mean! . . ." she had puffed to Smoke. "These people are equating my doughnuts to . . . that's disgusting!"

"Bear tracks, Sally," Smoke had told her. "Not what you're thinking."

She had refused to believe him.

And Smoke never would fully explain.

More fun letting her make up her own mind.

"My husband must have thought a lot of you, Pearlie," she said, watching the puncher eat, a doughnut in each hand. "He's not normally a trusting person."

"He's a fine man, Miss Sally," Pearlie said around a mouthful of bearsign. "And got more cold nerve than any man I ever seen."

"Can we win this fight, Pearlie?"

The cowboy pushed his battered hat back on his head. He took a slug of coffee and said, "You want a straight-out honest answer, ma'am?"

"That's the only way, Pearlie."

Pearlie hesitated. "It'll be tough. Right off, I'd say the odds are slim to none. But there's always a chance. All depends on how many of them nester friends of yourn will stand and fight when it gets down to the hardrock."

"A few of them will."

"Yes'um. That's what I mean." He stuffed his mouth full of more bearsign.

"Matlock will, and so will Wilbur. I'm pretty sure Colby will stand firm. I don't know about the others."

"You see, ma'am, the problem is this: them folks you just named ain't gunhands. Mister Tilden can mount up to two hundred riders. The sheriff is gonna be on his side, and all them gun-slingin' deputies he'll name. Your husband is pure hell with a gun—pardon my language—but one man just can't do 'er all."

Sally smiled at that. She alone, of all those involved, knew what her husband was capable of doing. But, she thought with a silent sigh, Pearlie was probably right . . . it would be unreasonable to expect one man to do it all.

Even such a man as Smoke.

"What does Mister Franklin want, Pearlie . . . and why?"

"I ain't sure of the why of it all, ma'am. As for me, I'd be satisfied with a little bitty part of what he has. He's got so much holdin's I'd bet he really don't know all that he has. What does he want?" The cowboy paused, thinking. "He wants everything, ma'am. Everything he sees. I've overheard some of his older punchers talk about what they done to get them things for Tilden Franklin. I wouldn't want to say them things in front of you, ma'am. I'll just say I'm glad I didn't have no part in them. And I'm real glad Mister Smoke gimme a job with ya'll 'fore it got too late for me."

"You haven't been with the Circle TF long, then, Pearlie?"

"It would have been a year this fall, ma'am. I drifted down here from the Bitterroot. I . . . kinda had a cloud hangin' over me, I guess you'd say."

"You want to talk about it?"

"Ain't that much to say, ma'am. I always been mighty quick with a short gun. Not nearabouts as quick as your man, now, but tolerable quick. I was fifteen and workin' a full man's job down in Texas. That was six year ago. Or seven. I disremember exact. I rode into town with the rest of the boys for a Saturday night spree. There was some punchers from another spread there. One of 'em braced me, called me names. Next thing I recall, that puncher was layin' on his back with a bullet hole in his chest. From my gun. Like I said, I've always been mighty quick. Well, the sheriff he told me to light a shuck. I got my back up at that, 'cause that other puncher slapped leather first. I tole the sheriff I wasn't goin' nowheres. I didn't mean to back that sheriff into no corner, but I reckon that's what I done. That sheriff was a bad one, now. He had him a rep that was solid bad. He tole me I had two choices in the matter: ride out or die.

"Well, ma'am, I tole him I didn't backpaddle for no man, not when I was in the right. He drew on me. I kilt him."

Pearlie paused and took a sip of coffee. Sally refilled his cup and gave him another doughnut.

"Whole place was quiet as midnight in a graveyard," Pearlie continued. It seemed to Sally that he was relieved to be talking about it, as if he had never spoken fully of the events. "I holstered my gun and stepped out onto the boardwalk. Then it hit me what I'd done. I was fifteen years old and in one whale of a pickle. I'd just killed two men in less than ten minutes. One of them a lawman. I was on the hoot-owl trail sure as you're born.

"I got my horse and rode out. Never once looked back. Over in New Mexico two bounty-hunters braced me outside a cantina one night. I reckon someone buried both of them next day. I don't rightly know, seein' as how I didn't stick around for the services. Then I was up in Utah when this kid braced me. He was lookin' for a rep, I guess. He didn't make it," Pearlie added softly. "Then the kid's brothers come a-foggin' after me. I put lead in both of them. One died, so I heard later on.

"I drifted on over into Nevada. By this time, I had bounty-hunters really lookin' for me. I avoided them, much as I could. Changed my name to Pearlie. I headed north, into the Bitterroot Range. Some lawmen came a-knockin' on my cabin door one night. Said they was lawmen, what they was was bounty-hunters. That was a pretty good fight, I reckon. Good for me, bad for them. Then I drifted down into Colorado and you know the rest."

"Family?"

Pearlie shook his head. "None that I really remember. Ma and Pa died with the fevers when I was eight or nine. I got a sister somewheres, but I don't rightly know where. What all I got is what you see, ma'am. I got my guns, a good saddle, and good horse. And that just about says it all, I reckon."

"No, Pearlie, you're wrong," Sally told him.

The cowboy looked at her, puzzlement in his eyes.

"You have a home with us, as long as you want to ride for the brand."

"Much obliged, ma'am," he said, his voice thick. He did not trust himself to say much more. He stood up. "I better

79

get back on the Sugarloaf East, ma'am. Things to do."

Sally watched him mount up and ride off. She smiled, knowing she and Smoke had made yet another friend.

12

Surprisingly, Smoke noted, the election went smoothly. There was one central voting place, where names were taken and written down in a ledger. There was no point in anyone voting more than once, and few did, for Tilden Franklin's men were lopsidedly out in front in the election count, according to the blackboard tally.

By noon, it was clear that Tilden's people were so far ahead they would not be caught.

Hunt, Haywod, Colton, and Ed had voted and vanished into the surging crowds. Preacher Morrow stayed with Smoke.

"You're not voting, Preacher?" Smoke asked.

"What's the point?" Ralph summed it up.

"You're a quick learner."

"It's not Christian of me, Smoke. But I took one look at that Tilden Franklin and immediately formed an acute dislike for the man."

"Like I said, a quick learner."

"The man is cruel and vicious."

"Yes, he is. All of that and more. Insane, I believe."

"That is becoming a catch-all phrase for those who have no feelings for other men's rights, Smoke."

Smoke was beginning to like the preacher more and more as time went by. He wondered about the man's past, but would not ask, that question being impolite. There were scars on the preacher's knuckles, and Smoke knew they didn't get there from thumping a Bible.

Then the call went up: the other candidates had withdrawn. Tilden Franklin's men had won. Within minutes, Monte Carson was walking the streets, a big badge pinned to his shirt.

Smoke deliberately stayed away from the man. He knew trouble would be heading his way soon enough; no point in pushing it.

He felt someone standing close to him and turned, looking down. Billy.

"What's up, Billy?"

"Trouble for you, Smoke," the boy said gravely.

Preacher Morrow stepped closer, to hear better. Haywood and Hunt were walking toward the trio. Smoke waved them over.

"Listen to what the boy has to say," Smoke said.

Billy looked up at the adults standing about him. "Some of the Circle TF riders is gonna prod you, Smoke. Push you into a gunfight and then claim you started it. They're gonna kill you, Smoke."

"They're going to try," Smoke said softly correcting him.

"Where did you hear this, boy?" Hunt asked.

"I was up in the loft getting ready to fork hay down to the horses when the men came inside the barn. I hunkered down in the loft and listened to them talk. They's five of them, Smoke. Valentine, Suggs, Bolton, Harris, and Wright."

"I've heard of Valentine," Smoke said. "He's a gunhawk. Draws fighting wages from Franklin."

"His name was mentioned too," the boy continued. "They said Mister Franklin told them to nip this matter in the bud and end it. If you was to die, they said, the other nests would crumble like a house of cards. They said the new law was on their side and Mister Franklin told them they didn't have nothin' to worry about from that end."

"I suggest we go see the new sheriff immediately," Hunt said. "Let him handle this matter."

Billy shook his head. "I don't know who you are, mister. But you don't understand the way things are. Monte Carson is Franklin's man. Franklin says frog, Carson jumps. Judge

Proctor is an old wine-head from over the Delores way. Franklin brung him in here to stick him in as judge. It's all cut and dried. All made up agin Smoke."

"Incredible!" Haywood said. "Oh, I believe you, son." He looked at Billy. "Activities of this sort are not confined solely to the West."

Billy blinked and looked at Smoke. "What'd he say?"

"Happens in other places too."

"Oh."

"If that is the case, Smoke," Hunt said, "then you must run for your life."

Smoke's eyes turned icy. He looked at the lawyer. "I don't run, Lawyer."

"Then what are you going to do?" Haywood asked.

"You've all three heard Billy's statement. A newspaper man, a lawyer, a minister." Smoke smiled with a grim wolf's baring of his teeth. "Take Billy's story down. I see a way to make Tilden Franklin eat crow on this matter and backpaddle."

"What are you going to do, Smoke?" Preacher Morrow inquired.

"Fight," Smoke said.

"But there's *five* of them!" Hunt protested. "Five against one of you."

"I've faced tougher odds, Lawyer." He looked at Billy. "Where is it going down, Billy?"

"They're gonna brace you in the stable."

Smoke nodded his head. "After these gentlemen take your story on paper, Billy, you get the horses out of there. I don't want to see a good horse die on account of trash like Tilden's men."

"Yes, sir!"

Smoke looked at the three men. "I'll be heading down that way in about an hour, boys. I would suggest you all hunt a hole."

Sally looked toward the eastern slopes of the Sugarloaf. Pearlie was not in sight. Bob Colby was working inside the barn, cleaning it out. She called for him.

"Yes'um?" He stuck his head out of the loft.

"Bob, look and see if you can spot Pearlie. He should be over there." She pointed.

Bob searched the eastern slopes of the Sugarloaf. "Nothing, ma'am," he called. "I can't spot him."

"All right, Bob. Thanks. He's behind a hill, I guess." She put Pearlie out of her mind and thought about what to fix for dinner — supper, as they called it out here, although she had never gotten used to that.

"Now what, boys?" Pearlie asked the half-dozen Circle TF riders facing him.

"I guess you know what, Pearlie," a puncher said. He shook out a loop in his rope.

"You boys is wrong," Pearlie said. "A man's gotta right to ride for the brand he chooses."

"You a turncoat, Pearlie. You should have knowed that no one shows his ass-end to Mister Franklin."

"He ain't God, Lefty."

"He is around here," Lefty responded.

"Then let him bring you back to life," Pearlie said. He jerked iron and blew Lefty out of the saddle, the slug taking the TF rider in the right shoulder, knocking him to the ground.

Pearlie spun his cutting horse and tried to make a run for it. He was just a tad slow. He felt the loop settle around him, and then another circled him and jerked him out of the saddle. He hit the ground hard, the breath knocked out of him.

Pearlie struggled to free himself of the stiff ropes, but he knew he was fighting a losing fight. He lifted his six-gun and thumbed the hammer back. He hated to do it, but he had to leave some proof of who had done this to him.

He shot a TF horse. The animal dropped almost immediately as the slug entered behind its left shoulder and shattered the heart. The rider cursed and jumped free, kicking the six-gun out of Pearlie's hand.

"Drag the son of a bitch!" the horseless rider yelled.

Pearlie was jerked along the ground. Mercifully, his head struck a rock and he was dropped into the darkness of unconsciousness.

"Did you hear a shot!" Sally called.

"Yes'um!" Bob called back. "Probably Pearlie shootin' a rattler, is all."

"Maybe," Sally muttered. She went back into the house and strapped on a pistol. She picked up a rifle and levered a round into the chamber of the Henry. Back outside, she called, "Bob! Are you armed?"

"Yes'um. Got a short gun on and my rifle is right down there." He pointed.

"Get your rifle and stay in the loft. Keep a look-out for riders. I think we're in for some trouble."

"Yes'um!"

"While you're getting your rifle, close and bar all the barn doors. I'll bring Seven inside and put him in a stall."

"Yes'um, Miss Sally."

Sally hurriedly fixed containers of water and a basket of food for the boy. She put in several boxes of ammunition and carried it to him in the barn. "We might be in for a long day, Bob," she told him. "And you might have to stay out here by yourself tonight."

"I ain't skirred, Miss Sally. I can knock the eye out of squirrel at a hundred yards with a rifle. If anybody comes to fight, we'll stand 'em off."

"Good boy. I'll be in the house. Let them come close, we'll catch them in a crossfire."

Bob grinned. "Yes, *ma'am!*"

It was as if some invisible messenger had passed the word. The town of Fontana grew quiet, then hushed almost entirely. Smoke walked across the street and stepped into the tent of Louis Longmont. Louis waved him to the bar.

"A pall has fallen over us, my young friend," Louis said.

"I'm sure it concerns you. Am I correct?"

"Uh-huh. Some of Franklin's men are setting me up for a killing."

"And naturally, you're going to leave town in a cloud of dust, right?"

"Sure, Louis. You know that."

"How many?"

"Five." Smoke named them.

"Valentine is a bad one. I know him. He's a top gun from down near the Tex-Mex border. Watch him. He's got a border roll that's fast as lightning."

"Yeah, I've heard he's good. How good?"

"Very good," the gambler said softly. "He beat Johnny North."

A smile passed Smoke's lips. "But Johnny North is still alive."

"Precisely."

So Valentine was cat-quick, but couldn't shoot worth a damn. Many quick-draw gunhands were blindingly fast, but usually missed their first shots.

Smoke almost never missed.

"I'll back you up if you ask, Smoke," Louis offered.

"It'll come to that, Louis. But not yet. Speaking of Johnny North, where is he?"

"A question I've asked myself a few times since coming here. He'll be here. But he's a strange one, Smoke. He hates Monte Carson."

"So I hear. I've never heard of him teaming up with anyone."

"Lone wolf all the way. Johnny must be . . . oh, about my age, I suppose. But age has not slowed him a bit. When do you meet these gentlemen, and where?"

Smoke opened his watch. "In about fifteen minutes. Down at the stables."

"Anything you need?"

"A shotgun and a pocketful of shells."

Louis reached over the bar and pulled out a sawed-off twelve-gauge express gun. He handed Smoke a sack of shells.

"I loaded these myself," the gambler said. "Full of ball-bearings."

Smoke loaded the express gun. "Got a taste of that scotch handy?"

Louis walked behind the long, deserted bar and poured two fingers of scotch for each of them. He lifted his glass. "To your unerring marksmanship."

"And hope I shoot straight too," Smoke said needling the man.

13

Pearlie opened his eyes. He could have sworn he opened his eyes. But he couldn't see a thing. Slowly, painfully, he lifted one hand and wiped his eyes. There. He could see . . . a little bit, at least.

He hurt all over. He wriggled his toes. Something was wrong. His boots were gone. He could feel the cool earth against his skin. His jeans were ripped and his shirt was gone. He carefully poked at himself. He was bruised and cut and torn from head to toes, but he didn't feel any broken bones sticking out. Lucky. Damn lucky.

Pearlie turned his head and felt something flop down over one ear. He carefully inspected his fingertips. A flap of skin was torn loose. He pressed it back against his head and took his bandana from around his neck, tying it around his head. Hurt like hell.

Only then did he think of the danger he might still be in. What if the TF riders were still hanging around?

He looked around him.

Nothing and nobody in sight.

He slowly drew himself up to his knees and looked around. He could clearly see where he had been dragged. He looked down where he had lain. A hole in the hard ground, blood beside it. He stuck a finger into the hole and pulled out the dirt. His fingers touched something hard. Pearlie dug it out and looked at it. A battered and mangled .44 slug. The bastards had shot him. They thought they'd killed him with a gunshot to the head. That would account for the flap of skin hanging down.

"Boy, you was lucky," he croaked, pushing the words out of a dry throat.

He looked back along the torn path he'd been dragged on. It ran for a ways back toward the cabin. He could see one boot standing all alone in the mangled path. He rose unsteadily to his feet and staggered back toward the boot, one solid mass of aches and pains and misery.

And mad.

Goddamn, was he mad!

He picked up the boot and wandered off in search of his other boot. Pearlie fell down more times than he cared to recall. He banged and bruised and battered his knees and hands each time he fell, but each time he hit the ground, his anger increased. He began cursing Tilden Franklin and all the TF riders who had dragged him and then left him for dead.

The verbal barrage seemed to help.

He found his other boot and sat down to rest, slipping on both his boots. Now he felt better. He could see, just barely, the fallen horse of the TF man. He walked and staggered and stumbled toward it. The animal had fallen on its left side; no way Pearlie could get to the rifle in the saddle boot. But he could salvage the canteen full of water. He sat on the rump of the dead horse and drank his fill. His eyes swept the immediate area. He spotted his six-gun and walked to it, picking it up. He brushed off the dirt, checked the action and the loads, and holstered the weapon. Now he felt better than ever. He dug in the saddlebags of the fallen horse and found a box of .44's, distributing them in his pockets.

Now, by God, just let me find some TF punchers! he thought. He managed to pull the other saddlebag from under the dead horse and rummage through it. Some cold biscuits and beef. As tired and as much as he hurt, he knew he had to have something to eat. Them bearsign was good eatin', but they didn't stay with a man.

He ate the beef and biscuits and washed them down with water. He looked toward the direction of the ranch. A good four or five miles off. With an explosive oath, Pearlie stood up and began walking. Miss Sally and the boy was probably in for a rough time of it. And by *God*, Pearlie was gonna be there to help out.

He put one boot in front of the other and walked and staggered on.

Drops of blood marked his back trail.

Smoke didn't know where all the people had gone, but the streets of Fontana were empty and silent as he walked along, keeping to the near side of the long street, advancing toward the stable.

But he could feel many eyes on him as he walked.

He slipped the thongs from his Colts as he walked, shifting the sawed-off express from right hand to left hand. He looked up as the batwing doors of a saloon swung open. Tilden Franklin and his foreman, Clint, stepped out to stare at Smoke. The new sheriff, Monte Carson, stood beside them, his large, new, shiny badge catching the late-morning rays of the sun.

"We don't like troublemakers in this town, Smoke," Monte said.

Smoke stopped and turned to face the men. With his eyes on Monte, he said, "What trouble have I caused, Sheriff?"

That took Monte aback. He stared at Smoke. Finally, he said, "Man walks around carrying a shotgun like that one there you got must be lookin' for trouble."

Smoke grinned. "Why, Sheriff, I'm just going down to the stables to see about my horse. Any law against that?"

Monte shook his head.

"Thanks. If there is nothing else, I'll just be on my way."

Tilden grinned at Smoke. His mean eyes shone with evil and power.

Smoke met the man's eyes. "How about you, Franklin? You got anything to say?"

"You talk mighty big standing there with that express gun in your hands," Tilden replied.

"Insurance, Franklin," Smoke said. "Since you're afraid to move without your trained dogs with you."

That stung Clint. His eyes narrowed and his hands balled

into fists. But he knew better than to prod Smoke; the gunfighter's rep was that his temper was volatile, and that express gun would turn all three of them into chopped meat at this distance.

"That's right, Clint," Smoke said, a nasty tone to his words. "I forgot. You'd rather make war against farmers and women and kids, wouldn't you?"

"Stand easy, Clint," Tilden quietly warned his foreman.

Smoke laughed and turned, continuing his walking down the street.

Billy darted from the corral and pressed against the side of a newly erected building. "They're all over the place, Smoke," he called in a stage whisper. "Two of 'em up in the loft."

Smoke nodded his thanks and said, "Get out of here, Billy. Hunt a hole."

Billy took off as if the devil was howling and smoking at his heels.

Smoke looked toward the corral. Horse was watching him, his ears perked up.

Smoke walked to the huge open doors and paused. He knew he would be blind for a few seconds upon entering the darkened stable. Out of habit, he rechecked the loads in the express gun and took a deep breath.

He slipped the thongs back on the hammers of his Colts and jumped inside the stable, rolling to his right, into an open stall.

Gunfire blasted the semi-darkness where Smoke had first hit the floor.

"Riders comin,' Miss Sally!" Bob called from the barn loft.

"How far off, Bob?" She called from the house.

"Bout a mile, ma'am. I can't make out no brand yet."

"If they're Circle TF, Bob," she called, "we'll blow them out of the saddle."

"Yes, *ma'am!*"

Woman and boy waited, gripping their rifles.

Pearlie found Lefty's horse and gently approached the

still-spooked animal. The horse shied away. Pearlie sat down on a large rock and waited, knowing that the horse would eventually come to him, desiring human company. In less than five minutes, while Pearlie hummed a low tune, the animal came to him and shoved at the puncher with its nose. Pearlie petted the animal, got the reins, and swung into the saddle. Lefty's rifle was in the boot and Pearlie checked it. Full. Pearlie pointed the animal's nose toward the ranch.

"Let's go boy," Pearlie said, just as the sounds of gunfire reached him. "I wanna get in a shot or two myself."

Sally's opening shot knocked a TF rider out of the saddle. Bob squeezed off a round, the slug hitting a TF gunhawk in the center of his chest. The puncher was dead before he hit the ground. With only three gunslicks left out of the original half a dozen, those three spun their horses and lit a shuck out of that area.

They ran right into Pearlie, coming at them at full gallop. With the reins in his teeth, his right hand full of Colt and his left hand full of Henry rifle, Pearlie emptied two saddles. The last TF rider left alive hunched low in the saddle and made it over a rise and out of range. He then headed for the ranch. They'd been told they were going up against Pearlie and one little lady. But it seemed that Pearlie was as hard to kill as a grizzly and that that little lady had turned into a bobcat.

Meanwhile, Pearlie reined up in a cloud of dust and jumped out of the saddle. "You folks all right?" he yelled.

"My God, Pearlie!" Sally rushed out of the house. "What happened to you?"

"They roped and drug me," Pearlie said. "Then shot me. But they made a bad mistake, ma'am."

She looked at him.

"They left me alive," Pearlie said, his words flint hard.

Smoke darted into the darkness of the first stall just as the lead tore smoking holes where he'd first hit. Rolling to one side, Smoke lifted the sawed-off express gun and eared back both hammers and waited.

"Got the punk!" someone hissed.

"Maybe," a calmer voice spoke from just above Smoke.

Smoke lifted the sawed-off and pulled both triggers. The express gun roared and bucked, and ball-bearing loads tearing a great hole in the loft floor. The "maybe" man was flung out of the loft, both loads catching him directly in the crotch, almost tearing him in half. He lay on the stable floor, squalling as his blood stained the horse-shit-littered boards.

Smoke rolled to the wall of the stall, reloaded the express gun, and jumped over the stall divider, into the next stall. His ears were still ringing from the tremendous booming of the sawed-off.

Quietly, he removed his spurs and laid them to one side.

He heard someone cursing, then someone else said, "Jensen shot him where he lived. That ain't right."

The mangled man had ceased his howling, dying on the stable floor.

Smoke waited.

As he had expected, Sheriff Monte Carson was making no effort to interfere with the ambush.

So much for the new law and order in Fontana.

Smoke waited, motionless, his callused hands gripping the express gun. His mentor, Preacher, had taught Smoke well, teaching him, among other things, patience.

One of Tilden's gunhands lost his patience and began tossing lead around where he suspected Smoke to be. He was way off target. But Smoke wasn't.

Smoke blew the man out of the loft, the loads taking him in the belly, knocking him backward. He rolled and thrashed and screamed the pain finally rolling him off the edge and dropping him to the ground floor.

Smoke heard one man jump from the loft and take off running. The others ran out the back and disappeared.

Smoke waited for a long ten-count, then slipped out the front door. He made sure all watching saw him reload the sawed-off shotgun. Then he walked straight up the dusty street to where Tilden and Monte were standing. Still in the street, Smoke wondered where Clint had gotten off to. No matter. Clint might ride for a sorry no-account, but the man was not a backshooter. Smoke knew that much about him.

Looking straight at Tilden, Smoke said, "Two of your men are on the stable floor. One is dead and I imagine the other won't live long the way he's shot. Your other hands lost their nerve and ran. Maybe you told them to ambush me, maybe you didn't. I don't know. So I won't accuse you of it."

Tilden stood still, smoking a thin cigar. But his eyes were filled with silent rage and hate.

Smoke looked at Monte. "You got anything you want to say to me, Sheriff?"

Monte wanted desperately to look at Tilden for some sign. But he was afraid to take his eyes off Smoke. He finally shook his head. "I reckon not."

"Fine." Smoke looked at Tilden. "See you 'round, Franklin." He knew the man despised to be called by his last name.

Smoke turned and walked to Louis Longmont's place. He handed Louis the shotgun and walked across the street to join the Easterners.

"Go get my horse, Billy. And stay out of the barn until someone cleans up the mess."

"Yes, sir!"

"Is that . . . it?" Hunt asked.

"That's it, Lawyer," Smoke told him. "Out here, for the time being, justice is very swift and short."

Smoke looked at Ed Jackson.

"I'd suggest you bear that in mind," Smoke told him.

14

Tilden sat at a table in a saloon. By himself. The kingpin rancher was in a blue funk and everybody knew it. So they wisely left him alone.

Those six gunhands he'd sent to ambush Jensen were among the best he'd had on his payroll. And they'd failed. And to make matters worse, Jensen had made Tilden look like a fool . . . in front of Monte and countless others who were hiding nearby.

Intolerable.

Tilden emptied his shot glass and refilled it from the bottle. Lifting the shot glass filled with the amber liquid to his lips, Tilden glanced down at the bottle. More than half empty. That too was intolerable. Tilden was not a heavy-drinking man, not a man who liked his thoughts muddled.

He set the shot glass on the table and pushed it from him. He looked up as one of his punchers—he couldn't remember the man's name and that irritated him further—entered the saloon and walked quickly up to Clint, whispering in the foreman's ear.

The foreman stiffened and gave the man a dark look, then cut his eyes to Tilden.

Tilden Franklin rose from the table and walked to Clint and the cowboy. "Outside," he said.

In the shade offered by the awning, the men stood on the boardwalk. "Say it," Tilden ordered the cowboy-gunhand.

"Lefty and five others went over to the Sugarloaf to drag Pearlie. Only one come back and he was shot up pretty bad.

95

He said they drug Pearlie a pretty fair distance and then shot him in the head. But he ain't dead, boss. And they was two people at Jensen's spread. Both of them trigger-pullers."

"Son of a *bitch*!" Tilden cursed low.

"And that ain't all, boss. Billy was over to our western range drivin' the beeves back to the lower slopes. He seen a campfire, smelled beans cookin'. Billy taken off over there to run whoever it was off the range. When he got there, he changed his mind. It was Charlie Starr."

Tilden thought about that for a few seconds. He didn't believe it. Last word he'd had of Charlie Starr was five, six year back, and that news had been that Starr had been killed in a gunfight up in Montana.

He said as much.

The puncher shook his head. "Billy seen Charlie over in Nevada, at Mormon Station, seven, eight years ago. That's when Charlie kilt them four gunslicks. Billy bought Charlie a drink after that, and they talked for nearabouts an hour. You've heard Billy brag about that, boss. It ain't likely he'd forget Charlie Starr."

Tilden nodded his head in agreement. It was not very likely. Charlie Starr. Mean as a snake and just as notional as a grizzly bear. Wore two guns, tied down low, and was just as good with one as the other. Charlie had been a number of things: stagecoach guard, deputy, marshal, gambler, outlaw, gunfighter, bounty hunter, miner . . . and a lot of other things.

Charlie was . . . had to be close to fifty years old. But Tilden doubted that age would have slowed him down much. If any.

And Charlie Starr hated Tilden Franklin.

As if reading his thoughts, Clint said, "You don't think . . ."

"I don't know, Clint." He dismissed the cowboy and told him to get a drink. When the batwings had swallowed the cowboy, Tilden said, "That was more than fifteen years ago, Clint. Seventeen years to be exact. I was twenty-three years old and full of piss and vinegar. I didn't know that woman belonged to Charlie. Damnit, she didn't tell me she did.

96

Rubbing all over me, tickling my ear. I had just ramrodded a herd up from Texas and was hard-drinkin' back then." He sighed. "I got drunk, Clint. I've told you that much before. What I haven't told you was that I got a little rough with the woman later on. She died. I thought she liked it rough. Lots of women do, you know. Anyway, I got the word that Charlie Starr was gunning for me. I ordered my boys to rope him and drag the meanness out of him. They got a little carried away with the fun and hurt him bad. He was, so I'm told, a long time recovering from it. Better part of a year. Word got back to me over the years that Charlie had made his brag he was going to brace me and kill me."

"I seen him up on the Roaring Fork nine, ten years ago," Clint said. "Luis Chamba and that Medicine Bow gunslick braced him. Chamba took a lot of lead, but he lived. The other one didn't."

"Where is Chamba?"

"Utah, last I heard."

"Send a rider. Get him."

"Yes, sir."

It was full dark when Smoke saw the lights shining from the windows of the cabin. He had pushed Horse hard, and the big stallion was tired, but game. Smoke rubbed him down, gave him an extra ration of corn, and turned him loose to roll.

When he opened the door to the cabin and saw Pearlie's battered and torn face, his own face tightened.

"He'll tell you over dinner," Sally said. "Wash up and I'll fix you a plate."

Over a heaping plate of beef and potatoes and gravy and beans flavored with honey, with bearsign for dessert, Pearlie told his story while Smoke ate.

"If there was any law worth a damn in this country I could have Tilden arrested," Smoke said, chewing thoughtfully.

"I don't even know where the county lines are," Pearlie said. He would have liked another doughnut, but he'd already eaten twenty that day and was ashamed to ask for another.

With a smile, Sally pushed the plate of bearsign toward him.

"Well," Pearlie said. "Maybe just *one* more."

"What county does our land lie in, Smoke?" Sally asked.

"I don't know. I'm not sure. It might be split in half. And that's something to think about. But . . . I don't know. You can bet that when it comes to little farmers and little ranchers up against kingpins like Tilden, the law is going to side with the big boys. Might be wiser just to keep the law out of this altogether."

"I thought you folks had bought most of your land and filed on the rest?" Pearlie said.

"We have," Smoke told him. "And it's been checked and it's all legal. But they surveyed again a couple of years ago and drew up new lines. I never heard anymore about it."

"Mister Smoke?" Bob asked, from a chair away from the adults.

"Yes, Bob?"

"Who is Charlie Starr?"

Smoke sopped up the last of his gravy with a thick hunk of bread and chewed for a moment. "He's a gunfighter, Bob. He's been a lot of things, but mostly he's a good man. But a strange one. I met him while I was riding with an old Mountain Man called Preacher. Why do you ask?"

"I heard them Jones boys talkin' last week. When we was all gathered over to the Matlocks' for Sunday services. That feller who sometimes works for Mister Matlock said Charlie Starr's been camped out around this country for a month or so."

"I can't believe Charlie is in here to hire his gun out to Tilden. He never has hired his guns out against a little man. He's done a lot of things, but he kinda backed into his rep as a gunslick. Maybe that fellow was mistaken?"

"Maybe, Mister Smoke."

Charlie Starr shifted his blankets away from his fire and settled in for the night. He smiled in the darkness, the sounds of his horse cropping grass a somehow comforting sound in the night. Since that puncher had come up on him, he'd moved his location — out of, he thought, the TF range. High up in the mountains, where snow was still capping the crests, above some place called the Sugarloaf. Nice-sounding name, Charlie thought.

Louis Longmont sat at a table playing stud, winning, as usual. Winning even though his thoughs were not entirely on the game. He'd just that evening heard the rumors that Charlie Starr was in the area, and heard too that Tilden Franklin had sent a rider to Utah to get Luis Chamba, the Sonora gunslick. And he'd heard that Tilden was building up his own forces by half a hundred riders.

Louis pulling in his winnings and excused himself from the game. His mind wasn't on it and he needed a breath of air. He walked outside, into the rambunctious, boom-town night air. The town was growing by hundreds each day. Most of the men were miners or would-be miners, but there was a lot of trash mixed in as well.

With this many people working the area, the town might last, Louis thought, six months — maybe less. There was a strong urge within the man to just fold his tent and pull out. Louis felt there would be a bloodbath before everything was said and done.

But Louis couldn't do that. He'd given his word to Preacher he'd look in on Smoke from time to time. Not that Smoke needed any looking after, Louis thought with a grin. But a man's word was his bond. So Louis would see it through. He tossed his cigar into the street and walked back into his gaming tent.

Tilden Franklin sat alone in his huge house, his thoughts as savage as much of the land that lay around him. His thoughts would have made a grizzly flinch. Tilden had never seen a woman that he desired more than Sally Jensen. Educated, aloof, beautiful. Tilden wondered how she'd look

99

with her dress on the floor.

He shook that thought from him.

Then, with a faint smile curving his lips, he thought about the nester Colby. More specifically, Colby's daughter. Velvet.

Tilden laughed. He thought he knew how to get rid of that nester, and let his boys have some fun in the process.

Yeah. He'd give it some extra thought in the morning. But it seemed like a pretty good idea.

Billy lay on the hay in the loft, in his longjohns, his new clothing carefully folded and stored on a little ledge. His thoughts were of Smoke. Billy wondered how it would be to have a pa like Smoke. Probably real nice. There was a streak of gentleness in the gunfighter that few adults could see. But a kid could see it right off. Smoke for a pa. Well, was something to dream about. One thing for sure, nobody would mess with you, leastways.

Ed Jackson lay by his wife's side and mentally counted all the money he was going to make. He'd hired some rough-looking men that day, promising them a grubstake if they'd build his store for him. They had accepted. Ed Jackson dreamed of great wealth. Ed Jackson dreamed of becoming a very important person. Maybe even someone like Tilden Franklin.

Now there was a *really* important man.

Paul Jackson lay in his blankets under a wagon. He was restless, sleep was elusive. He kept thinking about the way Bountiful had looked at him. Something was building between them, he just knew it. And Paul also knew that he wasn't going to hang around here with his stupid, greedy brother any longer than necessary. If he could find gold, that would really make Bountiful sit up and take notice of him.

He grinned.

Or lay down and take notice of him.

Dana lay by her husband, listening to him breathe as he slept. She wondered if they'd made a mistake in coming out West. Haywood didn't think so, but she'd wondered often about it, especially during the last few days. These men out here, they took violent death so . . . so calmly. It frightened her.

Colton closed up his tent and put his money, some of it in gold dust, into a lockbox and carefully stowed it away in the hidden compartment under the wagon. He was tired, but he'd made more money in just two days than most physicians back East made in a month—maybe two months. If this kept up, he'd have enough to travel on to California and set up a practice in real style. In a place that had some class, with a theater and opera and all the rest that civilized people craved. At this rate, he'd have far more than enough in a year's time.

He washed his hands and made ready for bed.

Hunt was wide awake, his thoughts many and most of them confused. True, he'd been busy all day handling gold claims, but no one had come to him for any legal advice concerning the many fights and stabbings and occasional shootings that occurred within the town of Fontana. He simply could not understand that. Didn't these people understand due process? All those fistfights and gunfights. It was positively barbaric. And so needless. All people had to do was come see him; then they could handle it in a proper court of law.

If, Hunt thought with a grimace, they could find the judge when he was sober.

15

Leaving Pearlie with Sally, Smoke escorted Bob back to his home. For the first time since arriving in the area, Smoke saw both Wilbur Mason and Colby armed with short guns and rifles. Dismounting, Smoke ground-reined Drifter and faced the farmer-ranchers.

"Seen any of the others?" Smoke asked.

"Nolan rode by yesterday evenin'," Colby said. "He's scared and admitted it."

"Ray and Betty sent word that they're with us all the way," Mason said.

"How about Peyton?"

Both men shrugged.

"I think he'll stand," Smoke said. "Way he talked to me the other day, he'll stick. How's your food supply?"

"Plenty. The old woman canned enough last summer to last us for a good long time. Potato bin's half full. What's your plans, Smoke?"

Smoke brought them both up to date. Then he said, "I'm staying close to home. Shifting my cattle to a different graze. But if I need something in the way of supplies, nothing or nobody will keep me out of Fontana."

"When you decide to go in," Colby said, "I'll take my wagon and go in with you. The two of us can get supplies for everybody."

"Sounds good. We don't want to leave the whole area without menfolks. I'm going to talk with the others today. Get a better idea of where they stand. I'll see you both later

102

on."

Velvet came out of the house and walked to the well. Smoke's eyes followed her. She was a young girl, but built up like a grown woman. And that worried Smoke. Tilden was ruthless, might do anything. And some of the gunslicks riding for the TF brand were nothing more than pure white trash. They'd do anything Tilden ordered. While most Western men would not bother a good woman, there were always exceptions.

Colby had followed Smoke's eyes. "I still think you're wrong, Smoke. She's just a child."

"Tilden Franklin is a sorry son of a bitch," Smoke told the men. "Don't put anything past him." He swung into the saddle. "See you boys later."

Smoke rode hard that day, stopping in to see all the small outfits he thought might throw in with him and the others. And he had been correct in his thinking. Steve and Mike and Nolan and Ray all agreed to toss in, forming an alliance among all the small spreads. If one got hit, the others would respond.

Their lives and money were sunk deep into this land, and with many, some of their blood as well. They were not going to run.

"What's this talk about Charlie Starr, Smoke?" Nolan asked.

"So far as I know, just that—talk." He told the man what he knew about Starr. "I think, if he is in this area, he's here to kill Tilden Franklin. Lots of bad blood between those two. Goes back years, so the story goes. I'm going to try to pin the rumor down. When I do, I'll get back with you. Stay loose, Nolan, and keep an eye on your womenfolk. I have no way of knowing exactly what Tilden has in mind, but whatever it is, it's bad news for us, that's for sure."

"I'm not going to put up with these miners tearing up my land, Smoke," the rancher said. "If I have to shoot two or three of them, I will."

"Check your land title, Nolan. You might not have

103

mineral rights. Ever think about that?"

The farmer-rancher cursed. "I never thought about that. Could someone buy those rights without my permission?"

"I think so. The law is still kind of raw out here, you know that. I checked on my title last night. I own the mineral rights to my land."

"I just didn't think about it. I'll do just that. See you, Smoke."

Smoke spent a week staying close to home. He received no news about what might be happening in Fontana. Then, on a fine, clear, late spring day, Smoke decided to ride his valley. He found several miners' camps high up, and told the men to clear out—right then.

"And if we don't?" one bearded man challenged him.

"I'll kill you," Smoke told him, ice in the words.

"You talk big, mister," another miner said. "But I'm wonderin' if you got the sand to back up your words."

"My name is Smoke Jensen."

The miners cleared out within the hour.

With the sun directly over his head, Smoke decided to stop in a stand of timber and eat the lunch that Sally had prepared for him. He was just stepping down from the saddle when the smell of wood smoke reached him.

He swung back into the saddle and followed the invisible trail. It took him the better part of an hour to find the well-concealed camp, and when he found it, he knew he had come face to face with one of the most feared men in all the West.

Charlie Starr.

"Mind some company?" Smoke asked, raising his voice to be heard over the hundred yards or so that separated the men.

"Is this your land?" the man called.

"Sure is."

"Light and sit then. You welcome to share what I got."

"Thanks," Smoke said, riding in and dismounting. "My wife fixed me a bait of food."

Charlie Starr looked hard at Smoke. "Ain't I seen you afores?"

"Yes," Smoke told him, unwrapping the waxed paper Sally had used to secure his lunch. "Long time ago, up in Wyoming. I was with a Mountain Man called Preacher."

"Well, I'll just be damned if that ain't the truth! You've growed a mite, boy."

There was a twinkle in his eyes as he said it. And Smoke knew that Charlie Starr knew all about him.

Charlie's eyes flicked to Smoke's guns. "No notches. That's good. Only a tinhorn cuts his kills, and half of them are lies."

Smoke thought of Colby's boy, Adam. "I told that to a boy just the other day. I don't think he believed me."

"He might not live to be a man, thinking like that." Charlie's eyes lit up as he spotted the bearsign in Smoke's sack. "Say, now!"

Smoke halved his doughnuts and Charlie put them aside for dessert. "Much obliged, Smoke. Have some coffee."

Smoke filled his battered tin cup and settled back to enjoy his lunch among the mountains flowers and trees and cool but pleasant breezes.

"You wonderin' why I'm squatted on your range?" Charlie asked.

"Stay as long as you're friendly, Charlie." Smoke spoke around a mouthful of beef and bread.

Charlie laughed. "And you'd brace me too, wouldn't you, young man?"

Younger eyes met older eyes. Both sets were flint hard and knowing.

"I'd try you, Charlie."

Charlie chuckled and said, "I killed my first man 'fore you was even a glint in your daddy's eyes, Smoke. Way before. How old do you think I am, Smoke?"

"You ain't no young rooster."

Again, the gunfighter laughed. "You shore right about that. I'm fifty-eight years old. I killed my first man when I was fourteen, I think it was. That's be, uh, back in '36, I reckon."

"I was fourteen when I killed an Indian, I think we were

105

in Kansas."

"You don't say? I'm be damned. Some folks would say that an Injun don't count, but I ain't one of them folks. Injuns is just like us . . . but different."

Smoke stopped chewing and thought about that. He had to smile. "You don't look your age, Charlie."

"Thank you. But on cold mornin's I shore feel it. Seen me a bunch of boomers headin' this way. They made it to No-Name yet?"

"No-Name is now Fontana. Oh, yeah, the boomers made it and are still coming in."

"Fontana," Charlie said softly. "Right pretty name." His voice had changed, becoming low-pitched and deadly. "Fontana. Now what do you think about that."

Smoke said nothing. Preacher had told him the story about Charlie's girl, Rosa Fontana, and about Tilden Franklin killing the girl and dragging Charlie.

The men ate in silence for a time, silently enjoying each other's company. While they ate, they eyeballed each other when one thought the other wasn't looking.

Smoke took in Charlie's lean frame. The man's waist was so thin he looked like he'd have to eat a dozen bearsign just to hold his britches up. Like most cowboys, his main strength lay in his shoulders and arms. The man's wrists were thick, the hands big and scarred and callused. His face was tanned and rugged-looking. Charlie Starr looked like a man who would be hard to handle in any kind of fight.

Then Smoke had an idea; an idea that, if Charlie was agreeable, would send Tilden Franklin right through the roof of his mansion in fits of rage.

"You always sit around a far grinnin', boy?" Charlie asked.

"No." Smoke had not realized he was grinning. "But I just had me an idea."

"Must have been a good'un."

"You lookin' for work, Charlie?"

"Not so's you'd notice, I ain't."

"My wife is one of the best cooks in the state."

"Keep talkin.' " He picked up a doughnut and nibbled at

it. Then he stuffed the whole thing in his mouth.

"Wouldn't be a whole lot to do. I got one hand. Name's Pearlie."

"Rat good with a gun, is he?"

"He'll do to ride the river with. Some of Tilden's boys hung a rope on him last week and dragged him a piece." Smoke kept his voice bland, not wanting Charlie to know that he knew about the bad blood between Starr and Franklin. Or why. "Then they shot him in the head. Pearlie managed to live and get lead in two of them. He's back working a full day now."

Charlie grunted. "Sounds like he'll do, all rat. What is he, half 'gator?"

"He's tough. I'll pay you thirty and found."

"Don't need no job. But . . ."

Smoke waited.

"Your wife make these here bearsign now and then, does she?"

"Once a week."

"I come and go as I please long as my work's caught up?"

"Sure. But I have to warn you . . . they'll probably be some shooting involved, and . . . well, with you getting along in years and all, I wouldn't blame you if you turned it down."

Charlie fixed him with a look that would have withered a cactus. Needles and all.

"Boy, are you out of your gawddamned mind or just born slow?"

"Well, no, Charlie . . . but they're gonna be broncs to bust, and with your age and all, I was just . . ."

Charlie threw his battered hat on the ground. "Gawd-damn, boy, I ain't ready for no old folks' home just yet!"

"Now, don't get worked up, Charlie. You're liable to have a heart attack, and I don't know nothing about treating heart attacks."

Charlie turned blue around the mouth and his eyes bugged out. Then he began to relax and chuckle. He wiped his eyes and said, "Shore tell Preacher had a hand in your up-bringin', Smoke." He stuck a hard, rough hand across the hat-sized fire. "You got you a man that'll ride the river with you, Smoke Jensen."

Smoke took the hand and a new friendship was born.

16

On the slow ride back to the ranch, Smoke discovered that Charlie and Preacher shared one common bond. They both liked to bitch.

And like Preacher's had been, Charlie's complaints were numerous . . . and mostly made up.

"I stayed in a hospital a week one time," Charlie informed him. "Them doctors found more wrong with me than a human body ought to have to suffer. I swear, if I'd stayed in there another week, I'd have probably died. They told me that no human bein' could be shot twenty-two times and still live. I told them I wasn't shot no twenty-two times, it was twenty-five times, but three of them holes was in a place they wasn't about to look at.

"Boy, was I wrong!"

Smoke was laughing so hard he had to wipe his eyes with a bandana.

"Nurse come in that first day. That was the homeliest-lookin' female I ever did see. Looked like a buffalo. Told me to hike up that gown they had me in. I told her that her and no two others like her was big enough to make me do that.

"I was wrong agin.

"I want to warn you now, Smoke. Don't never get around me with no rubber tubin'. Don't do it. I'm liable to go plumb bee-serk. Them hospitals, boy, they got a thing about flushin' out a man's system. Stay away from hospitals, boy, they'll kill you!"

Pearlie was clearly in awe. Not only was he working for Smoke Jensen, but now Smoke had done gone and hired Charlie Starr.

"Shut your mouth, boy," Charlie told him. "Afore you swaller a bug."

Pearlie closed his mouth.

Charlie was clearly taken aback when Sally came out of the cabin to meet him . . . dressed in men's jeans. With a pistol belted around her tiny waist.

Wimmin just didn't have no business a-runnin' around in men's pants. They'd be smokin' cigarette's 'fore long.

But he forgot all about that when she said, "Fresh apple pie for dessert, Mister Starr."

"Charlie, ma'am. Just Charlie."

The sun was just settling over the Sugarloaf when Sally called them in for dinner. Steaks, beans, potatoes, fresh-baked bread, and apple pie.

Smoke and Sally both noted that, for such a spare fellow, Charlie could certainly eat.

After Charlie had sampled his plate and pleased his palate, he said, "Bring me up to date, Smoke."

Smoke told him what he knew, and then what he guessed. Including Tilden's desires for Sally.

"That's his way, all right," Charlie said, Then he leveled with them, speaking slowly, telling them about Rosa. "Way I hear it, Tilden fancied that she was comin' up on him. But that was her job, hostess at a saloon. Rosa had part of the action, owned about twenty-five percent of it. When I come to in the hospital, after Tilden's boys drug me, Louis told me what really happened."

Smoke glanced at the man. "Louis!"

Charlie grinned grimly. "Louis Longmont. It was one of his places. And you know Louis don't tolerate no pleasure ladies workin' for him. That's more Big Mamma O'Neil's style. Louis was considerable younger then, and so was I. Louis said one of his bouncers saw it all . . . well, most of it. Tilden was so drunk he got it all wrong. And when Rosa tried to break a-loose from him, he started slappin' her around. Bad. The bouncers come runnin', but Tilden's

110

hands held them at bay whilst he took Rosa in the back room and . . ." He paused, looking at Sally. ". . . had his way with her. Then he killed her. Broke her neck with his bare hands. You see, one of them doctors in that damnable hospital told me, once I got to trust the feller, that Tilden ain't quite right in the head. He's got the ability to twist things all around, and make the bad look good and so forth. He shapes things the way he wants them to be in his mind. I disremember the exact word the doc used. That buffler-faced nurse come by 'bout that time with some rubber tubin' in her hands and things kinda went hazy on me."

"What nurse?" Sally asked.

"I'll tell you later," Smoke said.

Charlie said, "Me and Rosa was gonna get married in the spring. I was unconscious for several days; didn't even get to go to her buryin'." He sighed deeply. "Course, by the time I got on my feet, Tilden and his bunch was long gone. I lost track of him for a time, but by then the fires inside me had burned low. I still hated the man, but I had to make a livin' and didn't have no idea where he might be. I been knowin' he was in this area for some years. I've drifted in and out half a dozen times, stayin' low, watching that low-life build his little kingdom. Then I had me an idea. I'd wait until he got real big, real powerful, real sure of himself. And then I'd kill him . . . slow."

Charlie laid down his knife and fork, pushed his empty plate from him, and stood up. "Bes' grub I've had in many a moon, ma'am. I thank you. Reckon I'll turn in now. Tomorrow I wanna roam the range for a couple of days, learn all the twists and turns and ways in and out. I seen me a cookstove in the bunkhouse. I'll fix me a poke before I pull out in the mornin'. Night, folks."

After the door had closed softly and the sounds of Charlie's jingling spurs had faded, Pearlie said, "I think Tilden Franklin's string has just about run out."

"That hombre who just walked out the door," Smoke said, "I believe means every word he said.

"Story goes that Charlie's folks was kilt by Injuns when he was just a little boy. He was raised by the Cheyenne. If

Charlie says he's gonna kill Tilden Franklin slow, that is exactly what he means."

For two days, Charlie prowled the Sugarloaf, getting his bearings and inspecting the cattle and horses that Smoke and Sally were raising.

"You want it known that you're working for me?" Smoke asked him upon his return to the ranch house.

"Don't make no difference to me, Smoke," the gunfighter said. "My bein' here ain't gonna make Tilden backpaddle none. Man sets out to be king, only thing that's gonna stop him is dyin'."

Smoke nodded his agreement. "I'll be gone for several days, Charlie. You and Pearlie stay close to the house, all right?"

"Will do."

Smoke pulled out early the next morning, riding Drifter. It was not like Tilden to wait, once his intentions became known; Smoke wanted to find out what the kingpin had up his sleeve.

As he rode, the sounds of drilling and hammers against rocks and occasional blasting came to him. The miners were in full swing. And they were paying no attention to the No Trespassing signs the farmer-ranchers had posted around their property. Bad trouble was building; the smell of it was in the air.

Smoke figured he'd better check in with Lawyer Brook as soon as he hit town.

"Smoke," the lawyer informed him, "there is nothing your friends can do, not legally."

"But it's their land!"

"But they don't hold the mineral rights to it. The holder of those rights has given the miners permission to mine. The miners get fifty percent, the holder of the rights gets fifty percent."

Smoke leaned back in his chair and built one of his rare

112

cigarettes from the cloth pouch he carried in his vest pocket. He licked the tube and smoothed it, lighting and inhaling before speaking.

"Let me guess," Smoke said. "Tilden Franklin bought all the mineral rights."

"Well . . . if you don't hear it from me, you'll hear it from somebody else. Yes, that is correct."

"It's legal stealing, Hunt."

"I wouldn't phrase it quite like that," the lawyer said stiffly.

"I just did," Smoke told him. He walked out of the lawyer's new offices.

The long building containing the offices of the lawyer, the doctor, and the newspaper had been put up in hurry, but it was well built nonetheless. Across the street, the big store of Ed Jackson was in business and doing quite well, Smoke observed, eyeballing the many heavily loaded wagons lined up behind it, waiting to be unloaded. And, surprisingly enough, Ralph Morrow's church was up—nearly completed. He walked across the small field to the church and located the minister.

"You do all this yourself, Ralph?" Smoke asked.

"Oh, no! Mister Franklin donated the money for the church and paid the workmen to build it. He's really a very fine man, Smoke. I think you're wrong about him."

Slick, Smoke thought. Very slick on Tilden's part. "Well, I'm happy about your church, Ralph. I wish you a great deal of success."

"Thank you, Smoke." The minister beamed.

Smoke rode to the stable and located Billy. "Take care of him, Billy. Lots of corn and rub him down."

"Yes, sir!"

Smoke walked over to Louis's place and stepped inside. The gambler was sitting at a table, having breakfast. He waved Smoke over.

"Saw you ride in just as I was getting up. Care for a late breakfast?"

"Sounds good."

The gambler called for his cook and ordered breakfast for Smoke. Looking at Smoke, he asked, "Have you spoken to the minister yet?"

Smoke's smile gave him his silent reply.

"Nice move on Franklin's part, don't you think?"

"Very Christian of the man."

Louis enjoyed a laugh at the sarcasm in Smoke's voice. "Slick on his part about the mineral rights."

"I'll tell you the same thing I told Lawyer Brook—it's nothing but legal stealing."

"Oh, I agree with you, Smoke. But it is legal. Were I you, I'd advise the others to walk lightly and don't start any shooting."

"It's their land, Louis. They have a right to protect their herds."

Louis chewed for a moment, a thoughtful look on his face. "Yes, they do," he finally spoke. He took a sip of coffee out of one of the fanciest cups Smoke had ever seen. One thing about Louis Longmont. When he traveled, he went first class all the way, carrying a cook, a valet, and a huge bodyguard with him at all times. The bodyguard usually acted as bouncer in Louis's place, and was rarely seen— except when there was trouble. And then he was seen by the troublemaker only very briefly . . . seconds before the troublemaker died in Mike's bare hands. Providing Louis didn't shoot the troublemaker outright.

Louis buttered a piece of toasted bread and then spread preserves on top of that. The preserves, Smoke was sure, were imported. "Smoke, you know, or I hope you do, that I will back you to the hilt . . . in whatever you do. Regardless of whether I think you are right or wrong. Preacher saved my life a number of times, and besides that, you are a very good young man. But whether our newly elected law is worth a tinker's damn or not, in this mineral rights matter Tilden Franklin is legal. And the law is on his side. Smoke, the land can be repaired. Another hole in the ground is not worth a shooting or a hanging. Your herds? Well, that is quite another matter." He glanced at Smoke, a twinkle in his hard eyes. "There is no law out here that says a man can't hang or shoot a rustler or a horse thief—if you get my drift."

Smoke got it. And he would pass the word to the other

small farmer-ranchers. Then they would ride out and advise the miners that there would be no trouble, providing the herds of cattle and horses were left alone. But trample over someone's garden, stampede one herd, cut out one beeve, or steal one horse, and someone was going to die.

And then, if any or all those things happened, they would have to have the raw nerve to carry the threat through.

The French chef placed a plate before Smoke. Smoke looked at the food on the plate. Damned if he knew what it was. He said as much.

Then the chef reached down with a lighted match, set fire to the stuff, and Smoke jumped out of his chair.

Louis had a good laugh out of that. "Sit down, Smoke. Enjoy your breakfast."

"Hell, I can't eat *fire*!"

The flames abated and the chef departed, chuckling. Louis smiled. "Those are *crepes suzette*, my young friend. This dish." He tapped another plate with a knife blade. "Is an *au jambon*."

"Do tell?"

"An omelette, with bits of ham," Louis explained. "Now eat and enjoy."

Them crap susies was a tad too sweet for Smoke's taste, but the omelette was tasty. He made a mental note to tell Sally about what he had had for a late breakfast. Maybe she'd heard of them; damned if he ever had.

"Either way," Smoke said, "I think we're all looking at a lot of trouble just up the road."

"I share your feelings, Smoke. But why not postpone it as long as possible. You know this strike is not going to last. In six months it will have seen its heyday."

"I can't figure you, Louis. I never . . ." He bit off the words just at the last possible second.

The gambler-gunfighter did not take umbrage at what he suspected Smoke had been about to say. Instead, he smiled and finished it for him. "Never knew me to back off from trouble, Smoke?"

"I apologize for thinking it, Louis."

Louis smiled and shook his head. "No need for any of

that—not between friends." He sighed. "But you're right, Smoke. I am trying to avoid trouble. Not for my sake," he was quick to add. "But for yours."

Smoke laid down his fork. "My sake?"

"Listen to me, my young friend. How many guns do you have? A dozen? Maybe fifteen at the most? Tilden has seventy-five hardcases right now and can pull in two hundred more anytime he wishes, and will. Talk is that Luis Chamba is on his way here. And where Luis goes, Sanderson and Kane go with him. Think about it."

Smoke thought about it, and the more he thought about it the madder he got. Louis saw his expression change and tried to calm the young man down.

"No, Louis. No. Don't you see what Tilden is trying to pull?"

"Of course I do, boy! But give it time. In six months this area of the country will be right back where it was a month ago. Farm and ranch country. This town will dry up with only a few of the businesses remaining. I'm betting Tilden won't want to be king of nothing."

"He won't be king of nothing, Louis. For if we don't fight, he'll kill us all one by one. He'll make some grand gesture of buying out the widows or the kids—through some god-damned lawyer—and then he'll own this entire section of the state of Colorado. Everything!"

Louis nodded his head. "Maybe you're right, Smoke. Maybe you're right. If that's the case, then you've got to start hiring guns of your own. You and your wife have the means to do so; if you don't, let me advance you the money."

Suddenly, Smoke thought of something. In a way it was a cruel thought, but it was also a way for a lot of broke, aging men to gather in one final blaze of glory. The more he thought about it, the better he liked it, and his mood began to lighten. But he'd have to bounce it off Charlie first.

"Why are you smiling, Smoke?" Louis asked.

"Louis, you're one of the best gamblers around, aren't you?"

"Some say I am one of the best in the world, Smoke. I should think my numerous bank accounts would back up that claim. Why do you ask?"

"Suppose you suddenly learned you were dying, or suppose some . . . well, call it fate . . . started dealing you bad hands and you ended up broke and old—anything along that line—and then someone offered you the chance to once more live in glory. Your kind of glory. Would you take it, Louis, or would you think the offer to be cruel?"

"What an interesting thought! Say now . . . cruel? Oh, no. Not at all. I would jump at the opportunity. But . . . what are you thinking of, Smoke? I'm not following this line of questioning at all."

"You will, Louis." Smoke stood up and smiled. His smile seemed to Louis to be rather mysterious. "You will. And I think you'll find it to your liking. I really believe you will."

Long after Smoke had plopped his hat on his head, left the gaming room, and ridden out of town, Louis Longmont had sat at the table and thought about what his young friend had said.

Then he began smiling. Soon the smile had turned to chuckling and the chuckling to hard laughter.

"Oh . . ." he managed to say over the pealing laughter. "I love it!"

17

Smoke sat with Sally, Pearlie, and Charlie. Charlie listened to what Smoke had on his mind and then leaned back in his chair, a broad smile on his face. He laughed and slapped his knee.

"Smoke, that's the bes' idee I've heard of in a long, long time. Cruel? No, sir. It ain't cruel. What you're talkin' about is what they do bes'. You give me the wherewithal and I'll have an even dozen here in a week, soon as I can get to a telegraph and get hold of them and get some money to them."

"Name them, Charlie."

"Oh . . . well, there's Luke Nations, Pistol Le Roux, Bill Foley, Dan Greentree, Leo Wood, Cary Webb, Sunset Hatfield, Crooked John Simmons, Bull Flagler, Toot Tooner, Sutter Cordova, Red Shingletown . . . give me time and I'll name some more."

Pearlie said, "But all them old boys is *dead*!"

"No, they ain't neither," Charlie corrected. "They just retared is all."

"Well . . ." Pearlie thought a moment. "Then they mus' be a hundred years old!"

"Naw!" Charlie scoffed at that. "You jus' a kid, is all. They all in their sixties."

"I've met some of them. Charlie, I don't want to be responsible for any of them going to their deaths."

"Smoke . . . it's the way they'd want it. If they all died, they'd go out thankin' you for the opportunity to show the world they still had it in them. Let them go out in a blaze of glory, Smoke."

Smoke thought about it. That was the way Preacher would have wanted to go. And those old Mountain Men three years back, that's how they had wanted it. "All right, Charlie. We'll give you the money and you can pull out at first light. Me and Pearlie will start adding on to the bunkhouse. How many do you think will be here?"

"When the word gets out, I'd look for about twenty-five or so." Charlie said it with a smile. "You gonna have to hire you a cook to help Miss Sally. Or you'll work her to a frazzle, Smoke."

"All right. Do you know an old camp cook?"

"Shore do. Dad Weaver. He can cook and he can still pull a trigger too. One about as good as the other."

"Hire him. Oh, 'fore I forget." He looked at Sally. "I had a late breakfast with Louis Longmont. His chef fed me crap susies."

"Fed you *what*?" Sally said.

"The chef set it on fire before he served me. I thought he'd lost his mind."

"You didn't eat it, did you?" Pearlie asked.

"Oh, yeah! It was pretty good. Real sweet."

"*Crepes suzette*," Sally said.

"That's it," Smoke said. "Say it again."

"You pronounce it . . . *krehp sew-zeht*. You all try to say it." They all tried. It sounded like three monkeys trying to master French.

"I feel like a plumb idiot!" Charlie said.

"What're those damned nesters up to?" Tilden Franklin asked his foreman.

"I can't figure it," Clint said. "They've all rode out and told the miners there wouldn't be no trouble as long as the miners don't spook their herds or trample their crops. They was firm, but in a nice way."

"Damn!" Tilden said. "I thought Jensen would go in shooting."

"So did I. You want us to maybe do a little night-ridin'?"

"No. I want this to be all the nesters' doing. Wait a minute. Yeah, I do want some night-riding. Send some of the boys out to Peyton's place. Rustle a couple head and leave the butchered carcasses close to some miners' camps. Peyton is hot-headed; he'll go busting up in there and shoot or hang some of them. While we stand clear."

Clint smiled. "Tonight?"

"Tonight."

Sheriff Monte Carson and his so-called deputies kept only a loose hand on the rowdy doings in Fontana. They broke up fistfights whenever they could get to them in time, but rarely interfered in a stand-up, face-to-face shootout. Mostly they saw to it that all the businesses — with the exception of Louis Longmont, Ed Jackson, and Lawyer Hunt Brook — paid into the Tilden kitty . . . ten percent of the gross. And don't hold none back. The deputies didn't bother Doctor Colton Spalding either. They'd wisely decided that some of them just might need the Doc's services sooner or later . . . probably sooner.

And, to make matters just a little worse, the town was attracting a small group of would-be gunslicks; young men who fancied themselves gunfighters and looked to make a reputation in Fontana. They strutted about with their pearl-handled Colts tied down low and their huge California spurs jangling. The young men usually dressed all in black, or in loudly colored silk shirts with pin-striped trousers tucked inside their polished boots. They bragged a lot about who they had faced down or shot, and did a lot of practicing outside the town limits. They were solid looking for trouble, and that trouble was waiting just around the corner for a lot of them.

The town of Fontana was still growing, both in businesses and population. It now could boast four hotels and half a dozen rooming houses. Cafes had sprung up almost as fast as the saloons and the hurdy-gurdy girls who made their dubious living in those saloons . . . and in the dirty cribs in the back rooms.

The mother lode of the vein had been located, and stages were rolling into town twice a day, to carry the gold from the assay offices and to drop off their load of passengers. Tilden Franklin had built a bank, The Bank of Fontana, and was doing a swift business. Supply wagons rolled and rattled and rumbled twenty-four hours a day, bringing in much-needed items to the various businesses.

To give the man a small amount of credit, Tilden Franklin had taken a hard look at His Town and quietly but firmly begun rearranging the business district. There were now boundaries beyond which certain types could not venture during specific hours. The red-light district lay at one end of Fontana, and just behind a long row of saloons and greasy-spoon cafes. Those ladies who worked in the red-light houses — in God We Trust, All Others Pay Cash — were not allowed past the invisible line separating the good people from the less desirable people during the time between seven in the morning and four in the afternoon. Heaven forbid that a "decent woman" should have to rub shoulders with . . . that other kind of lady.

Peyton had found the butchered carcass of two of his beeves close to a miner's camp.

"Take it easy," Smoke said trying to calm the older man. "Those miners have hit a solid strike over there. No reason for them to have rustled any of your cows. Think about it, Peyton. Look here," Smoke said, pointing. "These are horse tracks around these carcasses."

"So?" Peyton angrily demanded. "What the hell has that got to do with it?"

"Those miners are riding mules, Peyton."

That news brought the farmer-rancher up short and silent. He walked over and sat down on a fallen log. He thought about that news for a moment.

"We're not actin' like Tilden would like," Peyton said softly. "So he's tryin' to prod us into doin' something to blow the lid off. I was about to play right into his game, and he would have sent those so-called deputies up to arrest me, wouldn't he, Smoke?"

"Probably." Smoke had told none of the others about the old gunfighters on their way in. Charlie had returned from his travels, all smiles and good news.

The aging gunfighters would begin arriving at any time, trickling in alone or in pairs as they linked up on the trails and roads.

"Go on home," Smoke told the older man. "I'll go see the miners."

Smoke watched the man mount up and leave. He swung into the saddle and rode up toward the miners' camp. He hailed the camp and was told to come on in.

Briefly Smoke explained, but he made no mention of Tilden Franklin.

"Who would try to cause trouble, Smoke?" a burly miner asked.

"I don't know. But I just put the lid back on what might have been real trouble. You boys be careful from here on in. Tempers are frayed enough around here. The slightest thing could lit the fuse."

"We will. Smoke, you reckon Peyton and some of the others would mind if me and the boys pitched in and kind of helped around their places? You know . . . we're all pretty handy with tools . . . maybe some repair work, such as that?"

"I think it would be a hell of a nice move on your part." Smoke grinned and the miners grinned back. "And it's gonna irritate whoever it is trying to stir up trouble. I'll tell the others to look for you. I bet y'all would like some home-cooked grub too, wouldn't you?"

That brought a round of cheers from the miners, many of whom had families far away.

Smoke wheeled his horse and rode back down the mountain. Smoke the gunfighter had suddenly become Smoke the peacemaker.

"Nothing," Clint told Tilden. "Smoke made peace with the

miners. He figured it all out somehow."

"What's it going to take to prod those goddamned nesters into action?" Tilden asked. "I'm about out of ideas."

Clint didn't like what he was about to suggest, but Clint rode for the brand. Right or wrong. "The Colby girl."

Although it had originally been Tilden's idea, the more he thought about it, the less he liked it. Bother a good woman out West and a man was in serious trouble . . . and it didn't make a damn who you were or how much or how little you had.

"Risky, Clint." He met the man's eyes. "You have a plan?"

"Yes," the foreman said, and stepped across that narrow chasm that separated good from evil, man from rabid beast.

"How long will it take you to set it up?"

"A few days. Them nesters got to be going into town for supplies pretty soon."

Tilden nodded his head. "Do it."

"You better get some sort of platform, Boss," Pearlie told Smoke.

"Platform? What are you talking about?"

"Some of them old gunhands is pullin' in. I swear to God there oughta be a hearse followin' along behind 'em."

Smoke stepped out of the barn just as Charlie was riding up from the Sugarloaf range.

Smoke had never seen a more disreputable, down-at-the-heels-looking bunch in all his life. Some of them looked like they'd be lucky to see another morning break clear.

"See what I mean about that platform, Boss? I swear that them ol' boys is gonna hurt themselves gettin' off their horse."

Smoke had to smile. He was fondly recalling a bunch of Mountain Men who, at eighty, were as spry as many men half their age. "Don't sell them short, Pearlie. I got a hunch they're gonna fool us all."

"Hi, thar, Buttermilk!" Charlie called.

"Aaa-yeeee!" the old man hollered. "You get uglier ever' time I see you, Charlie."

"Talks funny too," Pearlie said.

"I seen now why he's called Buttermilk."

"Why?"

"That's probably all he can eat. He don't have any teeth!"

18

"*That* is The Apache Kid?" Sally said, speaking to Smoke. "I have heard stories about The Apache Kid ever since I arrived in the West. Smoke, he looks like he might topple over at any moment."

"That's him," Smoke said. "Preacher told me about him. And I'll make you a bet right now that that old man can walk all day and all night, stop for a handful of berries and take a sip of water, and go another twenty-four hours."

"I ain't dis-pootin' your word, Boss," Pearlie said. "But I'm gonna have to see it to believe it."

Smiling, Smoke bent down and picked up a small chunk of wood. "Apache!" he called.

The old, buckskin-clad man turned and looked at Smoke.

"A silver dollar says you can't knock it out of the air."

"Toss 'er, boy!"

Smoke tossed the chunk high into the air. With fifty-odd years of gunhandling in his past, Apache's draw was as smooth and practiced as water over a fall. He fired six times. Six times the hardwood chunk was hit, before falling in slivers to the ground.

"Jesus!" Pearlie breathed.

"That's six silver dollars you owe me," Apache said.

Smoke laughed and nodded his head. The Apache Kid turned to talk with Charlie.

"That Jensen?" Apache asked, as the other old gunfighters

listened.

"That's him."

"He as good as they say?" Bowie asked.

"I wouldn't want to brace him," Charlie said, paying Smoke the highest compliment one gunhand could pay to another.

"That good, hey?" Luke Nations asked.

"He's the best."

"I heared he was that," Dan Greentree said. "Rat nice of him to in-vite us on this little hoo-raw."

Smoke and Sally had gone into the cabin, leaving the others to talk.

Pearlie shyly wandered over to the growing knot of men. He was expecting to get the needle put to him, and he got just that.

"Your ma know you slipped away from the house, boy?" a huge, grizzled old man asked.

Pearlie smiled and braced himself. "You be Pistol Le Roux?"

"I was when I left camp this mornin'."

"I run arcost a pal of yourn bout three years ago—up on the Utah-Wyoming line. South of Fort Supply. Called hisself Pawnee."

"Do tell? How was ol' Pawnee?"

"Not too good. He died. I buried him at the base of Kings Mountain, north side. Thought you'd wanna know."

"I do and I 'preciate your plantin' him. Say a word over him, did you?"

"Some."

"This is Pearlie, Pistol."

"Pleased. Join us, Pearlie."

Pearlie stood silent and listened to the men talk. Charlie said, "This ain't gonna be no Sunday social, boys. And I'll come right up front and tell you that some of you is likely to be planted in these here mountains."

The sounds of horses coming hard paused Charlie. He waited until the last of the old gunslicks had dismounted and shook and howdied.

Charlie counted heads. Twenty of the hardest, most-

126

talked-about, and most legendary men of the West stood in the front yard of the sturdy little cabin. Only God and God alone knew how many men these randy old boys had put down into that eternal rest.

The Apache Kid was every bit of seventy. But could still draw and shoot with the best.

Buttermilk didn't have a tooth in his head, but those Colts belted around his lean waist could bite and snarl and roar.

Jay Church was a youngster, 'bout Charlie's age. But a feared gunhawk.

Dad Weaver was in his mid-sixties. He'd opened him a little cafe when he'd hung up his guns, but the rowdies and the punks hadn't left him alone. They'd come lookin' and he'd given the undertaker more business. He'd finally said to hell with it and taken off for the mountains.

Silver Jim still looked the dandy. Wearin' one of them long white coats that road agents had taken to wearing. His boots was old and patched, but they shined. And his dark short coat was kinda frayed at the cuffs, but it was clean. His Colts was oiled and deadly.

Ol' Hardrock. Charlie smiled. What could he say about Hardrock? The man had cleaned up more wild towns than any two others combined. Now he was aging and broke. But still ready to ride the high trails of the Mountain Men.

Charlie lifted his eyes and spotted Moody. Ol' Moody. Standin' away from the others, livin' up to his name. Never had much to say, but by the Lord he was as rough and randy as they could come.

Linch. Big and hoary and bearded. Never packed but one short gun. Said he never needed but one.

Luke Nations. A legend. Sheriff, marshal, outlaw, gunfighter. Had books wrote about him. And as far as Charlie knew, never got a dime out of any of them.

Pistol Le Roux. A Creole from down in Louisiana. As fast with a knife as with a gun . . . and that was plenty fast.

Quiet Bill Foley. Wore his guns cross-draw and had a border roll that was some quick.

Dan Greentree. Charlie had ridden many a trail with Dan. Charlie wondered if these mountain trails around Fontana would be their last to ride.

Leo Wood. Leo just might be the man who had brought the fast draw to the West. A lot of people said he was. And a lot of so-called fast guns had died trying to best him.

Cary Webb. Some said he owned a fine education and had once taught school back East. Chucked it all and came West, looking for excitement. Earned him a rep as a fast gun.

Sunset Hatfield. Supposed to be from either Kentucky or Tennessee. A crack shot with rifle or pistol.

Crooked John Simmons. Got that name hung on him 'cause he was as cross-eyed as anybody had ever seen. Had a hair-trigger temper and a set of hair-trigger Colts.

Bull Flagler. Strong as a bull and just as dangerous. Carried him a sawed-off shotgun with a pistol grip on his left side, a Colt on the other.

Toot Tooner. Loved trains. Loved 'em so much he just couldn't resist holding them up back some years. Turned lawman and made a damn good one. Fast draw and a dead shot.

Sutter Cordova. His mother was French and his dad was Spanish. Killed a man when he was 'bout ten or eleven years old; man was with a bunch that killed his ma and pa. Sutter got his pa's guns, mounted up, and tracked them from Chihuahua to Montana Territory. Took him six years, but he killed every one of them. Sutter was not a man you wanted to get crossways of.

Red Shingletown. Still had him a mighty fine mess of flamin' red hair. He'd been a soldier, a sailor, an adventurer, a rancher . . . and a gunfighter.

And there they stood, Smoke thought, gazing at the men from the cabin. I'm looking at yet another last of a breed.

But did I do right in asking them to come?

Sally touched his arm. Smoke looked down at her.

"You did the right thing," she told him. "The trail that lies before those men out there is the one they chose, and if it is their last trail to ride, that's the way they would want it. And even though they are doing this for you and for Charlie, you know the main reason they're doing it, don't you?"

128

Smoke grinned, wiping years from his face. He looked about ten years old. All except for his eyes. "Ol' Preacher."

"That's right, honey. They all knew him, and knew that he helped raise you."

"What do you plan on having for supper?"

"I hadn't thought. Why?"

"How about making some bearsign?"

"It's going to run me out of flour."

"Well . . . I think me and Charlie and some of those ol' boys out there just might ride into Fontana tomorrow. We'll stop by Colby's and get him to take his wagon. Stock up enough for everybody. 'Sides, I want to see Louis's face when we all come ridin' in."

"Uh-huh," she said, poking him in the ribs and tickling him, bending him over, gently slapping at her hands. "But mostly you want to see Tilden Franklin's face."

"Well . . ." He suddenly swept her up in his arms and began carrying her toward the bedroom.

"Smoke! Not with all those . . ."

He kissed her mouth, hushing her.

". . . men out . . ."

He kissed her again and placed her gently on the bed.

"Who cares about those men out there?" she finally said.

It came as no surprise to Smoke to find the men up before he crawled out from under the covers. This high up, even the summer nights were cool . . . and this was still late spring. The nights were downright cold.

The men had gotten their bearsign the previous night, but Sally had been just a bit late with them.

Smoke dressed, belted on his Colts, and, with a mug of coffee in one hand, stepped out to meet the breaking dawn, all silver and gold as the sun slowly inched over the high peaks of Sugarloaf.

"Charlie, I thought a few of us would ride into town this morning and pick up supplies. We'll stop at Colby's place and he'll go with us in his wagon."

"Who you want to go in with you?"

"You pick 'em."

Adam Colby had been reading a dime novel about the life and times of Luke Nation, with a drawing of him on the cover, when he looked up at the sounds of horse's hooves drumming on the road. The boy thought he'd been flung directly into the pages of the dime novel.

He looked at the man on the horse, looked at the cover of the book, and then took off running for the house, hollering for his pa.

"Boy!" Colby said, stepping out of the house. "What in tarnation is wrong with . . ."

The man looked at the group of riders still sitting their horses in his front yard. Colby's eyes flitted from man to man, taking in the lined and tanned faces, the hard, callused hands, and the guns belted around the lean waists. Colby knew of most of the men . . . he just never imagined he'd see them in his front yard.

Adam approached Luke, the dime novel in his hand. He stood looking up at the famed gunfighter, awe in his eyes. He held out the book.

"Would you sign my book, Mister Nations?"

"I'd be right honored, boy," the gunfighter said. He grinned. "That's about all I can write is my name." He took the book and a stub of a pencil Adam held out to him and slowly printed his name, giving book and pencil back to the boy.

"Thank you, sir."

"You're welcome."

"We're riding into Fontana, Colby. Sally needs some supplies. Wanna get your wagon and come in with us?"

"Good idea. Wilbur and the boys will stay here. Give me a minute to get my shirt on. Adam, hook up the team, son."

Colby's wife Belle, daughter Velvet, and boys Adam and Bob stood with Wilbur and his wife Edna and watched the men pull out. They would stop at several other small spreads to take any orders for supplies. The men and women and kids left at Colby's place resumed their morning chores.

A mile away, hidden in the timber, a TF rider watched it all through field glasses. When the men had ridden and rumbled out of sight, the TF rider took a mirror from his saddlebags and caught the morning sun, signaling to another TF rider that everything was ready. He didn't know who them hard-lookin' old boys was with Jensen, but they didn't look like they'd be much trouble to handle. Most of 'em looked to be older than God.

Tilden Franklin wanted to make damn sure he was highly visible to as many people as possible until after Clint's plan was over. Tilden had taken to riding into Fontana every morning, early, with Clint and several of his hardcases for bodyguards. He and his foreman usually had breakfast at the best hotel in town and then took their after-meal cigars while sitting on the porch of the hotel, perhaps reading or talking or just watching the passing parade.

This morning, Tilden looked up from the new edition of the *Fontana Sunburst*, Haywood and Dana Arden's endeavor, just as a TF rider rode by. Without looking at either Tilden or Clint, the rider very minutely nodded his head as he passed.

With a slight smile, Tilden lifted the newspaper and once more resumed his reading.

In a way, Tilden thought, he was kind of sorry he was gonna miss out on the action with that built-up little gal of Colby's. Tilden would bet that, once she settled into the rhythm, Velvet would get to liking it. All women were the same when it came to that, Tilden felt. They liked to holler and raise sand, but they wanted it. They just liked to pretend they didn't for the look of things.

Women, to Tilden's mind, were very notional critters . . . and just like critters, not very bright. Pretty to have around, nice to pet, but that was about it.

One of Monte Carson's deputies rode up and looped the reins over the hitch rail in front of the hotel. Dismounting, he stood on the boardwalk facing Tilden.

"Charlie Starr ridin' in with that Smoke Jensen and the nester Colby, Mister Tilden."

Tilden felt his face stiffen and grow hot as the blood raced to flush his cheeks. He lowered the newspaper and stared at the deputy.

"Charlie *Starr*?"

"Yes, sir. And that ain't all. Smoke's got some mean ol' gunslicks with him, too. The Apache Kid, Sunset Hatfield, Bill Foley, Silver Jim, Moody, and Luke Nations. They ridin' like they got a purpose, if you know what I mean."

A young, two-bit, half-assed punk, who thought himself to be a bad man, was hanging around near the open doors of the hotel. He smiled and felt his heart race at the news. The deputy had just mentioned half a dozen of the most famous gunslingers in all the West. And they were coming into town—here!

Right here, the punk who called himself The Silver Dollar Kid thought, is where I make my rep. Right here, right out there in that street, that's where it all starts. He smiled and walked through the lobby, slipping out the back way. He wanted to change clothes, put on his best outfit before he faced one of those old gunhawks. There was a picture-taker in town; might be a good idea to stop by his studio and tell him about the old gunslicks so's he could have all his equipment set up and ready to pop.

The punk ran back to his tent and began changing into his very finest.

The news of the approaching gunfighters, still several miles out of Fontana, swept through the town like wildfire through a dry forest. Haywood heard it and walked rapidly toward the main business district. He found himself a spot on the boardwalk across the street from where Tilden Franklin sat, surrounded by his hardcases.

Shopkeepers had shooed customers outside, where they stood, lining the boardwalks and packed-dirt sidewalks, waiting for the event of the day.

Louis Longmont came out of his gaming tent to stand on the boardwalk, watching as he smoked his first cigar of the morning. So Smoke had done it, he thought. A smile curved his lips. He'd actually pulled in some of the randiest old boys still living in the West.

"Going to be interesting," Louis muttered. "Very, very interesting."

19

Smoke halted his small group on the edge of town. He looked at Charlie. "A whole passle of two-bit young punks who'll be looking for a reputation in town. They'll be on the prod for a fight."

Charlie spat on the dirt beneath his horse's belly. "They'll damn sure get more than they bargained for with this bunch," he replied.

"We'll ride straight through," Smoke said. "Stopping at Jackson's Mercantile. Colby, pull your wagon up to the loading dock by the side. If there's going to be trouble, let the other side start it. Let's go, boys."

Smoke and Charlie took the point, with Apache and Sunset riding to the left of the wagon, Bill Foley and Silver Jim to the right, and Moody and Luke Nations taking the drag. Smoke rode slowly, so the wheels of the wagon would not kick up much dust. The town had virtually come to a halt, the streets lined with citizens. They stood silently, watching the riders make their way along the street. Trouble hung in the air, as thick as dust.

The riders could practically feel the hate from Tilden Franklin's eyes boring into them as they rode past where he sat like a king on the hotel boardwalk. Smoke met the man's eyes and touched his hat brim in a gesture of greeting.

Tilden did not return the greeting.

They passed Louis Longmont's gaming tent. Most of the

old gunfighters knew the gambler and they greeted him. Louis returned the greeting and very minutely nodded his head in the direction Smoke was riding.

There was something or someone down there that Louis wanted Smoke to know about. Smoke's eyes searched both sides of the street. Then he saw them, the three of them, lounging in front of a newly erected tent saloon.

Luis Chamba, Kane, and Sanderson.

The Mexican gunfighter stood with his arms folded across his chest, his sombrero off his head, hanging down his back by the chin cord.

"See them?" Smoke whispered the words, just audible over the clop of hooves.

"I see them." Charlie returned the whisper. "That Chamba, he's a bad one. Kills for pleasure. Gets his kicks that way, you know?"

Smoke knew the type.

Then they were past the killers.

"Kane and Sanderson?" Smoke asked. He knew of them, but did not know them personally.

"Just as bad. They're all three twisted. And they'll kill anything or anybody for money."

"Look at those punks over to your left."

"Seen them too," Charlie said sourly. "Lookin' to make themselves a reputation. I hope they don't try none of this bunch. These guys are all on the shady side of their years, but Lord God, don't sell 'em short."

A young man with a smart-ass look to him and dressed like a San Francisco pimp stood glaring at the men. At least Smoke figured that's how a San Francisco pimp might dress, having never been there.

"Reckon it's time for us to start us a Boot Hill here in Fontana, boys!" the loud-mouthed, loudly dressed young man said, raising his voice so the riders could all hear him.

The Apache Kid favored the young man with a glance and dismissed him just as quickly.

Sunset openly laughed at the dandy.

"Yeah," another duded-up, two-gun-totin' young man agreed, his voice loud. "And them old boys yonder ain't got long to go no ways. Might as well start with them. How 'bout it?"

None of the aging gunfighters even acknowledged the punk had spoken. They rode on.

"Hell!" another would-be gunslinger yelled, fanning the air with his fancy hat. "They so goddamned old they done lost their balls, boys!"

"That one is mine," Luke said, just so his friends could hear.

"He means it, Smoke," Charlie said. "Don't interfere none."

"Far be it for me to interfere," Smoke answered.

Back in the high country, Velvet Colby, her chores done for the morning, thought it would be nice to take a walk through the woods.

"Stay close, Velvet!" her mother called.

"Yes, ma'am, I will."

Adam watched her go. He stuck his dime novel in his back pocket and picked up his .22 rifle, following Velvet but staying back, knowing how his sister enjoyed being alone.

While Ed Jackson and his brother loaded the wagon with supplies, Colby walked with Smoke over to Louis Longmont's place. He introduced them and Louis invited them inside. Smoke had no intention of trying to shepherd and play check-rein on Charlie and the others. They'd been without his advice for a combination of about three hundred and fifty years. They didn't need it now.

"A taste of the Glenlivet, gentlemen?" Louis asked.

"Huh?" Colby asked.

"Fine scotch whiskey," Smoke told him.

Three tumblers poured three fingers deep, Louis lifted his glass. "Here's to a very interesting summer, gentlemen."

They clinked glasses and sipped.

Louis smiled. "Shall we adjourn to what laughingly passes for a veranda and watch the show, boys?"

"Sure going to be one," Smoke agreed, moving toward the door.

Luke Nations had broken off from the others and was walking toward the knot of would-be gunslicks, walking directly toward the duded-up punk with the fat mouth. Luke stopped about twenty-five feet from him. He stood with the leather thongs off the hammers of his Colts. He stood with his feet slightly spread. He was big and bent and old and mean-looking. And the look in his eyes would have warned off a puma.

"You made a comment a minute or so ago, kid," Luke said, his voice flat and hard. "Well, now is your chance to back up your mouth. Either that . . . or tuck your fancy tail between your legs and carry your ass!"

His name was Lester. But he called himself Sundance. At this moment, he felt more like Lester than Sundance.

The Silver Dollar Kid had backed up against a wall. Unlike Lester, he wasn't afraid; he just wanted to see if the old men still had it in them. When he had studied them, then he would make his move.

"Goddamn you, boy!" Luke's voice was so sharp, it hurt. "Do you hear me?"

"Yeah, I hear you." Sundance surfaced, pushing Lester out of the way.

Monte Carson had come on the run when he heard the news of the impending shootout. He came to an abrupt halt, almost falling as his high-heeled boots dug into the dirt of the street. One of his deputies ran into him, and they both almost fell.

"What the hell?" the deputy said.

"Shut up and look around you!" Monte whispered hoarsely.

The Apache Kid was just across the street, standing alone, both hands to his sides, the palms very close to the butt of his Colts.

The deputy cut his eyes. Old Sunset was standing behind them, about thirty feet away.

Bill Foley stood just to their right, poised and ready for anything that might come his way.

"Ssshhittt!" Monte hissed, the breath whistling between his slightly gapped front teeth. He was looking eyeball to eyeball with Silver Jim, his long white duster brushed back, exposing the butts of the Colts, the leather hammer thongs off.

Back of them, facing Tilden Franklin and Clint, stood Moody. Moody said, "You boys come to watch or get dealt in?"

Tilden chewed his cigar soggy in a matter of a heartbeat. He felt no fear, for there was no fear in him. But he had grown up hearing stories about these old gunfighters. And at this distance, everybody was going to get lead in them. And there was something else too. Tilden knew, from hard experience, that when dealing with ballsy old men you'd best walk lightly. With their best years behind them, they had nothing to lose. Old men did not fight fair. Tilden had learned that the hard way too.

Clint cut his eyes. Louis Longmont, his tailored jacket brushed back over the butt of his guns, stood to Clint's right. Smoke was facing Tilden's other hands, and the other hands were looking a little green around the mouth.

And the gunslinger Johnny North had finally made his appearance. The blond-haired Nevada gunhand stood in the street, facing Luis Chamba and his two sidekicks. Johnny was smiling. And those that knew Johnny knew Johnny was not the smiling type.

All in all, as the *Fontana Sunburst* would later say in a column by its editor, it was a most exhilarating and tense moment. These legends of the Wild West, captivating an entire town with their bigger-than-life presence. A moment from the fading past that would be forever etched in the minds of all who had the opportunity to witness this fortuitous encounter of the last of the Bad Men.

Haywood did, on occasion, get a tad bit carried away with his writing.

But since the written word was scarce in the West, folks would read and enjoy nearabout anything. They might not understand what the hell they were reading, but read it they would.

"Do it, punk!" Luke shouted. He began walking toward the dandy. Luke had felt all along the dandy didn't have the cold nerve to pull iron. When he reached the young man, who was beginning to sweat, he balled his left hand into a hard fist and knocked the loud-mouth to the dirt. Lester-Sundance fell hard. He lay on the dirt, looking up at Luke through wide, scared eyes.

Luke reached down and plucked the pearl-handled Colts from the young man's holsters. He stepped to one side and wedged one barrel between a support block and the board-walk. With a swift jerk, he broke off first one barrel, and then the other. He tossed the ruined pistols to Lester-Sundance.

"I'll tell you something, boy," Luke said. "I wish somebody had done something like that to me when I was your age. I might have amounted to something."

Luke Nations turned his back to the sobbing, humiliated young man and walked away.

"I'll kill him for that," Lester-Sundance sobbed, but not loud enough for Luke to hear. "You just wait and see. I'll get him for that."

The Silver Dollar Kid walked across the street, in the direction Luke had taken.

"Well, boys!" Louis said. "How about the drinks on me? What say you all?"

Smoke looked at Tilden Franklin. "That includes you too, Franklin. Join us?"

His face flushed with rage and hate, Tilden turned his back on the invitation and stomped back up the street, Clint following like a dog behind him.

The TF puppies followed Clint.

Louis watched Tilden wheel around and stalk off. "The man is obviously of low degree," the gambler said.

Smoke, Colby, and the gunfighters had a laugh at that. Tilden had heard the remark, and his back stiffened with new anger. His rage was such that he could hardly see.

"Get the horses, Clint!" he snapped.

"Boss," Clint warned. "Hadn't we best stay in town?"

Tilden's big hands gripped a hitchrail and he trembled in

139

his hot fury. "Yes. Yes," he repeated, then cleared his throat. "You're right. Order your boys to take off their gunbelts, Clint."

"*What?*"

"You heard me, Clint. We're going to take that invitation for a drink. And then I'm going to stomp Smoke Jensen's goddamned guts out. With my fists and boots!"

20

"What the hell?" Billy said, eyeballing Tilden and Clint and the other TF rowdies removing their gunbelts and looping them on their saddle horns.

The livery stable-swamper darted across the street and into Louis Longmont's gaming place.

"Smoke!" he called. All heads turned toward the small boy in the doorway. "Tilden Franklin and them gunhands of his'n done dropped their gunbelts, and they're all headin' this way. I don't know what they're about, but I betcha it's bad trouble."

"I know what it is," Smoke said. He set his untouched tumbler on the bar. "Thanks, Billy."

"Come here, son," Louis said. "You get over there," he pointed, "and stay put. Andre!" he called for his chef. "Get this young man a sarsaparilla, *s'il vous plaît?*"

"But *monsieur . . . ou?*"

"Reasonable question," Louis muttered. "Where indeed? Lemonade?"

Andre's face brightened. *"Oui!"*

A big glass of cool lemonade in front of him, Billy slipped from the table to the eggs-and-cheese-and-beef end of the bar and filled a napkin with goodies. Eating and sipping, Billy sat back to watch the show.

Louis watched the boy's antics and smiled. His big bouncer, Mike, stood close by Billy, his massive arms folded across his barrel chest.

The chef, Andre, had beat it back to his kitchen. Let the

141

barbarians fight, he thought.

Boot heels drummed on the boardwalk and Tilden Franklin's bulk filled the doorway. "I thought I'd take you up on your offer, Gambler," he said.

"Certainly," Louis said. "Be my guest."

Tilden walked to the bar and poured a tumbler of whiskey. He toyed with the shot glass for a moment, then lifted the glass. "To the day when we rid the country of all two-bit nesters."

Tilden and his men drank. None of the others acknowledged the toast.

Tilden smiled. "What's the matter, boys? None of you like my toast?"

Smoke lifted his glass. "To the day when farmers and ranchers all get along."

Smoke's friends toasted that. Tilden, Clint, and the other TF men did not.

"What's the matter, Tilden?" Smoke asked. "You don't like my toast?"

Tilden's smile was thin. Toying with his empty shot glass, his eyes on the polished bar, he said, "I've always had this theory, Jensen . . . or whatever your name is. My theory is that most gunslicks live on their reputations, that without a gun in their hand, they're mighty thin in the guts department. What do you think about that?"

"I think you're mighty thin between the ears, Tilden. That's what I think. I think you sit on your brains. Now what do you think about that?"

"I'm not armed, Jensen," Tilden said, still looking down at the bar.

Smoke unbuckled and untied. He handed his guns to Colby. "Neither am I, Tilden. So the next move is up to you."

Tilden looked at his riders. "Clear us a space, boys."

Gaming tables and chairs were pushed back, stacked against one wall. The barroom floor was empty.

Tilden's smile was ugly and savage. "I'm gonna break you in half, Jensen. Then your wife can see for herself what a real man can do . . . when she comes to my bed."

Smoke laughed at that. "You're a bigger fool than I first thought, Tilden. Now make your move or shut your goddamned flapping mouth."

Tilden spun away from the bar railing and charged Smoke. All two-hundred-forty-odd pounds of him, like an enraged bull, charging at the smaller man.

Smoke stepped to one side, stuck out a boot, and tripped the big man, sending him crashing and sprawling to the barroom floor. Smoke stepped in and kicked Tilden in the side, bringing a grunt of pain from the man. Before Smoke could put the boots to him again, Tilden rolled away and jumped to his feet.

Smoke, weighing some fifty-odd pounds less than Tilden, faced the bigger man. Both men lifted their hands and balled their fists.

"I'm taking bets on Smoke!" Louis announced. "Any takers?"

Clint and the TF men bet on their boss.

Haywood, Colton, Hunt, Ralph, and Ed had quietly slipped into the gaming room, standing close to the front door.

Big Mamma O'Neil bulled her way past those at the door. "A hundred bucks on Tilden!" she yelled.

"Done!" Louis said.

"Barbaric!" Hunt muttered.

Big Mamma laughed and slapped the lawyer on the back, almost knocking him down. She stepped on past the men at the door and walked to a far wall.

Tilden flicked a right hand toward Smoke, a feeling-out punch. Smoke moved his head slightly, dodging the punch. He jabbed a hard left, catching Tilden in the mouth, snapping the man's head back.

With a roar, Tilden swung a roundhouse left that caught Smoke on the shoulder. A powerfully thrown punch, it brought a grunt of pain from the smaller man. Smoke countered with a right, hitting Tilden in the belly. It was like hitting a piece of hardwood. Tilden grinned at Smoke and the men went after each other, toe to toe, slugging it out.

Smoke realized that if he was to win this fight, and that

was something he had to do, for morale's sake if nothing else, there was no way he could stand up and match Tilden punch for punch. The man was bigger and stronger, and in excellent physical shape.

Smoke jumped to one side and lashed out with one boot, the toe of the boot catching Tilden on the kneecap. Tilden howled in pain and, for a second, dropped his guard. A second was all that Smoke needed.

Smoke hit the man twice, a left-and-right combination to the jaw. His punches were savage, and they rocked the bigger man, bringing blood from one side of his mouth. Tilden staggered under the combination, just for a second, his legs buckling.

Smoke hit the man flush on his mouth. Tilden's lips splattered under the hard-thrown punch, the blood spurting. Tilden grabbed Smoke in a bear hug, holding on until he could recover. Smoke experienced the man's massive strength as the air was crushed out of him. Tucking his head under Tilden's jaw, Smoke brought his head up savagely. Tilden's mouth snapped shut and he squalled in pain as the teeth caught his tongue and more blood was added to the flow from his battered mouth. The big man's grip eased and Smoke slipped out of the bear hug.

Pivoting, Smoke poured on the steam and hit Tilden in the gut with every ounce of strength he could muster. The right fist caught Tilden just above the belt buckle, and the wind whooshed out of the man as he involuntarily doubled over. Smoke stepped in close and grabbed Tilden's head and hair with both hands and brought the head down at the same time he was bringing a knee up. The knee caught Tilden smack on the nose and the nose crunched under the impact. Tilden was flung back against the bar.

The big man hung there, his eyes still wild but glazed over. Smoke stepped in close and went to work on the kingpin.

Smoke hammered at the man's belly and face with work-hardened fists. In seconds, Tilden's face was swollen and battered and bloody.

Clint stepped in to break up the fight and found himself

suddenly lying on the barroom floor, hit on the back of the head by The Apache Kid's rifle stock. Clint moaned once and then lay still, out cold.

Smoke went to work on Tilden's belly, concentrating all his punches there, and they were thrown with all his strength. It was a savage, brutal attack on Smoke's part, but Smoke knew, from having the old Mountain Man Preacher as his teacher, that there was no such thing as a fair fight. There was only a winner, and a loser.

He hammered at Tilden's mid-section, working like a steam-driven pile-driver.

Twice, Tilden almost slumped to the floor. Twice, Smoke propped him back up and went to work on him. He shifted his attention to Tilden's face, his punches ruining the man's once-handsome features. Smoke's flat-knuckled fists knocked out teeth and loosened others. His fists completely flattened Tilden's nose. One punch to the side of Tilden's head ripped loose an ear, almost tearing it off the man's head. Still Smoke did not let up. His fists smashed into Tilden's sides and kidneys and belly and face.

Smoke was fighting with a cold, controlled, dark fury. His fists battered the man; this man who had boasted he would take Smoke's wife; this man who had sworn to run Smoke and the others out of this part of Colorado; this man who dared impose his will on all others.

Then Smoke realized he was battering and smashing an unconscious man. He stopped his assault and stepped back, his chest heaving and his hands hurting. Tilden Franklin, the bully of the valley, the man who would be king, the man who would control the destiny of all those around him, slipped to the floor to lie among the cigarette and cigar butts. His blood stained the trash on the floor.

He was so deep in his unconsciousness he did not even twitch.

"I'd have never believed it," Big Mamma O'Neil was heard to whisper. "But I seen it. Lord have mercy, did I ever see it."

"That's a hundred dollars you owe me, Big Mamma," Louis said. "You can give it to Billy over there."

Louis looked at the Tilden riders. "You TF riders can pay

Big Mike."

"I have some medication at the office that will ease those swelling hands, Smoke," Colton said. "I'll be waiting for you."

Smoke leaned against the bar and nodded his head.

"Ain't you gonna see to Mister Franklin?" a TF rider asked.

"At the office," Colton said shortly. "I'll prepare a bed for him."

Smoke belted his guns around him and began working his fingers, to prevent them from stiffening any worse than he knew they would.

"Drag that cretin from my premises," Louis said, pointing at the prostrate Tilden Franklin.

Big Mamma O'Neil laid five twenty-dollar gold pieces on the table in front of Billy.

Billy looked up at her with a bit of egg sticking to his upper lip . . .

. . . and grinned!

Book Two

Now this is the law of the jungle — as old and as true as the sky. And the Wolf that shall keep it may prosper, but the Wolf that shall break it must die.

—Kipling

1

Twice, Adam thought he heard something back in the timber behind the Colby house. He lifted his head and concentrated. Nothing. He returned to his reading of the dime novel about the adventures of Luke Nations.

He was just getting to the part about where Luke rides into the Indian camp, both six-guns blazing, to rescue the lovely maiden when he heard kind of a muffled, cut-off scream from in the timber.

"Velvet!" he called.

Only the silence greeted his call. And then it came to him. The silence. The birds and the small animals around the place were used to Velvet's walking through the woods. They seldom stopped their singing and chattering and calling simply because she came gently walking through.

The boy picked up his single-shot .22-caliber rifle and put his dime novel in the hip pocket of his patched and faded work pants. "Velvet!" he shouted.

Nothing.

Not the singing of a bird, not the calling or barking of a squirrel.

Something was wrong.

Adam hesitated, started to go back to the house for Mister Wilbur. Then he shook his head. It would take too long, for Velvet had strayed a pretty good piece from the house.

There was movement from his left. Adam turned just as something hard slammed into the back of his head and sent him spinning into darkness. The darkness blotted out the sunlight filtering through the trees.

When he awakened, the first thing he noticed was that the

sunlight through the limbs had changed somewhat, shifting positions. Adam figured he'd been out a good thirty to forty-five minutes. Painfully, he got to a sitting-up position. His head was hurting something fierce and things were moving around like they shouldn't oughta.

He sat very still for a few moments, until his head began to clear and settle down. He thought he heard some sort of grunting sounds. Adam couldn't figure out what they might be.

He got to his feet, swaying for a moment. When things settled down, he looked around for his .22 rifle. He checked it, brushing the dirt from it, and checked the load. He kept hearing that grunting sound. Slowly, cautiously, the boy made his way through the timber toward that odd sound.

He came to a little clearing—must be two miles from the house—and paused, peering through the branches.

What he saw brought him up short and mad.

It was Velvet, and she didn't have no clothes on; her dress was torn off and tossed to one side. And a bunch of them TF riders was standing around, some of them bare-assed naked, some in their long-handles.

And there was money all over the ground. Adam couldn't figure out what all them greenbacks and silver dollars was doing on the ground.

But he knew what them men was doing. He'd never done it with no girl hisself, but he wasn't no fool.

It looked like to him that Velvet wasn't having no good time of it. It looked like to him she was out cold. He could see bruises on her face and her . . . on her chest. And there was dark marks on her legs where them riders had gripped at her with hard hands. Like that one was doing now. Pokin' at her. From behind. Like an animal.

Adam lifted his rifle and sighted in. It was not going to be a hard shot, but he had the rifle loaded with little shorts for squirrels. He sighted in and pulled the trigger.

It was a good shot, the little chunk of lead striking the rapist in his right eye. The rapist just fell backward, off Velvet, and lay on his back, his privates exposed.

Velvet sort of rolled off the log they'd had her bent over

and lay real still.

Adam quickly reloaded and sighted in again. But before he could pull the trigger, a short gun barked and something hard struck him in the chest. The slug knocked him backward. He lost his grip on his rifle. Adam knew he was bad hit, maybe going to die, but he lay still as the men ran up to him.

"Let's get outta here!" he heard one say.

"What about Steve?"

"Take him with us. We'll bury him proper."

"Little son of a bitch kilt him with a lousy .22," another spoke.

"Let's ride."

When the sounds of their horses had faded, Adam tried to reach his sister. He could not. The pain in his chest was getting worse and he was having a hard time seeing. He pulled his dime novel out of his pocket and took his worn stub of a pencil. Slowly, with bloody fingers, he began to print out a message.

A few minutes later, the boy laid his head down on the cool earth and closed his eyes. A moment later he was dead.

Smoke and the others arrived back a few hours before dark. They had pushed their horses hard. Colby and Charlie were about two hours behind.

Belle Colby met the men in the front yard.

"I can't find Velvet or Adam," she told Smoke. She had been crying, her eyes red-rimmed.

"Bob met us, Belle," Smoke said. "Charlie stayed with Colby just in case. They're a couple of hours behind us. Any idea where they might have gone?"

"No. The girl has her—what she calls her secret places in the timber where she goes to be alone."

The men dismounted. Smoke turned to The Apache Kid. "Apache, Preacher once told me you could track a snake over a flat rock."

"I'll find her trail," the old gunfighter said.

He moved out with a swiftness that belied his age. "Stay

behind me," he called to the others. "Jist stay back till I locate some sign. And don't come up to me when I do find it. I don't want none of it all mucked up."

He began moving in a criss-cross manner, looking to anyone who did not understand tracking like a man who had lost his mind. In less than five minutes, he called out. "I got it. Stay behind me."

Apache was following the girl's sign, not Adam's, so they found the girl first.

"Good Jesus Christ!" Silver Jim said. He peeled off his duster and wrapped it around the girl. She was conscious, but in some sort of shock. She seemed unable to speak.

"What's all this money doing piled up here?" Moody asked. "I don't understand none of this."

"Twenty-one dollars," Smoke said, counting the coin and greenbacks. "This isn't making any sense to me."

Then Apache found the body of Adam and called out. The men gathered around.

"They's words writ on this page here," Apache said. "My readin' ain't good enough to make 'em out." He handed the dime novel to Smoke.

Smoke looked at the bloody, printed words. "IT WAS TF RIDERS WHO DONE IT TO SIS. TF RIDERS WHO SHOT ME. GET THEM FOR ME LUKE. LUKE, GET"

Smoke read the message and then folded the book.

Luke Nations stood stony-faced. But there were tears running down his tanned, lined, leathery face.

"We play it legal-like, Luke, boys," Smoke said. "When that fails, then we go in shootin'."

"You play it legal-like, Jensen," Luke said, his words like chipped stone. "Me, I'll play my way."

He turned to go.

Smoke's hard voice stopped the old gunfighter. "*Luke!*"

The gunfighter turned slowly.

"Charlie told me when you signed on, you rode for the brand."

"I do."

"It's my brand."

That stung Luke. He stood for a moment, then slowly

nodded his head. "Right, Boss. We play it legal-like. But you know damned well how it's gonna come out in the long haul."

"Yes, I do. Or at least suspect. But when all the shooting is over and the dust settled, we're going to have United States marshals in here, plus all sorts of lawyers and other big-worded people. I don't want anyone to point the finger at us and be able to prove that we started a damn thing. That make sense to you?"

"Put that way, I reckon it do."

"Fine. I hate to ask any of you boys to ride back to town. But we need the sheriff out here first thing in the morning."

Wilbur Mason had walked up. "I'll go," he said quietly.

Smoke nixed that. "You'd be fair game, Wilbur. And you're no hand with a gun. No, I'll go. I'll take the book and give it to Lawyer Brook and tell him the story in the presence of Sheriff Carson. Damn!" he said.

"What's wrong?" Silver Jim said.

"I'll have to take the girl into town to Doctor Spalding. She's in bad shape. Wilbur, hitch up a wagon and fill the back with hay for her comfort. Luke, ride like hell for my place and tell some other men to come hard. They can catch up with me on the way in."

Luke nodded and ran, in his odd, bowlegged, cowboy way, back to his horse.

"I'll borrow a horse from Colby's stable and pick up mine on the way back. You boys tell Sally I'll be back when she sees me."

"You take 'er easy, Smoke," Silver Jim warned. "Them hands of yourn won't be fit for no quick draw for several days yet."

Smoke nodded and left.

Tilden Franklin had tried to sit a saddle. He fell off twice before he would allow himself to be taken back to his ranch in the back of a buckboard. If he was not blind crazy before, he was now. He knew it would be a week, maybe longer, before he was fit to do anything. He was hurt bad, and he

153

had enough sense to know it.

He also had enough sense to know, through waves of humiliation, that since he had started the fight, in front of witnesses, there was not a damn thing, legally, he could do about it.

Except lay in the back of the buckboard and curse Smoke Jensen.

Which he did, wincing with every bounce and jar along the rutted road.

Smoke had met Colby and Charlie on the trail and broken the news to the father. Colby and Wilbur had exchanged wagons and rolled on. Charlie had insisted on returning with Smoke. He didn't say it, but Smoke was glad the gunfighter was with him, for his own hands were in no shape for any standup gunfight.

It was long after dark when they rolled into Fontana and up to the doctor's office. Velvet still had not spoken a word. Nor uttered any sound.

Colton looked at Velvet, looked at Smoke, and silently cursed. He ordered the girl taken into his examining room and called for his wife to be present.

"Tell me what happened," he told Smoke. "As succinctly as possible."

"As what?"

Colton sighed. "Make it short."

Lawyer Hunt made his appearance, with his wife Willow. Mona asked her to assist her with Velvet. The women disappeared into the examining room.

Smoke had sent Billy for the sheriff as they passed the livery stable. For once, Sheriff Carson seemed genuinely concerned. He knew for an ironclad fact that nobody, but *nobody*, messed with a good woman and came off easy. Monte Carson was a hired gun, true, but he respected good womenfolk.

With everyone present, Smoke told his story, handing the bloody, damning dime novel, autographed by Luke Nations, to Lawyer Hunt.

Nobody heard Louis Longmont enter the office. He stood

off to one side, listening.

Lawyer Hunt read the message and looked at Monte. "Can you read, Sheriff?"

"Hell, yes!"

"Then read it and pick a side!" There was hard and genuine anger in the lawyer's voice. God*damn* people who would do this to a girl.

"Hey!" Monte said. "I don't pick sides. I'm the law around here."

"That remains to be seen, doesn't it?" Louis spoke from the darkness near the open door to the office.

Monte flushed and read the bloody words. Now, he thought, I *am* in a pickle.

Doctor Spalding stepped out of the examining room. "The girl's visible wounds will be easily treated. They're mostly superficial. But her mental state is quite another matter. She is catatonic."

Smoke lost his temper. He was tired, sore, hungry, disgusted, and could not remember when he wanted to kill anybody more than at this moment. "Now, what in the goddamn hell does all that jibber-jabber mean?"

"Settle down, Smoke," Louis said. Then the gambler explained the doctor's words.

Smoke calmed down and looked at Sheriff Carson. "You want a war on your hands, Monte?"

"Hell, no!"

"Somebody better hang for this, Monte," Smoke warned, his voice low and menacing. "Or that is exactly what you're going to have on your hands—a war."

Smoke stepped out into the night and walked toward the best of the hotels.

"You ever heard the expression 'caught between a rock and a hard place,' Sheriff?" Louis asked.

"Sure. Why?"

"Because that's where you are. Enjoy it." The gambler smiled thinly.

2

The news swept through the town of Fontana fast. Sheriff Monte Carson found Judge Proctor and jerked him away from the bottle on the bar, leading the whiskered man out of the batwings to the boardwalk.

Monte pointed a finger at the judge. He told him what had gone down, shaking his finger in the judge's face. "Not another drink until this is over," he warned the highly educated rummy. "If you don't think you can handle that, I can damn well put you in a cell and be shore of it."

Judge Proctor stuck out his chest and blustered. "You wouldn't dare!"

"Try me," Monte warned, acid in his voice.

Judge Proctor got the message, and he believed it. He rubbed a hand over his face. "You're right, of course, Sheriff. Goddamn Tilden Franklin! What was he thinking of authorizing something of this odious nature?"

Sheriff Carson shrugged. "Be ready to go at first light, Judge. No matter how the chips fall, we got to play this legal-like, all the way."

Judge Proctor watched the sheriff walk away into the night. "Should be interesting," he muttered. "A fair hearing. How quaint!"

Louis Longmont sat in his quarters behind his gaming

room and sipped hot tea. At first, the news of the money near where the girl was found puzzled him. Then his mind began working, studying all angles. Louis felt he knew the reason for the money. But it was a thin rope Tilden had managed to grab onto. The man really must be quite insane to authorize such a plan. Colby and Belle and their kids were all deeply religious folk—most farmers were. And the sheriff and judge were going to be forced to handle this right by the law books.

But, the gambler thought with a sigh, there was always the jury to consider. And money, in this case, not only talked, but cursed.

Big Mamma sat at the back of her bar and pondered the situation. In a case like this, wimmin oughta be allowed to sit on the jury . . . but that was years in the future. Even though Big Mamma was as cold-hearted and ruthless as a warlord, something like this brought out the maternal instinct from deep within her. She would have scoffed and cursed at the mere suggestion of that . . . but it was true.

She looked around her. It wouldn't take near as long to tear all this down and get gone as it had to put it all up. Damned if she wanted to get caught up in an all-out shootin' war. But sure as hell, that was what was gonna happen.

That Smoke Jensen . . . well, she had revised her original opinion of that feller. He was pure straight out of Hell, that one. That one was no punk, like she first thought. But one-hundred-and-ten-percent man. And even though Big Mamma didn't like men, she could respect the all-man types . . . like Smoke Jensen.

Ralph Morrow lay beside his wife, unable to sleep. He was thinking of that poor child, and also thinking that he just may have been a fool where Tilden Franklin was concerned. After witnessing that fight in the gaming room this very day, and seeing the brutal, calculating madness in Tilden's eyes, the preacher realized that Tilden would stop at nothing to attain his goals.

Even the rape of a child.

Hunt sat in his office, looking at the bloody dime novel. Like the gambler, Louis Longmont, Hunt felt he knew why the money had been left by the raped child. And, if his hunch was correct, it was a horrible, barbaric thing for the men to do.

But, his lawyer's mind pondered, did Tilden Franklin have anything to do with it?

"Shit!" he said, quite unlike him.

Of course he did.

Colton dozed on his office couch. Even in his fitful sleep he was keeping one ear out for any noise Velvet might make. But he didn't expect her to make any. He felt the child's mind was destroyed.

He suddenly came wide awake, his mind busy. Supplies! He was going to have to order many more supplies. He would post the letter tomorrow — today — and get it out on the morning stage.

There was going to be a war in this area of the state — a very bad war. And as the only doctor within seventy-five miles, Colton felt he was going to be very busy.

Ed Jackson slept deeply and well. He had heard the news of the raped girl and promptly dismissed it. Tilden Franklin was a fine man; he would have nothing to do with anything of that nature. Those hard-scrabble farmers and small ranchers were all trash. That's what Mister Franklin had told him, and he believed him.

There had been no rape, Ed had thought, before falling asleep. None at all. The money scattered around the wretched girl proved that, and if he was chosen to sit on the jury, that's the way he would see it.

Sleep was elusive for Smoke. And not just for Smoke. In the room next to his, he could hear Charlie Starr's restless pacing. The legendary gunfighter was having a hard time of it too. Mistreatment of a grown woman was bad enough, but to do what had been done to a child . . . that was hard to take.

War. That word kept bouncing around in Smoke's head. Dirty, ugly range war.

Smoke finally drifted off to sleep . . . but his dreams were bloody and savage.

Not one miner worked the next day . . . or so it seemed at least. The bars and cafes and hotels and streets and boardwalks of Fontana were filled to overflowing with men and women, all awaiting the return of Judge Proctor and Sheriff Monte Carson from the sprawling TF spread.

Luke Nations had stayed at the Sugarloaf with Sally and most of the other gunslicks. Early that morning, however, Pistol Le Roux, Dan Greentree, Bull Flagler, Hardrock, Red Shingletown, and Leo Wood had ridden in.

And the town had taken notice of them very quickly. The aging gunhawks made Monte's deputies very nervous. And, to the deputies' way of thinking, what made it all even worse was that Louis Longmont was solidly on the side of Smoke Jensen. And now it appeared that Johnny North had thrown in with Smoke too. And nobody knew how many more of them damned old gunfighters Smoke had brought in. Just thinkin' 'bout them damned old war-hosses made a feller nervous.

Just outside of town, Monte sat his saddle and looked down at Judge Proctor, sitting in a buckboard. "I ain't real happy about bringin' this news back to Fontana, Judge."

"Nor I, Sheriff. But I really, honestly feel we did our best in this matter."

Monte shuddered. "You know what this news is gonna do, don't you, Judge?"

"Unfortunately. But what would you have done differently, Monte?"

Monte shook his head. He could not think of a thing that could have been done differently. But, for the first time in his life, Monte was beginning to see matters from the *other* side of the badge. He'd never worn a badge before, never realized the responsibilities that went with it. And, while he was a long way from becoming a good lawman, if given a chance Monte might some day make it.

"Nothin', Judge. Not a thing."

Judge Proctor clucked to his team and rolled on.

Standing beside Smoke on the boardwalk, Lawyer Hunt Brook said, "Here they come, Smoke. Two went out, two are returning."

"That's about the way I figured it would be."

Judge Proctor halted his team in front of Hunt and Smoke. "Since you are handling this case for Miss Colby, Mister Brook," the judge said, "I'll see you in your offices in thirty minutes. I should like to wash up first."

"Certainly, your honor," Hunt said.

Smoke walked with the lawyer down the long, tightly packed street to his law office. Hunt went on into his personal office and Smoke sat out in the pine-fresh outer office, reading a month-old edition of a New York City newspaper. He looked up as Colby entered.

"It ain't good, is it, Smoke?" the father asked.

"It doesn't look good from where I sit. You sure you want to be here, listen to all this crap?"

"Yeah," the man said softly. "I shore do want to hear it. I left Belle with Velvet. This is hard on my woman, Smoke. She's talkin' hard about pullin' out."

"And you?"

"I told her if she went, she'd have to go by herself. I was stayin'."

"She won't leave you, Colby."

"Naw. I don't think she will neither. It's just . . . whatever the outcome today, Smoke, we gotta get back, get Adam into the ground. You reckon that new minister, that Ralph Morrow, would come up to the high country and say a few words over my boy?"

160

The man was very close to crying.

"I'm sure he would, Colby. Soon as this is over, I'll go talk to him."

"I'd be beholden, Smoke."

Judge Proctor and Sheriff Carson entered the office. The judge extended his hand to Colby. "You have my deepest and most sincere condolences, sir."

"Thank you, Judge."

Monte stood with his hat in his hand, looking awfully uncomfortable.

Hunt motioned them all into his office. When they were seated, Judge Proctor looked at them all and said, "Well, this is a bit irregular, and should this case ever come to court, I shall, of course, have to bring in another judge to hear it. But that event appears highly unlikely."

Smoke's smile was ugly.

Monte caught the mocking smile. "Don't, Smoke," he said quietly. "We done our best. And I mean that. If you can ever prove we slacked up even a little, you can have my badge, and I'm sayin' that in front of witnesses."

For some reason, Smoke believed the man. Queer feeling.

"Here it is," Judge Proctor said. He looked at Colby. "This is highly embarrassing for me, sir. And please bear in mind, these are the words of the TF men who were . . . well, at the scene."

"Just say it," the rancher-farmer said.

"Very well. They say, sir, that your daughter had been, well, shall we say . . . *entertaining* the men at that location for quite some time. They say this has been going on since last summer."

"What's been goin' on?" Colby blurted. "I ain't understandin' none of this."

Smoke had a sudden headache. He rubbed his temples with his fingertips and wished all this crap would be over. Just get all the goddamned lies over and done with.

"Sir," Judge Proctor said. "The TF men claim that your daughter, Velvet, has been entertaining them with sexual favors for some time. For money."

Colby sat rock still for a moment, and then jumped to his

feet. "That there's a damned lie, sir! My Velvet is a good girl!"

Smoke pulled the man back into the chair. "We know, Colby. We know that's the truth. It's all a pack of lies. Just like we figured it would be."

"Please, Mister Colby!" Judge Proctor said. "Try to control yourself, sir."

Colby put his face in his hands and began weeping.

Lawyer Brook wet a cloth from a pitcher on his desk and handed the cloth to Smoke, who handed it to Colby. Colby bathed his face and sighing, looked up. "Go on," he said, his voice strained.

The judge looked at the sheriff. "Would you *please* take a part in these proceedings, Sheriff? You explain. That's your job, not mine."

"Mister Colby," Monte said. "Them Harris brothers who ride for the TF brand, Ed and Pete? It was them and Billy and Donnie and Singer and . . . two or three more. I got their names writ down. Anyways, they claim that Miss Velvet was . . ." He sighed, thinking, Oh, shit! "Chargin' the men three dollars a turn. There would have been more than twenty-one dollars there this time except that not all the men got their turn."

"Dear God in Heaven!" Hunt Brook exclaimed. "Must you be so graphic, sir?"

"I don't know no other way to say it, Lawyer!" Monte said. "I'm doin' the bes' I can."

Hunt waved his hand. "I know, Sheriff. I know. Sorry. Please continue."

"They say Miss Velvet kep' her . . . earnin's in a secret place back in the timber. They told us where it was. We ain't been there, and you all know we ain't had the time to go to the ranch, into the high country, and back here by now. I'll tell y'all where they said it was. Y'all can see for yourselves.

"Anyways, Miss Velvet's brother come up there and started yellin' and hollerin' and wavin' that rifle of his'n around. Then he just up and shot Steve Babbin. That's for a fact. They buryin' Steve this afternoon. Shot him in the eye with a .22. Killed him. Little bitty hole. Had to have been a

.22. Them ol' boys just reacted like any other men. They grabbed iron and started shootin'. Killed the boy. They kinda got shook about it and took off. That's about it, boys."

Monte leaned back in his chair and looked at the newly carpeted floor.

"And you believe their story, Sheriff?" Lawyer Brook asked.

"It ain't a question of believin' or not believin', Lawyer. It's a matter of what can be proved. I don't like it, fellers. I just don't like it. But look at it like this: even if Miss Velvet could talk, which she cain't, it'd still be her word agin theirs. And that's the way it is, fellers."

Smoke stood up and put his hat on his head. "And that's it, huh, boys?"

"I'm afraid so, Mister Jensen," Judge Proctor said. "I don't like it. But we played this straight by the book. If you could bring me evidence to the contrary, I'd certainly listen to it and act accordingly."

"So will I, Smoke," Monte said softly. "Believe it."

"Oddly enough, I do believe you. Come on, Colby. Let's go."

Lawyer Hunt Brook was so angry he was trembling. "This is terrible!" He practically shouted the words. "This is not justice!"

"The lady is blind, Mister Brook," Judge Proctor said. "I shouldn't have to remind you of that." He stood up. "Come, Sheriff."

Stepping outside, the judge almost ran into Pistol Le Roux. "Good Lord!" Proctor said. "It's been years, Pistol. You're looking quite well."

"Thanks. How'd it go in yonder, Judge?"

"Not to anyone's liking, I'm afraid. Are you going to be in town long?"

"I work for Smoke Jensen."

"Oh, my!" the judge said. "How many of you, ah, men did Mister Jensen hire, Pistol?"

Pistol smiled. "Twenty or so."

Judge Proctor suddenly felt weak-kneed. "I see. Well, it's been nice seeing you, Pistol."

"Same here, Judge."

As they walked off, Monte asked. "How come it is you know that old gunslick, Judge?"

"I was up in the Wyoming country hearing a case of his when he was marshal of a town up there. Four pretty good gunhands braced him one afternoon."

"How'd it come out?"

"Pistol killed them all."

"And they's *twenty* of them old gunhawks workin' for Jensen?"

"Yes. Rather makes one feel inadequate, doesn't it, Sheriff?"

"Whatever that means, Judge."

The judge didn't feel like explaining. "You know, Monte, you could be a good lawman if you'd just try."

"Is that what I been feelin' lately, Judge?"

"Probably. But since you — we — are in Tilden Franklin's pocket, what are we going to do about it?"

"We wasn't in his pocket in this one, Judge."

"That is correct. And it's rather nice feeling, isn't it, Sheriff Carson?"

"Damn shore is, Judge Proctor. Would you like to join me in a drink, Judge?"

"No, Sheriff, I think not. I just decided to quit."

3

When Smoke and Sally and Pearlie and most of the other aging gunhawks rode up to Colby's place the following morning, they were all amazed to see the hills covered with people.

"What the hell?" Pearlie said.

"They're showin' Tilden Franklin how they feel," Luke said. "And rubbin' his nose in it."

"Would you look yonder?" Jay said. "That there is Big Mamma. In a *dress*!"

"Musta been a tent-maker move into town," Apache said.

"Who is that pretty lady beside the . . . large lady I presume you men are talking about?" Sally asked.

Smoke and Sally were in a buckboard, the others on horseback.

"That's Big Mamma's wife, Miss Sally," Silver Jim explained.

Sally looked up at him. "I beg your pardon, Silver Jim?"

"They was married 'bout three year ago, I reckon it was. Big Mamma had to slap that minister around a good bit 'fore he'd agree to do it, but he done 'er."

Sally turned her crimson face forward. "I do not wish to pursue this line of conversation any further, thank you."

"No, ma'am," Silver Jim said. "Me neither."

The service was a short one, but sincerely given by Ralph. Adam's forever-young body was buried on a hillside overlooking the Colby ranch.

And while most knew the TF riders were watching from the hills, no TF rider showed his face at the funeral. The mood of the crowd was such that if any TF riders had made an appearance, there most likely would have been a hanging.

Belle Colby and Velvet sat in the front yard during the service. Velvet had yet to speak a word or utter any type of sound.

Tilden sat on the front porch of his fine ranch house. He hurt all over. Never, *never*, in his entire life, had he been so badly torn up. And by a goddamned two-bit gunslinger.

Clint walked up to the porch. "Twelve hands pulled out last night, Boss."

"You pay 'em off?" The words were hard to understand and even harder for Tilden to speak. His lips were grotesquely swollen and half a dozen teeth were missing. His nose had yet to be set because it was so badly broken and swollen hideously.

"No. They just packed it all up and rode off. Told Pete Harris they hired their guns to fight men, not to make war on little kids."

"How noble of them. Hell with them!"

"Some of the others say they'll ride for brand—when it comes to punchin' cows. But they ain't gettin' involved in no war."

"Hell with them too. Fire 'em!"

"Boss?"

"Goddamn you! I said fire them!"

Clint stood his ground. He put one boot up on the porch and stared square at Tilden. "Now you listen to me, Boss. We got a hell of a big herd out yonder. And we need punchers to see to that herd. Now I feel sick at my stomach over what I ordered them men to do to that Colby girl, but it's done. And I can't change it. I reckon I'll answer to the Lord for that. If so, that's 'tween me and Him. But for now, I got a herd to look after. Are you so crazy mad you can't understand that?"

Tilden took several deep breaths—as deeply as he dared, that is. For Smoke had broken several of his ribs. He calmed himself. "All right, all right, Clint! You've made your point. I want a tally of how many men are going to fight for me. Those that want to punch cows, do so. But for every one that won't fight, hire two that will. Is that understood?"

"Yes, sir."

"Let's face it. You made a mistake by suggesting what was done to the Colby bitch; I made a mistake by going along with it. All right. Like you say, it's done. I understand that Colby brat wrote in that stupid book about Luke avenging him, right?"

"Yes, sir."

"I figured by now that old bastard would have come storming in here, fire in his eyes and his guns smoking. Maybe he's lost his balls."

Clint shook his head. "You never knew Luke Nations, did you, Boss?"

"Can't say as I ever had the pleasure."

"I do," Clint said softly. "He's . . ." The foreman searched for a word. "Awesome. There ain't a nerve in his body, Boss. He'll be comin' in smokin', all right. Bet on that. But he'll pick the time and place."

"Hire the gunnies!" Tilden ordered, his voice harsh. "And then tell our gunhawks it's open season on nesters."

Clint hesitated. "Can I say something, Boss?"

"What is it, Clint?"

"Why don't we just drop the whole damned thing, Boss? Call it off? If word of this war gets to the governor's ears, he's liable to send in the Army."

"Hell with the governor. We got the sheriff and the judge in our pockets; how's anything goin' to get out?"

"I don't know about Monte and the judge no more, Boss. They was both pushin' real hard yesterday about that Velvet thing."

"I got them elected, I can get them un-elected."

Clint's smile was rueful. "You're forgettin' something, Boss."

"What?"

"The *people* elected 'em. For four years."

Clint turned around and walked off, leaving Tilden alone on the porch . . . with his hurting body.

And his hate.

Two weeks passed with no trouble . . . none at all. Between Tilden and the smaller spreads, that is. There was still minor trouble in town. But Monte and his men put that down quickly and hard. And the now-sober Judge Proctor hit the offenders with such stiff fines and terms in the new jailhouse that it seemed to deter other potential lawbreakers.

And Monte stopped collecting graft from the saloons and other businesses. He was being paid a good salary as sheriff, and decided that was enough. Any deputy that didn't like the new rules could leave. A few did, most stayed. All in all, it was a good job.

Monte looked up as the front door to his office opened. Johnny North stood there, gazing at him.

"You decide to make your move now, Johnny?" Monte asked.

"I don't know," the gunfighter said. "Mind if I sit down?"

Monte pointed to a chair. "Help yourself."

Johnny first poured himself a cup of coffee. He sat and looked at the sheriff. "What the hell's the matter with you, Monte? You got religion or something?"

Monte smiled. "I ain't got religion, that's for sure. Maybe it's the something. Why do you ask?"

"I been waitin' for you to come brace me for two damn weeks. You forgot we're supposed to hate each other?"

"No, I ain't. But I'll tell you this: I can't remember what we're supposed to hate each other for!"

Johnny scratched his chin. "Come to think of it, neither can I. Wasn't it something about a gal?"

Monte started laughing. "I don't know! Hell, Johnny. Whatever it was it happened so many years ago, what difference does it make now?"

Johnny North joined in the laughter. "You et yet?"

"Nope. You buyin'?"

"Hell, why not? it's gettin' too damn hot outside for a gunfight anyways."

Laughing, the old enemies walked to a cafe.

A few of Tilden Franklin's hands were lounging in a tight knot outside a saloon. These were not the gunhawks employed by the TF brand, but cowboys. And to show they were taking no sides in this matter, they had checked their guns with the bartender inside the saloon.

Monte Carson had made it clear, by posting notices around the town, that TF gunhawks had better not start any trouble in his town, or in any area of his jurisdiction. He'd had to get the judge to spell all the words.

The judge had done so, gleefully.

"Looks like Johnny North and the Sheriff done kissed and made up," one cowboy remarked.

"That's more trouble for Tilden," another observed. There was just a small note of satisfaction in the statement.

Another TF puncher sat down on the lip of a watering trough. "It's May, boys. Past time to move the herds up into the high country for the summer."

"I been thinkin' the same thing."

"I think I'll talk to Clint when we get back to the ranch. Kinda suggest, nice-like, that we get the herds ready to move. If he goes along with it, and I think he will, that'll put us some thirty-five miles from the ranch, up in the high lonesome. Take a hell of a pistol to shoot thirty-five miles."

"Yeah. That'd put us clean out of any war, just doin' what we're paid to do: look after cows."

Another cowboy sat down on the steps. He looked at the puncher who had suggested the high country. "You know, Dan, sometimes you can show some signs of havin' a little sense."

"Thank you," Dan said modestly. "For a fact, my momma didn't raise no fool for a son."

"Is that right?"

"Yeah," Dan said with a smile. "I had a sister."

The aging gunfighters were having the time of their lives.

They were doing what most loved to do: work cattle. Smoke's bulls had been busy during the winter, and his herd had increased appreciably now that the calving was over. It was branding time, and the gunfighters were pitching in and working just as hard as Smoke or Pearlie. Some had gone to other small spreads in the area, helping out there, their appearance a welcome sight to the overworked and under-staffed ranchers.

It appeared that the area was at peace. Smoke knew, from riding the high country, that Tilden Franklin's punchers were busy moving the TF herds into the high pastures, and doing so, he suspected, for many reasons, not all of them associated with the welfare of the cattle. That was another sign that Tilden had not given up in his fight to rid the area of all who would not bend to his will. Those TF hands who were not gunslicks but cowboys were clearing out of the line of fire.

He said as much to Charlie Starr.

The gunhand agreed. "It ain't even got started good yet, Smoke. I got word that Tilden is hirin' all the guns he can, and they're beginning to trickle in. It's shapin' up to be a bad one."

"They any good?"

"Some of them are bad hombres. Some of them are just startin' to build a rep. But they're alive, so they must be fair hands with a gun."

Smoke looked around him, at the vast, majestic panorama that nature had bestowed on this part of Colorado. "It's all so foolish," he said. "There is more than enough room for us all."

"Not to a man like Tilden," Luke Nations said, walking up, a tin cup of coffee in his hand. He was taking a break from the branding. "Tilden, least for as long as I've known of him, has always craved to be the bull of the woods. He's crazy."

All present certainly agreed with that.

"What'd Colby say or do when you give him that money we found in that holler tree?" Charlie asked Smoke.

"Sent it to Tilden by way of the Sheriff. Wrote him a note

too. Told him where to put the money. Told him to put it there sideways."

Charlie and Luke both grinned at that, Luke saying, "I sure would have liked to seen the look on Tilden's face when he got that."

"How's his health?" Charlie asked.

"Coming along," Smoke said with a grin. "Doc Colton goes out there several times a week. 'Bout the only thing wrong with Tilden now—other than the fact he's crazy—is that he don't have any front teeth and his ribs is still sore."

"I figure we got two, maybe three more weeks before Tilden pulls all the stops out," Luke said. "He's not goin' to do nothin' until he's able to sit a saddle and handle a short gun. Then look out."

And they all agreed with that.

"I figure he'll save us for last," Smoke said. "I figure he'll hit Peyton first. That's the ranch closest to his range, and the furtherest from us. I've warned Peyton to be careful, but the man seemed to think it's all over now."

"Is he a fool?" Luke asked.

"No," Smoke said softly. "Just a man who tries to see the best in all people. He thinks Tilden has 'seen the light,' to use Peyton's own words."

"He's a fool then," Charlie opined. "There isn't one ounce of good in Tilden Franklin. That little trick with Velvet should have convinced Peyton."

"Speakin' of Velvet . . ." Luke let it trail off into silence.

"No change," Smoke said. "She eats, and sits. She has not uttered a sound in weeks."

"Her pa?"

"Colby has turned real quiet-like," Smoke told the men. "Never speaks of her. But I don't like the look in his eyes. Belle told me he takes his pistol out every day and practices drawing and firing."

"He any good?"

"No," Smoke said flatly. "He just doesn't have the eye and hand coordination needed to be any good. He's slow as molasses and can't hit jack-crap with a short gun."

"Then he's headin' for trouble," Luke said. "You want I

should go talk to him?"

"Can if you want. But it won't do any good. I tried talking to him. He just turned his back and walked away."

Charlie spat on the ground. "The fool is diggin' his own grave, Smoke."

"Yeah. I know it. But he's all tore up with grief. I'm thinkin' he's gonna brace the Harris Brothers if he ever gets the chance."

"They'll kill him," Luke said. "Them boys is real good."

Smoke nodded his head. He summed up his feelings by saying, "I think Colby wants to die."

4

Paul Jackson walked into his brother's office at the general store and told Ed he was quitting.

Ed looked at his brother as if he was looking at a fool. "To do what?"

"I staked me out a claim. Looks promisin' too. You're makin' all the money here. Hell with you!"

"Fine. But remember this: you'll not get a penny's worth of credit from me."

"I got money of my own." He walked out of the office.

"You're a fool!" Ed shouted after his brother.

His brother turned around and made a very obscene gesture. It was intended for Ed, but Ed's wife caught it as well.

Peg stamped her foot.

Paul laughed and walked on out, feeling as though he had just had a great weight lifted from his shoulders. He swung into the saddle and trotted out, toward the high lonesome, where he had staked his claim.

Paul would show them all. He'd come back a rich man and take Bountiful from that namby-pamby preacher and then, just like in one of them dime novels, the both of them would ride off into the sunset, to be forever together.

Or something like that.

"What side of this fracus is Utah Slim on?" Johnny North asked Monte over coffee one bright early summer morning.

"I can't figure it, myself. He don't appear to be on neither side. And he ain't hurtin' for money. He's always got a wad of greenbacks."

"Gamble?"

Monte shook his head. "No. I ain't never seen nor heard of him gamblin'."

"He's on somebody's payroll," the gunslinger opined. "You can bet on that. Utah don't do nothin' for nothin'. He's here for a reason."

"You find out, you let me know?"

"Why not? I sure ain't got no axes to grind in this here fight."

"Tilden's hirin', you know."

"Screw Tilden Franklin. I got me a little claim staked out and got guys workin' it for shares. 'Bout five years back, I started puttin' back a little bit of money ever' time I had some to spare. Got it in a bank up in Boulder. With the gold I get out of this claim, I aim to start me a little ranch; maybe do a little farmin' too. Hang up my guns."

Monte started grinning.

"What are you grinnin' about, you ape?" Johnny asked.

"Gonna do a little bit of ranchin' and a little bit of farmin', hey?"

"Yeah! What's wrong with that?"

"Nothin'. Nothin' at all. But what happens if you run into some big rancher like Tilden when you decide to settle down?"

"Well . . . I reckon I'll fight."

Monte suddenly felt better. He started chuckling. "Oh, yeah, Johnny, you got an axe to grind in this war—you just ain't realized it yet."

Johnny thought about that, then he too started chuckling. "By God, Monte, you right. I think I'll go see if that feller Colby needs a hand. Might do me some good to do some hard work for a change."

"He can't pay you nothin'."

"I ain't askin' for nothin'."

Boot heels drummed on the boardwalk and someone was hollering for the sheriff.

Monte jumped up and headed for the door, Johnny right behind him. A wild-eyed miner almost collided with them both.

"Come quick, Sheriff! That nester Colby is about to draw down on a TF gunnie named Donnie. Hurry, Sheriff, hurry!"

"Crazy farmer!" Monte yelled, running toward a saloon. He could see a crowd gathered on both sides of a man standing out in the street. He recognized the man as Colby, and with a sick feeling realized he was not going to be able to stop it. He just knew that Colby had started it, and if that was the case, he would not interfere. It was an unwritten rule in the West—and would be for about a decade to come—that a man broke his own horses and killed his own snakes. If one challenged another to a gunfight, and it was a fair fight, few lawmen would interfere.

The gunslick, Donnie, was standing on the boardwalk, laughing at the farmer. Colby was standing in the street, cursing the TF rider.

Monte stopped some distance away, halting both Johnny and the miner. "Who started it?"

"That farmer. He called Donnie out and started cussin' him. Ain't you gonna stop it, Sheriff?"

"There is nothin' I can do, mister," Monte told the man. "If Colby wants to back off, I'll see that he gets that chance. But I can't stop it. There ain't no city or county law agin a one-on-one fight."

"Colby's gonna get killed," the miner said.

"I reckon," Monte agreed.

"What's the matter, Pig-farmer?" Donnie taunted the older man. "You done lost your nerve?"

"No," Colby said, his voice firm. "Anytime you're ready, draw!"

Donnie and his friends laughed. "Hell, Nester," Donnie said. "I ain't gonna draw on you. You called me out, remember?"

"You raped my Velvet and killed my boy."

"I didn't rape nobody, Nester. Your daughter was sellin' and we'uns bought. Cash money for merchandise. Your boy

175

busted up in there and started throwin' lead around. We fired back. And that's the way it happened."

"You're a goddamned liar!" Colby shouted.

"Now that tears it, Nester," Donnie said, his hands over the butts of his guns. "You make your play." He grinned nastily. "Sorry 'bout Velvet, though. She shore liked it, the more the merrier."

Colby went for his old Navy Colt .36. Grinning, Donnie let the man fumble and then with a smooth, practiced motion drew, cocked, and fired, the slug taking Colby in the right shoulder. The farmer spun around, dropping his Navy Colt onto the dirt of the street.

Colby reached for the gun with his left hand and Donnie fired again, the slug striking Colby in the stomach. The farmer was tossed to one side and Donnie's Colt roared again, the slug taking Colby flush in the face, just above the nose and below the eye sockets. Colby's face was shattered. He trembled once and was still.

"That's it!" Monte shouted. "Holster your gun and ride out of town, Donnie. Right now. Git gone, boy, or face me. Make your choice."

"Hey, I'm leavin', Sheriff." Donnie grinned, returning his Colt to leather. "I mean, you saw it — I didn't start it."

Louis Longmont had watched the whole sickening show from across the street. But, like the sheriff, he had made no attempt to stop it. Such was the code demanded of those who braved the frontier.

Longmont tossed his cigar into the street and walked back to his gaming tent. Then a truth made its way into the light of his mind: he was sick of the whole damned mess. Tired of late hours and tired of taking other people's money — even if his games were honest — tired of sweat-stinking miners and cowboys, tired of the violence and dust and heat and intense cold. Tired of it all. Just plain tired of it.

The gambler realized then that this was to be his last boom town.

That thought made him immensely happy.

From his table in his gaming room, Louis watched the undertaker's black hack rumble past.

He heard a voice saying, "This poor wretch have any family?"

He could not hear the reply.

Louis poured a tumbler of scotch and lifted the glass, silently toasting the dead Colby.

"Not much money in his pockets." The undertaker's voice came to Louis.

"Mike!" Louis called.

The bouncer stuck his big head around the corner. "Yeah, Boss?"

"Go tell the undertaker to prepare Colby's body and do it up nice—the best he can offer. I'm paying."

"Yes, sir."

"And tell Johnny North to come see me."

"Yes, sir."

A few minutes later, Johnny North stepped into the gaming tent. "You wanna see me, Louis?"

The two were not friends, but then neither were they enemies. Just two men who were very, very good with a gun and held a mutual respect for each other.

"You know where Colby's spread is located, Johnny?"

"I can probably find it."

"Someone needs to ride up there and tell his wife that she's a widow."

"You tellin' me to do it, Louis?"

"No." The gambler's left hand worked at a deck of playing cards on the table. His right hand was not visible. "But I am asking."

"If that's the case . . . fine. I'll go."

"Ask her . . . no, ride on to Smoke's place and tell him what happened, if you will, please. Ask him to arrange for a wagon to come for Colby's body."

"I'll do that too, Louis. Louis?"

The gambler looked at the gunfighter.

"It wasn't right . . . that shootin'. But we couldn't interfere."

"I know. But the West is changing, Johnny. Going to ranch and farm a bit with the savings you have up in Boulder, Johnny?"

177

That shook the blond-haired Nevada gunslick. "How in the hell . . ."

"I own part of the bank, Johnny," Louis said with a very slight smile.

Johnny returned the smile. "I think I might just ask the Widder Colby if she needs some help up there, Louis. Not today, now, that wouldn't be fitten. But later on."

"That would be a very decent act on your part, Johnny. I think Belle would appreciate that very much."

"I'll get goin' now. See you, Louis."

"See you. Thanks, Johnny."

As the sounds of Johnny's big California spurs faded on the boardwalk, Andre stuck his head out of the kitchen. "A snack, sir?" the chef asked.

"I think not, Andre. Just coffee, please."

The chef hesitated. "It is a dismal and barbaric place, is it not, *monsieur?*"

"For a while longer, Andre. But it will change as time passes, and time will pass."

"*Oui, monsieur.*"

Johnny North caught up with Donnie about five miles out of town. The young gunslick had several of his friends with him, but numbers had never bothered Johnny North before, and didn't this time.

Johnny North made all the gunslicks and so-called gunslicks of this group nervous. They all kept their hands in plain sight, and as far away from their guns as could be humanly arranged.

"I ain't lookin' for no truck with you, Johnny," Donnie said, his voice sounding a bit shrill.

"Peel off from your friends, Donnie," Johnny told him.

"Why?"

"We're gonna take a ride, just you and me."

"Where we goin'?"

"To deliver a death message."

"I'll be damned if I'm goin'!"

Johnny smiled grimly. "Do you prefer dead to damned,

178

Donnie?"

"Huh?"

"You can either ride to the Colby place with me, and tell the widder how you gunned down her man, or you can be taken back to the TF spread . . . acrost your saddle. It's up to you, Donnie."

"They's five of us, Johnny," a TF gunhawk said.

"There won't be when the smoke clears."

Donnie and the others thought about that for a moment. "I reckon I'll ride with you, Johnny," Donnie said.

"Fine. You others hightail it back to the TF. You tell Tilden Franklin that from now on I'll be workin' out at Colby's place. Tell him to keep his ass and your asses off that range. You got all that?"

"Yes, sir, Johnny," a young TF gunnie said.

"Yes, sir, *Mister North*!"

"Yes, sir, Mister North!"

"Ride!"

The TF gunnies laid the spurs to their horses and left in a cloud of dust and drumming hooves. None of them was lookin' forward to delivering this news to Tilden Franklin. But none of them wanted to tangle with Johnny North neither. Lesser of two evils, they figured.

"You ride in front of me, Donnie," Johnny said. "Move out."

There was a lot of things Donnie wanted to say. Wisely, he said none of them. Just silently cussed.

5

"There was five of you!" Tilden shouted at the men. "Five of you! I'm paying you men good money, fighting wages. But so far, I've seen damn little fighting. But a hell of a lot of running. What does it take to put some backbone in you men?"

The gunslicks stood and took it in silence. Luis Chamba and his sidekicks, Kane and Sanderson, stood by the corner of the big house and smiled at the dressing-down Tilden was giving his gunhands.

When the chastised men had departed, Luis said, "Perhaps, *señor*, it is time for some night-riding, *si*?"

Tilden shifted his cold eyes to the Mexican gunfighter. "I'll pass the word, Luis. You're in charge. The others take orders from you. *Cooriente?*"

Luis smiled his reply.

"Make your plans, Luis."

"This game, *señor* . . . what are the limits?"

"No limits, Luis. Let the chips fall."

"I like this game, *señor*," Luis said with a smile.

"I rather thought you would," Tilden said tightly.

Belle Colby stood in her front yard, Bob by her side, and listened to Donnie haltingly tell what had happened. The TF gunslick's face was flushed with anger, but he told it all, leaving nothing out.

When he had finished, Johnny said, "If I ever see you on this range, Donnie, I'll kill you. Now ride, punk—ride!"

Donnie wheeled his horse and galloped out.

Bob said, "Are you really Johnny North?"

"Yes. Ma'am?" He looked at Belle. "I'll be ridin' over to the Sugarloaf. I should be back by sundown. I'll bunk in the barn if that's all right with you."

"That will be fine, Mister North."

She had taken the news of her husband's death calmly. Too calmly for Johnny. He sat his horse and looked at her.

"You're wondering why I'm behaving in such a calm manner, Mister North?"

"The thought did pass my mind, ma'am."

"My husband told me before dawn this morning, as he was belting on a gun, that he was going into town. I felt then that I would never seen him alive again. I did my grieving this morning."

Johnny nodded his head. He sat looking at the woman for a moment longer. Nice-looking woman; kind of trail worn, but that was to be expected, for this was a hard life for a woman. Then he thought of all the dance-hall floozies and hurdy-gurdy girls he had known down through the long and bloody years. Belle Colby, with her worn gingham dress, sunburned face, and work-hardened hands, seemed beautiful compared to them.

Johnny cleared his throat and plopped his hat back on his head. "You gonna need help around here, ma'am," he said. "If'n it's all right, I'll stick around and pull my weight and then some."

"That would be nice, Mister North," Belle said with a tired smile. "Yes. I'd like that."

Johnny returned the smile and wheeled his horse, heading for the Sugarloaf.

The crowd was respectable at Colby's burying, but not near so many people showed up as had Adam's planting.

181

Most men, whether they would say it aloud or not — and it was the latter if they were married, felt that Colby had done a damn fool thing. And while most of them didn't condone what Donnie had done, they probably would not have interfered. They might have done something similiar had they been in Colby's boots, but it would have been done with a sawed-off express gun in their hands, not with a pistol in a fast-draw type of situation.

Out here, a man had damn well best know his limitations and capabilities.

And behave accordingly.

Once again the Reverend Ralph Morrow conducted the funeral services, and once again he and Bountiful and lots of others stayed for lunch. That was no problem, for everyone who attended the services had brought some sort of covered dish.

Like hangings, funerals also served as quite a social event.

Louis Longmont was there, all fancied up in a tailored black suit . . . carefully tailored to hide the shoulder-holster rig he wore under the jacket.

The aging gunfighters were all in attendance, gussied up in their best. They made no attempts to conceal their Colts, wearing them openly, low and tied down.

Pearlie had stayed behind at the Sugarloaf, just in case some TF riders decided to use the occasion to come calling. With a funeral of their own in mind.

Monte Carson and Judge Proctor were there, and so were Hunt and Willow Brook, Colton and Mona Spalding, Haywood and Dana Arden.

Ed Jackson did not show. He figured he might lose a dollar or so by closing his store.

Besides, Ed felt that Colby had gotten exactly what he deserved. And the next time he saw that Smoke Jensen, Ed just might give him a good piece of his mind about the totally uncalled-for beating of a fine man like Tilden Franklin. Well . . . he'd think about doing that, anyways.

"Going to stay on up here for a time?" Monte asked Johnny.

"Thought I might. Belle has her hands full all day just tryin' to look after Velvet, and I think me and Bob can pretty well handle it. And some of them old gunslingers come over from time to time, Belle says. Them old boys know a lot about farming and such."

Monte and Judge Proctor said their goodbyes to Belle and returned to Fontana.

By late afternoon, most of those attending had left for home, since many had traveled miles to get there. About half of the old gunslicks had left, returning to the Sugarloaf to give Pearlie a break.

Louis had returned with Monte and Judge Proctor, riding a magnificent black stallion.

"Like to ride over and spend the night at our place?" Smoke asked Reverend Morrow. "It's a lot closer than town, and we have the room. 'Sides, I'd like for Sally and Bountiful to get to know each other."

After consulting with his wife, the young couple agreed. Those returning to the Sugarloaf made their way slowly homeward, Smoke and Sally and Ralph and Bountiful in buckboards, the rest on horseback.

"It's so beautiful up here," Bountiful said, squeezing her husband's arm. "So peaceful and lovely and quiet. I think I would like to live up here."

"Might have a hard time supporting a church up here, Bountiful."

"Yes, that's true. But you could do what you've always wanted to do, Ralph."

He looked at her, beautiful in the sunlight that filtered through the trees alongside the narrow road.

"You would be content with that, Bountiful? A part-time preacher and a full-time farmer?"

"Yes."

"You're sure?"

"I'm sure of several things, Ralph. One is that I'm not cut out to be a preacher's wife. I love you, but that isn't enough. Secondly, I'm not so sure you're cut out to be a preacher."

"It's that obvious, Bountiful?"

"Ralph, nothing happened back East. It was a harmless flirtation and nothing more. I think you're always known that. Haven't you?"

"I suspected. I should have whipped that scoundrel's ass while I was feeling like it."

He spoke the words without realizing what he had really said.

Bountiful started laughing.

"What is so . . ." Then Ralph grinned, flushed, and joined his wife in laughter.

"Ralph, you're a good, decent man. I think you're probably the finest man I have ever known. But you went into the ministry out of guilt. And I think that is the wrong reason for choosing this vocation. Look at us, Ralph. Listen to what we're saying. We've never talked like this before. Isn't it funny, odd, that we should be doing so now?"

"Perhaps it's the surroundings." And for a moment, Ralph's thoughts went winging back in time, back almost eight years, when he was a bare-knuckle fighter enjoying no small amount of fame in the ring, open-air and smokers.

The young man he'd been fighting that hot afternoon was good and game, but no match for Ralph. But back then, winning was all that Ralph had on his mind, that and money. And he was making lots of money, both fighting and gambling. The fight had gone on for more than thirty rounds, which was no big deal to Ralph, who had fought more than ninety rounds more than once.

And then Ralph had seen his opportunity and had taken it, slamming a vicious left-right combination to the young man's head.

The young man had dropped to the canvas. And had never again opened his eyes. The fighter had died several days later.

Ralph Morrow had never stepped into another ring after that.

He and Bountiful had known each other since childhood, and it was taken for granted by all concerned that they would some day marry. Bountiful's parents were relieved when Ralph quit the ring. Bountiful was a bit miffed, but managed to conceal it.

Both had known but had never, until now, discussed the obvious fact that Ralph simply was not cut out to be a minister.

"What are you thinking, Ralph?"

"About the death I caused."

"It could just as easily have been you, Ralph," she reminded him. "You've told me a thousand times that the fight was fair and you both were evenly matched. It's over, Ralph. It's been over. Stop dwelling on it and get on with the matter of living."

Quite unlike the strait-laced minister, he leaned over and gave Bountiful a smooch on the cheek. She blushed while the old gunfighters, riding alongside the buckboards, grinned and pretended not to notice.

After supper, the young couples sat outside the cabin, enjoying the cool air and talking.

"How many acres do you have, Smoke?" Ralph asked.

"I don't really know. That valley yonder," he said, pointing to the Sugarloaf, "is five miles long and five miles wide. I do know we've filed on and bought another two thousand acres that we plan to farm. Right now we're only farming a very small portion of it. Hay and corn mostly. Right over there—" again he pointed, "is seven hundred and fifty acres of prime farm land just sittin' idle. I think we overbought some."

"That acreage is just over that little hill?" Bountiful asked.

"Yes," Sally said, hiding a smile, for it was obvious that the minister and his wife were interested in buying land.

"We'll ride over in the morning and take a look at it, if you'd like," Smoke suggested.

"Do you have the proper saddle for Bountiful?" Ralph asked.

"We're about the same size," Sally told him. "She can wear some of my jeans and ride astride."

Bountiful fanned her suddenly hot face. She had never had on a pair of men's britches in her life. But . . . this was the West. Besides, who would see her?

"I don't know whether that would be proper for a minister's wife," Ralph objected.

"Don't be silly!" Sally said, sticking out her chin. "If it's all right for a man, why should it be objectionable for a woman to wear britches?"

"Well . . ." Ralph said weakly. Forceful women tended to somewhat frighten him.

"Have you ever read anything by Susan B. Anthony, Bountiful?" Sally asked.

"Oh, yes! I think she's wonderful, don't you?"

"Yes. As well as Elizabeth Cady Stanton. You just wait, Bountiful. Some day women will be on an equal footing with men."

"Lord save us all!" Smoke said with a laugh. He shut up when Sally gave him a dark look.

"Do you think the time will come when women will be elected to Congress?" Bountiful asked.

Ralph sat stunned at the very thought.

Smoke sat grinning.

"Oh my, yes! But first we have to work very hard to get the vote. That will come only if we women band together and work very hard for it."

"Let's do that here!" Bountiful said, clapping her hands.

"Fine!" Sally agreed.

"But how?" Bountiful sobered.

"Well . . . my mother knows Susan B. very well. They went to school together in Massachusetts. I'll post a letter to Mother and she can write Miss Anthony. Then we'll see."

"Wonderful!" Bountiful cried. "I'm sure Willow and Mona and Dana would be delighted to help us."

Smoke rolled a cigarette and smiled at the expression on Ralph's face. The man looked as though he might faint at any moment.

The ladies rose and went chattering off into the cabin.

"My word!" Ralph managed to blurt out.

186

Smoke laughed at him.

"Boss!" Pearlie stilled the laughter and sobered the moment. "Look yonder." He pointed.

In the dusk of fast-approaching evening, the western sky held a small, faint glow.

"What is that?" Ralph asked. "A forest fire?"

"No," Smoke said, rising. "That's Peyton's place. Tilden's hands have fired it."

6

There was nothing Smoke could do. Peyton's spread was a good twenty-five miles away from Sugarloaf, his range bordering Tilden's holdings.

It was not long before the fire's glow had softened, and then faded completely out.

"Peyton refused our offer of help," Buttermilk said. "Some of us offered to stay over thar with him. But he turned us down flat."

"We'll ride over in the morning," Smoke said. "At first light. There is nothing we can do this evening."

"Except wonder what is happening over there," Ralph stated.

"And how many funerals you gonna have to hold," Luke added.

Peyton, his wife June, and their kids had been forced to retreat into the timber when it became obvious they were hopelessly outnumbered and outgunned. The family had made it out of the burning, smoking area with the clothes on their backs and nothing else.

They had lain quietly in the deep timber and watched their life's work go up, or down, in fire. They had watched as the hooded men shot all the horses, the pigs, and then set the barn blazing. The corral had been pulled down by ropes, the garden trampled under the hooves of horses. The Peyton family was left with nothing. Nothing at all.

They could not even tell what spread the men had come from, for the horses had all worn different or altered brands.

The family lay in the timber long after the night-riders had gone. They were not hurt, not physically, but something just as important had been damaged: their spirit.

"I tried to be friends with Tilden," Peyton said. "I went over to his place and spoke with him. He seemed to be reasonable enough, thanked me for coming over. Now this."

"They turned the wagon over," June said, her eyes peering into the darkness. "Broke off one wheel. But that can be fixed. There's lots of land to be had just north of here. I won't live like this," she warned. "I will not. And I mean that."

"I got a little money. I can buy some horses. We'll see what we can salvage in the morning."

"Nothing," June said bitterly. "Nothing at all."

"And you don't have any idea who they were?" Smoke asked Peyton.

Dawn had broken free of the mountains only an hour before. Smoke and some of his old gunhawks had left the Sugarloaf hours before first light, stopping along the way at the other small spreads.

"No," Peyton said, a note of surrender in his voice.

The Apache Kid returned from his tracking. "Headin' for the TF spread," he said. "Just as straight as an arrow that's where they're headin'."

"So?" June demanded, her hands on her hips. "So what? Prove that them riders come from the TF. And then even if you do that, see what the law will do about it."

"Now, June," Peyton said.

The woman turned around and walked off, her dress dirty and soot-covered.

"What are you gonna do?" Smoke asked Peyton.

"Pull out. What else is there to do?"

"We'll help you rebuild, just like we're doing with Wilbur Mason."

"And then what?" Peyton demanded. "What happens after

that? I'll tell you," he blurted out. "The same thing all over again. No. I'll find me some horses, fix that busted wheel, and take off. This land ain't worth dyin' over, Smoke. It just ain't."

"That's not what you told me a few weeks back."

"I changed my mind," the man replied sullenly. "I don't feel like jawin' about it no more. My mind is made up. We're taking what we can salvage and pullin' out. Headin' up north of here. See you men." He turned and walked off, catching up with his wife.

"Let him go," Charlie said to Smoke. "He's not goin' to last anywhere out here. First time a drought hits him, he'll pack up and pull out. The locust come, he'll head out agin, always lookin' for an easy life. But he'll never find it. You know yourself it takes a hard man to make it out here. Peyton's weak, so's his woman. And them kids are whiners. He'll leave the land pretty soon, I'm figurin'. He'll get him a job in some little store, sellin' shoes and ribbons, and pretty soon he'll find something wrong with *that* job. But it ain't never gonna be his fault. It'll always be the fault of someone else. Forget him, Smoke. He ain't got no good sand bottom to him."

Smoke hated to say it, but he felt Charlie was right in his assessment of Peyton. Tilden had burned Wilbur Mason out; that had just made Wilbur and his family all the more determined to stay and fight.

"Good luck, Peyton!" Smoke called.

The man did not even turn around. Just waved his hand and kept on walking.

Somehow that gesture, or lack of it, made Smoke mad as hell. He wondered if he'd ever see Peyton or his family again. He thought, if he didn't, he wouldn't lose any sleep over the loss.

The few other small rancher-farmers in the high country met that afternoon on a plateau just about halfway between Smoke's Sugarloaf and the beginning of the TF range. And it was, for the most part, a quiet, subdued gathering of men.

Mike Garrett and his two hands; Wilbur Mason and Bob Colby; Ray Johnson and his hired hand; Nolan Edwards and his two oldest boys; Steve Matlock, Smoke and his gunhands.

And Reverend Ralph Morrow, wearing a pair of jeans and checkered shirt.

"Ralph is gonna buy some land from me," Smoke explained. "Farm some and ranch a little. Preach part time. The minister come up with a pretty good idea, I'm thinking. But we'll get to his idea in a minute. Anybody got any objections to Ralph joinin' our group?"

"I ain't got no objections," Ray said. "I'm just wonderin' if, him bein' a preacher and all, will he fight?"

Ralph stepped forward. "Some of you might know me. For five years, I went by another name. I fought under the name of the Cincinnati Kid."

Matlock snapped his fingers. "I read about you in the Gazette. You kilt a man . . ah . . ."

He trailed off into an uncomfortable silence.

"Yes," Ralph said. "I killed a man with my fists. I didn't mean to, but I did. As to whether I'll fight. Yes. For my family, my land, my friends. I'll fight."

And everyone there believed him. Still, one had to say, "But, Reverend Morrow, you're a minister; you can't go around shootin' folks!"

Ralph smiled . . . rather grimly. "Smoke and Charlie and some of the boys are going to help me build my cabin, first thing in the morning. You let some sucker come around and start trouble, you'll see how fast I'll shoot him."

The laughter helped to relieve the tension.

And Reverend Ralph Morrow suddenly became just "one of the boys."

"How about that other idea, Smoke?" Wilbur asked.

Smoke walked to the edge of the flats. He pointed down at the road. "That road, right there, connects Danner and Signal Hill. Seven, eight miles further down, you got to cut south to get to Fontana. Right?"

All agreed that was true. So?

"Pearlie is ridin' hard to the county seat right now. The

Reverend and his wife, Bountiful, come up with this idea at noonin'. Right here, boys, right here on this plateau, but back yonder a ways, there's gonna be a town. We don't need Fontana. The land the town will be built on is gonna be filed on by Pearlie; he's carrying the money to buy some of it outright. When that surveyor was through here last year, he left a bunch of his markings and such at the house. Never did come back for them. Sally remembered 'em this morning. Everything is gonna be legal and right. My wife is puttin' up the money to build a large general store. I figure that once I explain it all to Louis Longmont, he'll see the humor in it and drop some of his money in. I'm hopin' he will. Pretty sure. Pearlie is carryin' a letter to the bank at the county seat; me and my wife have some money there." He grinned. "She has a heap more than I do. Wilbur Mason and his wife is gonna run the store for us. Wilbur owned a store back east of here at one time. So they both know what to do.

"Day after tomorrow, there's gonna be wagons rolling in here. Lumber, and a lot of it. We're gonna have several buildings here, including a sheriff's office and a jail."

Everybody was grinning now. Some of the men were laughing outright.

"We're gonna have a saloon, 'cause you all know that a saloon is just as much a meetin' place as it is a place to drink. We're gonna have us a cafe, with home-cookin'. The women will see to that. It'll bring in some money—and I know you all could use that. A church too, where we can all go to services come Sunday morning. And . . . a school. Both Sally and Bountiful are schoolmarms. And I'm gonna tell y'all something: once the wives of Beaconfield and Jackson hear about this town, with a church and proper schoolhouse, don't you think they won't be putting the pressure on their husbands to lean toward us."

"Who's gonna be the sheriff?" Matlock asked.

"Charlie Starr," Smoke said with a grin. "He's still got an old badge he wore some years back down close to Durango. I think he'd make a damned good one. Any objections?"

None.

"Now we want this to be kept secret as long as possible. Soon as the wagons start rolling in, though, the cat's gonna be out of the bag. But by that time, there won't be a damned thing Tilden Franklin can do about it except cuss. Now here is something else. There ain't no post office in Fontana. Never has been. We've always had to ride over to either Danner or Signal Hill to the post office. We can post a letter on the stage that comes through Fontana, but that don't always mean it'll get where it's goin'. Sally wrote a letter this morning to the proper people up in Denver and also to her folks who have a lot of high-up connections back East. So I think we'll get us a post office.

"Now the name. That come pretty easy too. Last evenin', as Ralph and Bountiful was ridin' along, talkin', they come to this point, right down there." He pointed. "And she said, 'Oh, look at that beautiful big rock'."

Smoke grinned. "Big Rock. Big Rock, Colorado!"

7

"The son of a bitch is doing *what*?" Tilden Franklin screamed the question at Clint.

"Buildin' a town," Clint said woefully. "Big Rock, Colorado."

Tilden sat down. "Well, he can't do that," he said with something very close to a pout. "*I* done built a town. A proper one."

"Maybe he can't, Boss. But somebody forgot to tell him that. Him and that goddamned preacher and their wives. And lemme tell you something about that preacher man. He's done up and bought some land from Smoke Jensen and his cabin is damn near complete. And maybe you oughta know this too: that preacher is more than just a preacher. He fought for some years under the name of the Cincinnati Kid."

Tilden stared at his foreman as if the man had lost his mind. Then he slowly nodded his head. "I read about him. He killed a man with his fists right before he was scheduled to fight . . . somebody big-named. Iron Mike or something like that. What's the point of all this, Clint? What does Jensen hope to prove by it?"

Clint sat down, rather wearily, and plopped his hat down on the floor beside the chair. "Damned if I know, Boss. I figured with his reputation, when we burned Mason out, he'd come shootin'. He didn't. I figured when we . . . they done it to Velvet and killed Adam, Smoke would come a-shootin'. He didn't. Luis and his bunch burned out Peyton. And Smoke builds him a town. I can't figure it."

"I won't even ask if the town is legal."

"It's legal, and that Lawyer Hunt Brook and his wife done moved his practice out of Fontana and up to Big Rock. I spied on them some this morning. Then I nosed around Big Rock myself. That's a mighty fine store that's goin' up. And the smells from that cafe got my mouth waterin'. Some of the nesters' wives and older girls is doin' the cookin'. And them miners is swarmin' all over the place. They got 'em a saloon too. Big Rock Saloon. No games, no girls. A nice church and school combination goin' up too. And a jail."

"And I guess they elected themselves a sheriff, did they?"

"Shore did. Charlie Starr is the sheriff, and Luke Nations is his deputy."

Tilden pounded his fists on the desk and cursed. He looked and behaved like a very large, spoiled, and petulant child.

Clint waited patiently. He had seen his boss act like this before.

When Tilden had calmed down, Clint said, "Herds look good."

Tilden fixed him with a baleful look. "That's wonderful, Clint. I can't tell you how impressed I am. I'm making thousands of dollars a week on gold shares. I should be making several more thousands in kickbacks, except that goddamned sheriff I put into office has turned holy-roller on me. I am paying several thousands of dollars a month for some of the finest gunhands in the West, and they can't seem to rid the country of one Smoke Jensen. The son of a bitch rides all over the country, usually by himself, and my so-called gunslicks can't or won't, tackle him."

Clint sat quietly, knowing his boss was not yet through.

"Now Johnny North has taken up with a damned nester woman. Judge Proctor hasn't had a drink in weeks; he's turned just as righteous as Monte Carson. My men are afraid, *afraid*, to go into *my goddamn town!*"

Tilden rose from behind his desk to pace the study. He turned to face Clint's back.

"Turn around and look at me!" he ordered. "Tell Luis to take his men into town and rid it of Monte and Proctor.

Right now, Clint. Right now!"

Clint retrieved his hat and stood up. "Boss," he said patiently. "Are you talkin' about treein' a town?"

"Exactly."

Clint sighed and shook his head. He wished Tilden would get Smoke Jensen out of his mind and just get on with the business of ranching. The big foreman wished a lot of things, but he knew that Smoke Jensen had become an obsession with Tilden. He wasn't even talkin' much about Sally no more. His hatred of Smoke had nearly consumed the man.

And Clint felt—no, *knew*—somehow that Tilden wasn't goin' to win this fight. Oh, he would succeed in runnin' out the nesters who were weak to begin with. Like Peyton. But Peyton was long gone. And them that remained was the tough ones. Not cold-eyed tough like Luis Chamba and Kane and Sanderson and Valentine and Suggs and them other gunslicks Tilden had on the payroll, but tough like with stayin' power.

And now Tilden wanted to tree a Western town. He lifted his eyes, meeting the just-slightly-mad eyes of Tilden Franklin.

"Are you not capable of giving those orders, Clint?"

"Don't push on me, Boss," Clint warned. "Don't do it."

Tilden face softened a bit. "Clint . . . we've been together for years. We've spent more than a third of our lifetimes together. We've had rough times before. You own ten percent of this ranch. You could have taken your profits and left years ago, started your own spread, but you stayed with me. Just stay with me a while longer, you'll see. Things will be like they were years ago."

"Boss, things ain't *never* gonna be like they was. Not ever agin."

Tilden picked up a vase and hurled it against a far wall, breaking the vase, showering the carpet with bits of broken ceramic. "It will!" he screamed. "You'll see, Clint. Just get rid of Smoke Jensen and those nesters will fold up and slink away. Now get out, Clint. Carry out my orders. *Get out*, damn you!"

Crazy! Clint thought. He ain't just obsessed . . . he's plumb crazy. *He's* the one who's livin' in a house of cards. Not them nesters, but Tilden Franklin.

"All right, Boss," Clint said. There was a different note in his voice, a note that Tilden should have picked up on. But he didn't. "Fine. I'll get out."

Clint left the big house and stood for a moment on the front porch. His eyes swept the immediate holdings of Tilden Franklin. Thousands and thousands of acres. Too goddamn much for one man, and that silly bastard isn't content with it. He wants more.

But not with my help.

Clint walked to his own quarters and began packing. He would take only what he had to have to travel light. One pack horse. Clint had money. Being a very frugal man, he had banked most of his salary and the profits from selling the cows over the years.

He smiled, not a pleasant smile. Tilden didn't know that he owned land up on the Gunnison, up near Blue Mesa. Owned it under the name of Matthew Harrison. Everybody around here knew him as Clint Harris. He'd changed his name as a snot-nosed boy, when he'd run off from his home down in Texas, after he'd shot his abusive stepfather. Clint never knew whether he'd killed the man, or not. He'd just taken off.

And that was what he was going to do now. Just take off.

The foreman—no! he corrected that—ex-foreman . . . had not had a good night's sleep since that . . . awfulness with Velvet Colby. He sat down at his rough-hewn desk and slowly wrote out instructions on a piece of paper. Finished with the letter, he walked to the door and opened it, calling for a puncher to get over there.

"Billy, can you read and write?"

"Yes, sir, Mister Clint," the cowboy said. "I finished sixth grade."

"Fine. Come on in." With the cowboy inside Clint's quarters, Clint pointed to the letter. "Sign your name where it says Witness."

"Yes, sir, Mister Clint." The cowboy did not read the

letter; that wasn't none of his business. He signed his name. "You want me to date this, Mister Clint?"

"Yes. Good thought, Billy."

After Billy had gone, Clint looked around his spartan living quarters. Looked around for one last time. He could see nothing left that he wished to take. Outside, he rigged the pack horse and swung onto his own horse. Looking around, he spotted several punchers just down from the high country. They walked over to him.

"Where you goin', Mister Clint?" a puncher called Rosie asked.

"Haulin' my ashes, Rosie. And if you got any sense about you, you will too." He looked at the others. "All of you."

"You got a new job, Mister Clint?" a cowboy named Austin asked.

"Yeah, I do, Austin. And I'm hirin' punchers. I'm payin' forty a month and found. You interested?"

They all were.

Clint figured he could run his place with four hands, including himself. At least for a time.

"Pack your warbags, boys. And do it quiet-like. Meet me just north of Big Rock, south of Slumgullion Pass."

He swung his horse's head and moved out.

The punchers moved quietly to the bunkhouse and packed their meager possessions. One by one, they moved out, about thirty minutes behind Clint. None of them knew why the foreman was pullin' out. But with Clint gone, damned if they was gonna stay around with all these lazy-assed, overpaid gunhands.

As they rode over and out of TF range, they met other TF punchers—not hired guns, cowboys. The punchers looked at those leaving, put it all together, and one by one, silently at first, made their plans to pull out.

"I ain't seen my momma in nigh on three years," one said. "I reckon it's time to head south."

"I got me a pard works over on the Saguache," another said. "Ain't seen him in two, three years. It's time to move on anyway."

"I know me a widder woman who owns a right-nice little

farm up near Georgetown," yet another cowboy said. "I'm tared of lookin' at the ass end of cows. I think I'll just head up thataway."

"I ain't never seed the ocean," another cowboy lamented. "I think I'll head west."

Clint rode into Big Rock and tied his horses at the post outside the Big Rock Saloon. As he was stepping up onto the still-raw-smelling boardwalk, he saw Johnny North and that Belle Colby woman coming out of the general store. They stopped to chat with Lawyer Hunt Brook.

Clint removed his gunbelt and walked slowly over to them. Johnny saw the man coming at him and instinctively slipped the thongs off the hammers of his Colts. Then he noticed that Clint was not armed. His eyes found the packhorse.

"What the hell . . ." he muttered.

Clint had some papers in his right hand.

Clint stopped about twenty-five feet from the trio. "I'm friendly," he said.

"Come on," Johnny said.

Clint held the papers out to Belle. Slowly, she took them. Clint said, "It won't make up for what was done to your daughter and your husband, but it's something I'd like to do." He turned and walked back to his horses.

Belle, Johnny, and Hunt watched him swing into the saddle and ride out of their lives.

"Let me see those papers, Belle," Hunt said. The lawyer quickly scanned first one paper, then the others—older, slightly yellowing around the edges. He began to smile.

"What is it, Mister Brook?" Belle asked.

"Why, Belle . . . you own ten percent of the TF Ranch. I think you have just become a very wealthy woman."

Tilden called for his houseboy.

"Yes, sir?"

"Get Clint for me, boy."

"Yes, sir."

The houseboy returned a few minutes later. "Sir? Mister Clint is gone."

"Gone . . . where, damnit?"

"He packed up and rode out. His quarters is empty, and so is the bunkhouse. Old Ramon at the stable says all the punchers packed up and left. Following Mister Clint."

"Get out!" Tilden said, real menace in his voice.

"Yes, sir," the houseboy said. "I most certainly will do that, Mister Tilden."

Thirty minutes later, the servant had packed his kit and was walking toward Fontana.

In his study, Tilden called for his houseboy. "Bring me a cup of coffee, boy!"

The big house creaked in empty silence.

"Boy!" Tilden roared. "You bring me a cup of coffee or I'll take a whip to your lazy greaser ass!"

Silence. And Tilden Franklin, the man who would be king, knew he was alone in his large, fine home.

He walked to a large window and looked out. His thoughts were savage. "I'm gonna kill you, Jensen. I'm gonna bring Fontana to its knees first. Then I'm gonna burn your goddamn Big Rock to the ground. Then I'm gonna kill you and have your woman."

He walked to a rack and took down his gunbelt, buckling it around his hips. He put his hat on his head and walked outside.

"Ramon?" he yelled.

"*Si, señor?*" the old man called.

"Bring me my horse. Then you find your mule and get Luis for me."

"*Si, señor.*" Son of a bitch! he silently added.

8

The houseboy heard the thundering of hooves long before he saw them. He did not know what they meant, other than a lot of riders were in a big hurry. He shifted his heavy satchel to his other hand and trudged on, walking along the side of the rutted dirt road. As the thunder grew louder, he turned around, fear and panic on his face.

"Ride the insubordinate bastard down!" he heard Tilden Franklin scream, his voice just carrying over the steel-shod thunder.

The houseboy tried to run. He dropped his belongings and leaped to one side. He was too slow.

The rushing shoulder of a horse hit him in the back, tossing him to the road. Pain filled him as he heard his bones break. He looked up in time to see Tilden's crazed face and his stallion rear up, the hooves flashing in the hard sunlight.

The houseboy screamed.

His screaming was cut off as the steel hooves came down on his face, crushing his skull. The riders galloped on, leaving the houseboy lying in the road, his blood staining and dampening the dust.

They were fifty-odd strong, drunk not with alcohol, but with the power given them by Tilden Franklin. Raw, unbridled, killing power. He was paying them good money, and offering them immunity and total impunity.

From the law. None of them was taking Smoke Jensen into consideration as any form of punishment. They should have.

One deputy saw them coming hard and ran for his horse. He hauled his ashes, leaving everything he owned behind him in Fontana. If it ever calmed down, he might be back. If not, to hell with it!

Yet another deputy, nicknamed Stonewall, saw the riders coming and ran across the street to the sheriff's office. "Monte!" he hollered, jumping into the office and running to the shotgun rack. "Tilden and his gunhawks comin' fast. Get ready."

A third deputy ran inside the office-jail just as gunfire ripped the street. Like Monte and Stonewall, he grabbed a Greener from off the rack and stuffed his pockets full of shells.

"Take the back, Dave," Monte said, his voice calm. "Where are the others?"

"I seen Slim haulin' his ashes outta here," Dave told him. "I think Joel is out in the county somewheres servin' a notice from Judge Proctor."

"Stay calm," Monte told his men. "We got some food, and we got a pump for water. Tilden wanted this place built of stone for strength, so that's gonna work agin him. It'd take a cannon to bring these walls down."

"Hey!" a miner back in lockup hollered. "What about me?"

"Turn him loose and give him a shotgun," Monte ordered. "If he tried to get of here, those gunnies would cut him to rags."

The miner looked out at the angry group of heavily armed riders. "Who the hell is all them people?"

"That's your buddy, Tilden Franklin, and his gunhands," Stonewall told him. "Would you like to go out and kiss him hello?"

"Would you like to kiss another part of me?" the miner challenged.

Stonewall laughed and handed the man a sawed-off shotgun and a sack of shells.

Monte called out through an open but barred window. "As Sheriff I am ordering you to break this up and leave this town or you'll all under arrest."

"That's gonna be a good trick," Dave muttered.

A TF gunhand made the mistake of firing into the jail. Monte lifted his express gun and blew the rider clear out of the saddle.

The street erupted in gunfire, the hard exchange returned from those in the fortlike jail.

Blood dropped onto the dusty street as the shotguns cleared half a dozen saddles of living flesh, depositing dead, dying, and badly wounded men into the dirt.

Monte reloaded his express gun and lined up a gunhand he knew only as Blackie. He gave Blackie both barrels full of buckshot. The double charge lifted the gunhand out of the saddle, a hole in his chest so large it would take a hat to cover it.

The screaming of frightened and bucking horses filled the gunsmoke air. The riders were hard pressed to control their mounts, much less do any fighting.

Louis Longmont stepped out of his gaming tent, a Colt in each hand. As calmly as in a seconded duel, Louis lifted first one Colt and then the other, firing coolly and with much deliberation. He emptied two saddles and then paused, not wanting to shoot a horse.

The man who owned and cooked at the Good Eats Cafe stepped out of his place with a Sharps .50. The man, a Civil War veteran with four hard years of fighting as a Union cavalryman, lifted the Sharps and emptied yet another saddle.

Big Mama ran out of her place and literally jerked one gunhand off his horse. She began smashing his face with big, hard fists, beating the man into bloody unconsciousness.

Billy, up in the loft of the stable with his newly bought .22 caliber rifle, grinned as he took careful aim at the big man on the big horse. Gently he squeezed the trigger.

And shot Tilden Franklin smack in one cheek of his ass.

With a roar of rage, Tilden wheeled his horse around and

took off at a gallop, out of town, the gunhands following closely.

Nobody treed a Western town in the 1870's. Nobody. Nearly every man in every town was a combat veteran of some war, whether it be against Indians, outlaws, the Union Blue, or the Rebel Gray. But nobody treed a Western town.

Two years prior to the formation of Fontana, back in September of 1876, Jesse James and his outlaw gang had tried to collar Northfield, Minnesota. They were shot to rags by the townspeople.

The dust settled slowly, and a quiet settled over Fontana. Only the moaning of the badly wounded TF gunslicks could be heard. Doctor Spalding came wheeling up in his buggy, sliding to a halt in the street. His unbelieving eyes took in the carnage before him. He began counting. He stopped at ten, knowing there were several more scattered about in the dirt and dust.

Monte and his deputies stepped out of the jail building. "Get 'em patched up, Doc," he said. "Them that is able, bunk 'em in yonder." He jerked his thumb toward the jail. "You!" His eyes found a man lounging about. "Git the undertaker on down here."

The photographer was coming at an awkward run, his tripod-and-hood camera-and-flash container a cumbersome burden. He set up and began taking pictures.

"Sheriff!" Doc Spalding called. "Most of these men are dead. Several more are not going to make it much longer."

"Good," Monte said. "Saves the town the expense of a trial."

Tilden Franklin lay on his belly, in bed, while the old camp cook probed and poked at his buttock, finally cutting out the small .22 slug. He dropped the bloody pellet into a pan.

"Somebody was a-funnin' you with that thing," the cook observed.

Tilden swore, loud and long.

News of the attempted collaring of Fontana was quick to reach Big Rock and the small spreads scattered out from it. When Smoke took the news to Ralph, the minister sat down on a log he was hewing and laughed.

"Billy shot Tilden Franklin in the ass!" he hollered, then started laughing again.

Bountiful came on the run, sure something was wrong with her husband. Sally was with her. The ladies had been working, making a list of prospective members for the Big Rock Women for Equal Rights Club.

"What's wrong?" Bountiful asked.

"Billy shot Tilden Franklin in his big ass!" Ralph again hollered, then bent over with laughter.

The laughter was infectious; soon they were all howling and wiping their eyes.

Judge Proctor was furious. Since he had begun his program of alcohol abstention, he had realized he was supposed to help maintain law and order, not make a mockery of it by drunken antics.

The judge signed arrest warrants for Tilden Franklin and as many of the TF gunslicks that people on the street could recall being present during the shooting spree.

Louis Longmont put up five thousand dollars reward for the arrest and conviction of Tilden Franklin, and the judge had Haywood's printing press cranking out wanted posters for Tilden Franklin. He then had them posted throughout the county.

Louis thought it all hysterically amusing.

Now everybody, or most everybody, knew that no one was really going to try to arrest Tilden Franklin. Or, for that matter, any of the TF gunhawks. But it did keep them out of Fontana and Big Rock and, for the most part, confined to the TF ranges. Punching cattle. Which pissed off the gunslicks mightily.

"You got no choice," Tilden said to his new foreman, Luis Chamba. Tilden was unshaven, and sitting on a pillow. "Not if you want to stay alive. All them damned old gunslingers have ringed my range. They're just waiting for you or me or some of the others to step off of this range. Anyway, what are you boys bitching about? You're all drawing top wages for sitting around really doing nothing." Tilden did manage a rueful smile. "Except herdin' beeves, that is."

Luis did not see the humor in it. He stalked out of the great house. But Luis was no fool. He knew that, for the time being, he was stuck. Herding cattle.

And then two things happened that would forever alter the histories of Fontana and Big Rock and the lives of most of those who called them home.

Belle Colby, accompanied by Johnny North and Lawyer Hunt Brook, claimed her ten percent of the TF.

And Utah Slim finally made his move, setting out to do what he had been paid to do.

Kill Smoke Jensen.

9

"Riders coming, Boss!" Luis Chamba hollered through an open window of the large home.

"Who are they?" Tilden shouted returning the holler. He was sitting in his study, drinking whiskey. The interior of the home was as nasty as Tilden Franklin's unwashed body and unshaven face.

"Can't tell yet," the gunslinger called. "But there's a woman in a buckboard, I can tell that much."

Tilden heaved himself up and out of his chair. For a moment, the big man swayed unsteadily on his booted feet. He stumbled to a water basin and washed his face. Lifting his dripping face, he stared into a mirror. He was shocked at his appearance. A very prideful man, Tilden had always been a neat dresser and almost fastidious when it came to washing his body.

He could smell his own body odors wafting up to assail his nostrils. With a grimace, he called to Luis.

"Tell them I'll be out in fifteen minutes, Luis."

"*Sí*, Boss."

Hurriedly, Tilden washed himself best he could out back of the great house and toweled himself dry. He had water on the stove heating for shaving. He shaved, very carefully, noting his shaking hands. Somehow, he managed not to nick his face.

For some reason, his crazed mind felt that the woman in

the buckboard was Sally Jensen, coming to see him.

Tilden splashed Bay Rum on his face and sprinkled some on his body, then dressed in clean clothes. He was shocked when he stepped out onto the porch and saw it was not Sally Jensen.

The woman was Belle Colby. With her was Johnny North, the lawyer Hunt Brook, Sheriff Monte Carson, and someone Tilden had never seen before. A man dressed in a dark suit, white shirt, and string tie. His face was tanned and his eyes were hard. A drooping moustache.

He cleared up who he was in a hurry. "My name is Mitchell," he said. "United States Marshal. I don't know who started the war in this part of the country, Franklin, and I don't much care. But I'm delivering two messages today. One to you, another to Smoke Jensen. The war is over. If I have to come back in here, I'll bring the Army with me and declare a state of martial law. You understand all that?"

"Yes . . . sir," Tilden said, the words bitter on his tongue. He glared at Carson.

"Fine," Mitchell said. "Now then, Lawyer Brook is here representing Mrs. Colby. Me and Sheriff Carson will just sit here and see that the lady gets her due."

"Her . . . *due*?" Tilden questioned.

Briefly, Hunt Brook explained. He further explained that the papers given Belle Colby were now part of court records.

"I want to see your books, Mister Franklin," Hunt told Tilden. "When that is done, I shall determine how much is owed Mrs. Colby. She has confided in me that she is willing to sell her ten percent back to you. Once a fair price is determined. By me. Shall we get to it, Mister Franklin?"

Speaking through an almost blind rage, Tilden started to choke out his reply. Then some small bit of reason crept into his mind. He did not want these people inside his smelly house. That would not look good, and the word would get around.

"I'll get my books. We'll go over them on the porch. All right?"

"Fine, Mister Franklin," the lawyer said.

Luis Chamba had discreetly disappeared into the bunk house. He had known who Mitchell was at first sighting. And while the Mexican gunfighter felt he could best him, no one in their right mind killed a federal marshal. He told his men to stay low and out of sight.

Chamba felt, along with many of the other gunhands, that Tilden Franklin had just about come to the end of his string. But as long as he could pay the money, they would stay. Anyways, Luis wanted his chance at Smoke Jensen. Now that the elusive gunfighter had finally surfaced, a lot of gunslicks wanted to try their skills against his.

Tilden was seething as the lawyer went over his books. As far as the money went, the money to buy out Belle Colby, Tilden had that much in his safe inside the house. It wasn't the money. It was the fact that Clint had given his percentage to this trashy nester woman. Husband not even cold in the grave and she was probably hunchin' and bumpin' the gunslinger Johnny North. Trash, that's all she was.

Tilden listened as the lawyer quoted an absurdly high figure. But Tilden wasn't going to quibble about it. He just wanted his holdings intact, and this hard-eyed U.S. marshal out of the area. Mitchell was damn sure wrong on one count, though: the war was not over. Not by a long shot.

"All right," Tilden said, agreeing to the figure.

The lawyer reached into his case and handed Tilden what the man knew was a binding note. He signed it, Belle signed it, and then Mitchell and North both witnessed it. Belle Colby was now a woman of some means.

Tilden Franklin sat in a chair and watched them leave. Slowly, the gunfighters began to once more gather around the porch.

"Play it close to the vest for a time," Tilden said. "Let that damned marshal get clear of this area. Then you'll all start earning your wages. I don't care who you have to kill in order to get to him, but I want Smoke Jensen dead. Dead, goddamnit . . . *dead*!"

U.S. Marshal Mitchell looked at the legendary gunfighter

Smoke Jensen. He was even younger than Mitchell had been led to believe. The man was still a ways from thirty.

"If I tried real hard, Jensen, I probably could come up with half a dozen arrest warrants for you. You know that, don't you?"

Smoke grinned boyishly. "But findin' people to stand up in court, look me in the eyes, and testify against me might give you some problems."

Smart too, Mitchell thought. The marshal returned Smoke's smile. "There is always that to consider, yes."

"The war is not over, Marshal. You must know that."

"I mean what I say, Jensen. If I have to, I'll bring the Army in here. The Governor of the State of Colorado is tired of hearing about this place. In terms of blood."

"Tilden Franklin is a crazy man, Marshal. I don't know why he hates me, but he does. He will never rest until one of us is dead."

"I know that," Mitchell said. "But don't sell him short, Jensen. Not even Luis Chamba is as fast as Tilden Franklin. He's poison with a short gun."

"He thought he was poison with his fists too," Smoke replied, again with that boyish grin.

"So I heard." The marshal's reply was very dry. "That beating you gave him didn't help matters very much."

"It gave me a great deal of satisfaction."

"I really hope I never see you again, Jensen. But somehow I feel I will."

"I didn't start this, Marshal. But if it comes down to it, I'll damn sure finish it."

The marshal looked at Smoke for a moment. "Other than Tilden Franklin, you know anyone else who might pay a lot of money to have you killed?"

Smoke thought about that for a moment. Then he shook his head. "No, not right off hand."

Time took him winging back more than three years, back to the ghost town of Slate, where Smoke had met the men who had killed his brother and his father, then raped and killed his wife Nicole, and then killed Nicole and Smoke's son Arthur.

Mitchell, as if sensing what was taking place in Smoke's mind, stood motionless, waiting.

"Them old mountain men is pushin' us toward Slate," a gunhand said.

The one of the Big Three who had ordered all the killing, Richards, smiled at Smoke's choice of a showdown spot. A lot of us are going to be ghosts in a very short time, he thought.

As the old ghost town loomed up stark and foreboding on the horizon, located on the flats between the Lemhi River and the Beaverhead Range, a gunslick reined up and pointed. "The goddamn place is full of people."

"Miners," another of the nineteen men who rode to kill Smoke said. "Just like it was over at the camp on the Uncompahgre."

The men checked their weapons and stuffed their pockets full of extra shells and cartridges.

They moved out in a line toward the ghost town and toward the young gunfighter named Smoke.

"There he is," Britt said, looking up the hill toward a falling-down store.

Smoke stood alone on the old curled-up and rotted boardwalk. The men could just see the twin .44's belted around his waist. He held a Henry repeating rifle in his right hand, a double-barreled express gun in his left hand. Suddenly, Smoke ducked into the building, leaving only a slight bit of dust to signal where he once stood.

"Two groups of six," Richards said. "One group of three, one group of four. Move out."

Smoke had removed his spurs, hanging them on the saddlehorn of Drifter. As soon as he'd ducked out of sight, he had run from the store down the hill, staying in the alley. He stashed the express gun on one side of the street in an old store, his rifle across the weed-grown street.

He met the gunslick called Skinny Davis in the gloom of what had once been a saloon.

"Draw!" Skinny hissed.

Smoke put two holes in his chest before Davis could cock his .44's.

"In the saloon!" someone yelled.

Williams jumped through an open, glassless window of the saloon. Just as his boots hit the old warped boards, Smoke shot him, the .44 slug stopping him and twisting the gunhawk back out the window to the boardwalk. Williams was hurt, but not out of it. He crawled along the side of the building, one arm broken and dangling, useless.

"Smoke Jensen!" the gunnie called Cross called. "You ain't got the sand to face me."

"That's one way of putting it," Smoke muttered. He took careful aim and shot the man in the stomach, doubling him over and dropping him to the dirty street.

The miners had hightailed it to the ridges surrounding the old town. There they sat, drinking and betting and cheering. The old Mountain Men, Preacher among them, watched expressionless.

The young man called Smoke, far too young to have been one of that rare and select breed of adventuring pioneers called Mountain Men, had, nonetheless, been raised, at least in part, by Preacher, so that made Smoke one of them. Indeed, the last of the Mountain Men.

A bullet dug a trench along the old, rotting wood, sending splinters flying, a few of them striking Smoke in the face, stinging and bringing a few drops of blood.

Smoke ran out the back, coming face to face with Simpson, the outlaw gunfighter having both his dirty hands filled with .44's.

Smoke pulled the trigger on his own .44's, the double hammer-blows of lead taking Simpson in the lower chest, knocking him dying to the ground.

Smoke reloaded, then grabbed up Simpson's guns and tucked them behind his belt. He ran down the alley. A gunslick stepped out of a gaping doorway just as Smoke cut to his right, jumping through a windowless opening. A bullet burned his shoulder. Spinning, he fired both Colts, one slug taking Martin in the throat, the second striking the outlaw just above the nose, almost removing the upper part of the man's face.

Smoke caught a glimpse of someone running. He dropped to one knee and fired. His slug shattered the hip of Rogers, sending the big man sprawling in the dirt, howling and cussing. Another gunslick spurred his horse and charged the building where Smoke was crouched. He smashed his horse's shoulder against the old door and came thundering inside. The animal, wild-eyed and scared, lost its footing and fell, pinning the outlaw to the floor, crushing the man's stomach and chest. The outlaw, Reese, cried in agony as blood filled his mouth and darkness clouded his eyes.

Smoke slipped out the side door.

"Get him, Turkel!" a hired gun yelled.

Smoke glanced up roof-level high; he ducked as a rifle bullet flattened against the building. Smoke snapped off a shot and got lucky, the slug hitting Turkel in the chest. He crashed through an awning, bringing down the rotting awning. The hired gun did not move.

A bullet removed a small part of Smoke's right ear; blood poured down the side of his face. He ran to where he had stashed the shotgun, grabbing it up and cocking it, leveling the barrels just as the doorway filled with gunslicks.

Smoke pulled both triggers, fighting the recoil of the 12-gauge. The blast cleared the doorway of all living things.

"Goddamn you, Jensen," a hired gun yelled, his voice filled with rage and frustration. He stepped out into the street.

Smoke dropped the shotgun and picked up a rifle, shooting the gunhand in the gut.

It was white-hot heat and gunsmoke for the next few minutes. Smoke was hit in the side, twisting him into the open doorway of a rotting building where a dead man lay. Smoke picked up the man's bloody shotgun and stumbled into the darkness of the building just as spurs jingled in the alley. Smoke jacked back both hammers and waited.

The spurs came closer. Smoke could hear the man's heavy breathing. He lifted the shotgun and pulled both triggers, blowing a bullet-sized hole in the rotting pine wall.

The gunslick stumbled backward, and slammed into an outhouse. The outhouse collapsed, dumping the dying gun-hand into the shit-pit.

Smoke checked his wounds. He would live. He reloaded his own Colts and the guns taken from the dead gunnie. He listened as Fenerty called for his buddies.

There was no response.

Fenerty was the last gunslick left.

He called again and Smoke pinpointed his voice. Picking up a Henry, Smoke emptied the rifle into the storefront. Fenerty came staggering out, stumbled on the rotting steps, and pitched face-forward into the street. There, he died.

Smoke laid down the challenge to Richards, Potter, and Stratton. "All right, you bastards!" he yelled. "Face me in the street if you've got the balls!"

The sharp odor of sweat mingled with blood and gun-smoke filled the summer air as four men stepped out into the death-street.

Richards, Potter, and Stratton stood at one end of the block. A tall, bloody figure stood at the other. All guns were in leather.

"You son of a bitch!" Stratton lost his cool and screamed, his voice as high-pitched as an hysterical girl's. "You ruined it all!" He clawed for his .44.

Smoke drew, cocked, and fired before Stratton's pistol could clear leather.

Screaming his outrage, Potter jerked out his pistol. Smoke shot him dead with his left-hand Colt. Holstering both Colts, Smoke faced Richards and waited.

Richard had not moved. He stood with a faint smile on his lips, staring at Smoke.

"You ready to die?" Smoke asked him.

"As ready as I'll ever be." There was no fear in his voice that Smoke could detect. Richards was good with a short gun, and Smoke kept that in mind. Richards's hands were steady. "Janey gone?"

"Took your money and pulled out."

Richards laughed. "Well, it's been a long run, hasn't it Smoke?"

214

"It's just about over."

"What happens to all our—" He looked down at his dead partners. "—*my* holdings?"

"I don't care what happens to the mines. The miners can have them. I'm giving all your stock to decent honest punchers and homesteaders."

A puzzled look crawled over Richards's face. "I don't understand. You mean, you did all . . . *this!*" He waved his left hand. "For nothing?"

Someone moaned, the sound painfully inching up the bloody, dusty, gunsmoke-filled street.

"I did it for my pa, my brother, my wife, and my baby son. You, or your hired guns, killed them all."

"But it won't bring them back!"

"Yeah, I know."

"I wish I had never heard the name of Jensen."

"After this day, Richards, you'll never hear it again."

"One way to find out," he replied with a smile, and went for his Colt. He cleared leather fast and fired. He was snake-quick, but he hurried his shot, the lead digging up dirt at Smoke's feet.

Smoke shot him in the right shoulder, spinning the man around. Richards drew his left-hand gun and Smoke fired again, the slug striking the man in the left side of his chest. He struggled to bring up his Colt. He managed to cock it before Smoke's third shot struck him in the belly. Richards sat down in the street, the pistol slipping from suddenly numbed fingers.

He opened his mouth to speak, and tasted blood on his tongue. The light began to fade around him. "You'll . . . meet . . ."

Smoke never found out, that day, who he was supposed to meet. Richards toppled over on his side and died.

Smoke looked up at the ridge where the Mountain Men had gathered.

They were gone, leaving as silently as the wind.

And to this day, he had never seen or heard from any of them again.

"You been gone a time, boy," Marshal Mitchell said.

Smoke sighed. "Just a few years. Bloody ones, though." He told the marshal about that day in the ghost town.

"I never knew the straight of it, Smoke. But you did play hell back then. That person Richards told you you'd meet?"

"Yeah?"

"He was talkin' about the man who will be faster than you. We who live by the gun all have them in our future."

Smoke nodded his head. "Yeah, I know. And yeah, I know who would pay to see me dead."

"Oh?"

"My sister. Janey."

10

"Your own sister would pay to have you killed!" Bountiful said, appalled at just the thought. "How dreadful. What kind of person is she?"

Ralph and Bountiful were having supper with Smoke and Sally. "She must have a lot of hate in her heart," Ralph said.

"I reckon," Smoke said. "Well, I'll just have to be more careful and keep looking over my shoulder from now on." He smiled. "That's something I'm used to doing."

Then he remembered Utah Slim. The man had aligned with no side in the mountain country war. No, Smoke thought, he didn't have to. He already had a job.

U.S. Marshal Mitchell had told Smoke that his office had received word that a gunslick had been paid to kill Jensen. But none of their usual sources could, or would, shed any light on who that gunslick might be.

Or why.

Smoke felt he knew the answer to both questions.

Utah Slim.

"You've got a funny look in your eyes, Smoke," Sally said, looking at her husband.

"I'm not going to sit around and wait for a bullet, Sally. I just made up my mind on that."

"I felt that was coming too."

"What are you two talking about?" Bountiful asked.

"A showdown," Smoke told her, buttering a biscuit. He chewed slowly, then said, "Might as well brace him in the morning and get it over with."

Ralph and Bountiful stopped eating and sat staring at the young gunfighter. Ralph said, "You're discussing this with no more emotion than if you were talking about planting beets!"

"No point in gettin' all worked up about it, Ralph. If I try to avoid it, it just prolongs the matter, and maybe some innocent person gets caught up in it and gets hurt. I told you and your friends a time back that we do things differently out here. And I'm not so sure that it isn't the best way."

"In the morning?"

"In the morning."

"I'll go in with you," the minister-turned-farmer said. His tone indicated the matter was not up for debate.

"All right, Ralph."

Ralph was a surprisingly good horseman, and Smoke said as much.

"I was raised on a farm," he said. "And I'm also a very good rifle shot."

"I noticed you putting the Henry in the boot this morning."

The morning was very clear and very bright as the two men rode toward Fontana. As they worked their way out of the mountains and toward the long valley where Fontana was located, the temperature grew warmer.

"Ever shot a man, Ralph?"

"No."

"Could you?"

"Don't ever doubt it."

Smoke smiled faintly. He didn't doubt it for a minute.

The town of Fontana seemed to both men to be a bit smaller. Ralph commented on that.

"The easy pickings have been found and taken out, Ralph. For however long this vein will last, it's going to be hard work, dirty work, and dangerous work. Look yonder. One whole section of Fontana is gone. Half a dozen bars have pulled out."

"Why . . ." Ralph's eyes swept the visibly shrinking town

218

that lay below them. "At this rate, there will be nothing left of Fontana by the end of summer."

"If that long," Smoke said, a note of satisfaction in his statement. "If we all can just settle the matter of Tilden Franklin, then we can all get on with the business of living."

"And it will have to be settled by guns." Ralph's remark was not put in question form. The man was rapidly learning about the unwritten code of the West.

"Yes."

Smoke reined up in front of Sheriff Monte Carson's office. The men dismounted and walked toward the bullet-scarred stone building. As they entered, Monte smiled and greeted them.

His smile faded as he noted the hard look in Smoke's eyes.

"I've had that same look a few times myself, Smoke," Monte said. "Gonna be a shootin'?"

"Looks that way, Monte. I'd rather not have it in town if I can help it."

"I'd appreciate that, Smoke. But sometimes it can't be helped. I got to thinkin' after talkin' with that marshal. It's Utah Slim, ain't it?"

"Yeah." Smoke poured a tin cup of coffee and sat down. "I got a strong hunch my sister hired him to gun me."

"Your . . . *sister?*"

Smoke told him the story of Janey. Or at least as much as he knew about her life since she'd taken off from that hard-scrabble, rocky, worthless farm in the hills of Missouri. Back when Smoke was just a boy, after their ma had died, when their pa was off fighting in the War Between the States. And Smoke had had to shoulder the responsibilities of a boy forced into early manhood.

It was a story all too common among those who drifted West.

It sounded all too painfully familiar to Monte Carson, almost paralleling his own life.

"I seen Utah early this mornin', sittin' on the hotel porch." He smiled. "The only hotel we got left here in Fontana, that is."

"Won't be long now," Smoke told him. "How many businesses are you losing a day?"

"Half a dozen. As you know, up there in Big Rock, the stage is runnin' twice a day now, carryin' people out of here."

"Seen some TF riders in town as we rode in," Smoke said. "And didn't see any of those flyers the Judge had printed up. What happened?"

"Some state man was on the stage three, four days ago, from the governor's office. He looked at the charges I had agin Tilden and his men and told me to take them dodgers down. They wasn't legal." He shrugged. "I took 'em down."

Smoke grinned. "It was fun while it lasted, though, wasn't it?"

"Damn shore was."

Conversation became a bit forced, as both Monte and Smoke, both gunfighters, knew the clock was ticking toward a showdown in the streets of Fontana. Stonewall and Joel came into the office.

"Git the people off the boardwalks," Monte told his deputies. "And have either of you seen Utah Slim?"

"He's standin' down by the corral, leanin' up agin a post," Joel said. "He's got a half dozen of them punk gunslingers with him. They lookin' at Utah like he's some sort of god."

"Run 'em off," Monte ordered. "I'll not have no mis-matched gunfight in this town."

The deputies left, both carrying sawed-off express guns.

Monte looked at Smoke after the office door had closed. "Utah is fast, Smoke. He's damn good. I'd rate him with the best."

"Better than Valentine?"

"He don't blow his first shot like Valentine, but he's just as fast."

Ralph looked out a barred window. "Streets are clear," he announced. "Nobody moving on the boardwalks."

Smoke stood up. "It's time." He slipped the leather thongs from the hammers of his Colts and put his hat on his head. "I'd like to talk to Utah first, find out something about my sister. Hell, I don't even know if she's the one behind this. I'll give it a try."

Smoke walked out onto the shaded boardwalks outside the

220

sheriff's office. He pulled his hat lower over his eyes and eased his Colts half out of leather a few times, letting them fall back naturally into the oiled leather. He stepped out into the street and turned toward the corral.

As he walked down the center of the street, his spurs jingling and his boots kicking up little pockets of dust, he was conscious of many unseen eyes on him, and even a few he could associate with a body.

Stonewall and Joel were on opposite sides of the broad street, both still carrying shotguns. The duded-up dandies who fancied themselves gunslingers had gathered as close to the corral as the deputies would allow them. Smoke saw the young punk Luke had made eat crow that day. Lester Morgan, Sundance. He had himself some new Colts. And that kid who called himself The Silver Dollar Kid was there, along with a few other no-names who wanted to be gunfighters.

Smoke wondered how they got along; where did they get eating money? Petty thievery, probably.

Louis Longmont had stepped out of his gaming tent. "How many you facing, Smoke?" he asked, as Smoke walked by.

"Just one that I know of. Utah Slim. I think my sis, Janey, sent him after me."

Louis paced Smoke, but staying on the boardwalk. "Yes, it would be like her."

"Where is she, Louis?"

"Tombstone, last I heard. Runnin' a red-light place. She's worth a lot of money. Richards's money, I presume."

"Yeah. Richards ain't got no use for it. I never heard of no Wells Fargo armored stage followin' no hearse."

Louis laughed quietly. "I'll watch your back, Smoke."

"Thanks."

Smoke kept on walking. He knew Louis had fallen back slightly, to keep an eye on Smoke's back trail.

Then the corral loomed up, Utah Slim standing by the corral. Smoke's eyes flicked upward to the loft of the barn. Billy was staring wide-eyed out of the loft door.

"Billy!" Smoke raised his voice. "You get your butt outta

that loft and across the street. Right now, boy—move!"

"Yes, sir!" Billy hollered, and slipped down the hay rope to the street. He darted across the expanse and got behind a water trough.

"That there's a good kid," Utah said. "Funny the other week when he shot Tilden in the ass."

"Yeah, I'd like to have seen that myself."

"I ain't got nothin' personal agin you, Jensen. I want you to know that."

"Just another job, right, Utah?"

"That's the way it is," the killer said brightly.

"My sister hire you?"

"Damned if'n I know. Some woman named Janey, down in Tombstone paid me a lot of money, up front." He squinted at Smoke. "Come to think of it, y'all do favor some."

"That's my darlin' sister."

"Make's me proud I ain't got no sister."

"Why don't you just get on your horse and ride on out, Utah. I don't want to have to kill you."

The killer looked startled. "Why, boy! You ain't gonna kill me."

"You want to wager on that?" Louis called.

"Yeah." Utah smiled. "I'll bet a hundred."

"Taken," Louis told him.

"How much did she pay you, Utah?" Smoke asked the man.

"Several big ones, boy." He grinned nastily. "She's a whoor, you know."

"So I heard." Smoke knew the killer was trying to anger him, throw him off, make him lose his composure.

"Yeah, she is," Utah said, still grinning. "I tole her, as part of the payment, I'd have to have me a taste of it."

"Is that right?"

"Shore is. Right good, too."

"I hope you enjoyed it."

"I did for a fact." This wasn't working out the way Utah had planned it. "Why do you ask?"

Smoke drew, cocked, and fired twice. Once with his right-hand Colt, that slug taking Utah in the chest and staggering him backward. The second slug coming from his left-hand gun and striking the gunslick in the stomach, dropping the killer to his knees, his left arm looped around the center railing of the corral.

Smoke holstered his left-hand Colt and waited for Utah. The killer managed to drag his Colt out of leather and cock it. That seemed to take all his strength. He pulled the trigger. The slug tore up the dirt at his knees.

Utah dropped the Colt. He lifted his eyes to Smoke. Just as the darkness began to fade his world, he managed to gasp, "How come you axed me if I enjoyed it?"

" 'Cause you damn sure ain't gonna get no more, Utah."

Utah died hanging onto the corral railing. He died with his eyes open, staring at emptiness.

Smoke holstered his pistol and walked away.

11

The undertaker's hack rumbled past Louis Longmont's tent just as the gambler and the gunfighter were pouring tumblers of scotch.

Louis lifted his glass. "May I pay you a compliment, Smoke Jensen?"

"I reckon so, Louis."

"I have seen them all, Smoke. All the so-called great gunfighters. Clay Allison, John Wesley Hardin, Bill Longley, Jim Miller. I've drank with Wild Bill Hickok and Jim, Ed, and Bat Masterson. I've gambled with Doc Holliday and Wyatt Earp. I've seen them all in action. But you are the fastest gun I have ever seen in my life."

The men clinked glasses and drank of the Glenlivet."

"Thank you, Louis. But I'll tell you a secret."

Louis smiled. "I'll bet you a double eagle I already know what it is."

"No bets, Louis, for I imagine you do."

"You wish you were not the faster gun."

"You got that right."

The men finished their drinks and stepped out onto the boardwalk. The photographer had set up his equipment at the corral and was taking his shots of Utah Slim. The duded-up dandies had gathered around, managing to get themselves in almost every shot the man took.

"Fools!" Smoke muttered.

"Look at them with their hands on the butts of their guns," Louis pointed out. "They'll be bragging about that picture for the rest of the lives."

"However short they may be," Smoke added.

"Yes."

Ralph walked up, joining the gambler and the gunfighter. Louis smiled at him.

"I would offer you a drink, Mister Morrow, but I'm afraid I might offend you."

"I'm not adverse to a cool beer, Mister Longmont."

Louis was more than slightly taken aback. "Well, I'll just be damned!" he blurted.

"Oh, I think not, sir," Ralph replied. He met the man's cool eyes. "How is your orphanage up in Boulder doing? Or that free hospital out in San Francisco?"

Louis smiled. "For a man of the cloth, you do get around, don't you, Ralph?"

"But I wasn't always a preacher, Mister Longmont," he reminded the gambler.

"Tell me more," Smoke said with a grin, looking at Louis.

"Don't let the news of my . . . philanthropic urges get out," the gambler said. "It might destroy my reputation."

Smoke looked at him and blinked. "Hell, Louis! I don't even know what that means!"

Laughing, the men entered the gaming tent for a cool one.

And the photographer's flash pan popped again.

And Utah Slim still clung to the corral railing.

The town of Fontana had begun to die, slowly at first, and then more rapidly as the gold vein began to peter out. More businesses shut down, packed up, and pulled out. The rip-roaring boom town was not yet busted, but a hole had been pierced in the balloon.

Those who elected to stay until the very end of the vein had been found were slowly shifting their trading to the new town of Big Rock. But since the Mayor of Big Rock, Wilbur Mason, refused to allow gaming and hurdy-gurdy girls in, the town of Fontana soon became known as the pleasure palace of the high country.

But that was both a blessing and curse for Sheriff Monte Carson and his three remaining deputies. A curse because it kept them on the run at all hours; a blessing because it kept them all in steady work, and doubly so for Monte, because it gave him a new direction in life to pursue. One that he found, much to his surprise, he enjoyed very much.

Louis had, of course, noticed the change in Monte, and in his quiet way tried to help the man, as did Judge Proctor, Louis helping the man with his reading and Proctor loaning him books on the law.

And Tilden Franklin maintained a very low profile, as did most of his gunslicks. Tilden wanted the area to settle down, stop attracting the governor's attention. More importantly, he wanted that damned hard-eyed U. S. marshal to stay out of the high country.

But both Tilden and Smoke knew that the undeclared war in the high country was not over, that the uneasy truce was apt to break apart at any time. And when it did, the high lonesome was going to run red with blood.

Someone was going to come out on top, and Tilden was making plans for that someone to be named Tilden Franklin. And he had not given up on his plans to possess Sally Jensen. Not at all. They had just been shelved for a time. But not forgotten.

The festering blot on the face of the high country began to leak its corruption when Paul Jackson rode into Fontana after a lonely six weeks in the mountains. Paul had heard talk of the new town of Big Rock, but had never seen it. He had heard talk of Fontana slowly dying, but had given it little thought. Paul had been busy digging gold. Lots of gold. More gold than even he had ever imagined he would ever find. His saddlebags were stuffed with the precious dust. His packhorses were loaded down.

He rode slowly into Fontana and could not believe his eyes. He had remembered a town, just six weeks past, full of people.

Place looked dead.

No, he corrected that. Just dying.

And where had the good people gone? Place looked to be full of whores and gamblers and pimps and ne'er-do-wells.

Made Paul feel kind of uncomfortable.

He reined up in front of the bank. But the damn bank was closed. He saw a deputy and hailed him.

Stonewall ambled over. "Something wrong, Paul?"

"Where's the bank?"

"Ain't got no bank no more, Paul," the deputy informed him. "It shut down when the gold began to peter out."

Paul, not a bright person to begin with, had to think about that for a minute or so.

"The gold is petering out?"

Now Stonewall never figured himself to be no genius, but even he was a shining light compared to this yoyo sitting his horse in front of the empty bank building.

"Yeah, Paul. The vein is about gone. If you got gold, we can store it at the jail until you can figure out what to do with it."

"I plan on taking my woman and my gold out of here," Paul said. "We are going to San Francisco and becoming man and wife."

"Your . . . woman?"

"Yes. I should like to see Bountiful now. So if you'll excuse me . . ."

"The minister's wife . . . Bountiful?" Stonewall asked.

"Yes."

"Paul . . . they don't live here in Fontana no more. The preacher quit his church and took to farmin'. He bought hisself some land up near the Sugarloaf. He preaches ever' Sunday morning at the new church up in Big Rock."

"Bountiful?"

Stonewall was rapidly losing patience with this big dumbbell. "Why, hell, man! She's with her husband."

"Not when she sees me," Paul said, then swung his horses and rode slowly out of town, toward the high lonesome and the town of Big Rock.

And Bountiful.

"What the hell was all that about?" Monte asked, walking

up to his deputy.

Stonewall took off his hat and scratched his head. "Sheriff, I don't rightly know. That Paul Jackson never was too bright, but I think the time up in the mountains has flipped him over the edge."

He told Monte the gist of the conversation.

"Strange," Monte agreed. "But Paul is gonna be in for a surprise if he tries to mess with Ralph's wife. That preacher'll whip his butt up one mountain and down the other."

"Surely Paul ain't *that* dumb!"

"Don't bet on it. Did he really have them horses loaded with gold?"

"Said he did."

"Outlaws workin' the high country; he'll be lucky if he makes it to Big Rock."

"Bountiful," Paul said, sitting his horse in front of the Morrow cabin. "I've come for you."

Bountiful blinked her baby blues. "You've . . . *come* for me?"

"Yes. Now get your things. I'm a rich man, Bountiful. We can have a beautiful life together. I'll buy you everything you ever dreamed of."

"Paul, everything I have ever dreamed of is right here." She waved her hand. "What you see is what I want. I have it all."

"But . . . I don't understand, Bountiful. The way you looked at me . . . I mean . . . I was sure about your feelings."

It had been that way all her life; men were constantly misreading her. Mistaking friendliness for passion. It was very difficult for a beautiful woman to have men friends.

"Paul, I like you. You're a good man. And I'm happy that you found gold. I hope it brings you a lot of happiness. And you'll find a nice lady. I just know it. Now you'd better leave."

Smoke and Ralph rode into the yard. Sally stepped out of the cabin where she had been helping Bountiful make

228

curtains.

"Hello, Paul," Ralph said. "How have you been?"

"Very well, thank you, Ralph. I've come for your wife."
Ralph blinked. "I beg your pardon?"

Bountiful looked at Sally and shook her head. Sally knew
the story; Bountiful had told her that Paul was infatuated
with her.

"Leave, Paul," Sally told the man. "You've got everything
all mixed up in your mind. It isn't the way you think it is."

"Is too!"

"Now, Paul," Ralph said soothingly. "You don't want to
make trouble for us. Why don't you just leave?"

Paul shook his head and dismounted. With a knife, he cut
open one saddlebag, the yellow dust pouring out onto the
ground.

"See, Bountiful?" Paul cried. "See? It's all for you. I did it
for you. You can have it all."

"I don't want it, Paul," Bountiful said softly. "It's yours.
You keep it."

Paul stood like a big, dumb ox, slowly shaking his head. It
was all so confusing. He had thought he had it all worked
out in his mind, but something was wrong.

Then he thought he knew what would bring Bountiful to
him. "I know," he said. "You're afraid to leave because of
Tilden Franklin. I can fix that for you, Bountiful. I really
can."

"What do you mean, Paul?" Smoke asked.

Paul turned mean eyes toward Smoke. "You stay out of
this. You're one of the reasons Bountiful won't go with me."

Smoke blinked. "Huh?"

"I can use a gun too," Paul said, once more looking at
Bountiful. "I'll show you. I'll show you all."

Smoke looked at Paul's pistol. It was in a flap-type holster,
the flap secured. Smoke figured he could punch Paul out
before any real damage was done—if he went for his gun.

"I'll come back a hero, Bountiful," Paul said. "I'll be the
hero of the valley, Bountiful." He cut the saddlebags loose
and let them fall to the ground. He tossed the reins of the
packhorses to the ground. "You keep this for me, Bountiful.

229

Play with it. It's not as pretty as you. But it's pretty. I'll be back, Bountiful. You go on and pack your things. Wait for me."

Paul swung awkwardly into the saddle and rode off.

"Paul is not very bright," Ralph said. "What in the world do you suppose he's going to do?"

No one would even venture a guess.

Smoke squatted down and fingered the dust and the nuggets. He looked at them closely. Then he stood up with a sad smile on his face.

"It's all fool's gold."

"If it wasn't so pitiful, it would be funny," Ralph said. "But Paul really believes, after he does whatever in the world he plans to do, that Bountiful is going with him. I wonder what he has in mind."

"What was that about Tilden Franklin?" Sally asked.

"He said I was afraid to leave because of Tilden Franklin," Bountiful said. "But that's silly. Why should I be afraid of that man?"

No one could answer that.

And in a few hours, it wouldn't matter to Paul either.

Paul said it. It was just as you said. "Just the plainly. I'll be back the rather. You ride on and pick your things. Wait for me."

12

"Rider comin', Boss," Valentine called to Tilden.

Tilden stepped out onto the porch and squinted his eyes against the sun. It was that fool shopkeeper's brother, Paul Jackson. "What in the hell does he want?"

"That one ain't playin' with a full deck," Slim said. "That's the one used to foller the preacher's wife around with his tongue a-hangin' out like a big ugly hound dog."

"He looks like a hound dog," Donnie observed. "A goofy one."

The gunfighters had a good laugh at that remark; even Tilden laughed. But for some reason he could not explain, the big man slipped the thongs off his six-guns.

Luis Chamba noticed the movement. "What's wrong, Boss?"

"I don't know. Just something about the way he's riding that bothers me."

"You want me to kill him?" Donnie asked.

Tilden waved that off. "No. Let's see what he's got on his mind."

Paul rode up to the house and sat his weary horse. "May I dismount?"

"Ain't he po-lite?" a gunfighter said, laughing.

"Sure, Jackson," Tilden said. "Climb down. What can I do for you?" Tilden noticed that the flap on the military-type holster was missing. Looked like it'd been freshly cut off. Paul's gun was riding loose.

"I've come to meet you man to man, Mister Franklin,"

Paul said.

"Well, Jackson, here I am. Speak your piece and then carry your ass off my range."

"I've come to kill you," Paul stated flatly.

"Is that so? Why?"

"Personal reasons."

"Don't I deserve better than that?" Tilden asked. This stupid sod was beginning to irritate him.

Several of the gunhands were beginning to giggle and titter and circle in the area of their temples with their forefingers.

Paul looked at the giggling gunslicks. "You men seem to find this amusing. Why?"

That brought them all down laughing. Tilden joined in the laughter. "Get off my range, you silly bastard!"

"Draw, goddamn you!" Paul shouted, and began fumbling for his gun.

Tilden drew, cocked, and fired with one blindingly fast motion. His slug hit Paul in the right shoulder, knocking the man to the dirt.

"You stupid son of a bitch!" Tilden snarled at the man, cocking the .44.

As Paul struggled to get to his feet, Tilden shot him again, this time the slug hitting the man in the right leg. Paul's feet flew out from under him and he landed hard in the dirt.

Screaming his rage at the rancher, Paul tried to claw his pistol out of leather. Tilden shot him in the other shoulder, rendering the man helpless.

Laughing, Tilden cocked and fired, the bullet striking Paul in the stomach.

"Tie him on his goddamned old nag and send him on his way," Tilden ordered, punching out the empties and reloading.

The gunslicks tied Paul upright in his saddle and slapped the already spooked horse on the rump. Paul went bouncing and swaying down the road, unconscious.

It was almost breaking dawn when Charlie Starr knocked on Smoke's cabin door. "Charlie Starr, Smoke. Got news for you."

In his longhandles, a Colt in his right hand, Smoke lifted the latch and peered out. "Mornin', Charlie. Come on in. I'll make us some coffee."

"Put your pants on first," Charlie said drily. "You ain't no sight to see first thing in the mornin'."

Smoke put on coffee to boil, visited the outhouse, then sat down at the kitchen table. "What's wrong, Charlie?"

"Paul Jackson was found late yesterday afternoon by some miners. He was tied to his horse. Somebody had a good time putting a lot of unnecessary lead in the fool. He's alive, but just barely. He told Doc Spalding he braced Tilden Franklin out at the TF ranch house. Then he went into a coma. Doc says he probably won't come out of it. My question is, why'd he do it?"

Sipping coffee, Smoke told Charlie about Paul's visit the day before.

"But there ain't nothin' between Bountiful and Paul Jackson. Is there?"

"No. It was all in Paul's mind."

"Fool's gold," Charlie muttered. "Finding that and thinkin' it was real might have been what pushed him over the edge."

"Probably was. How many times was he shot, Charlie?

"Both shoulders, leg, and stomach. Me and Monte been up all night talkin' about it. He admitted goin' out there and bracin' Tilden. Tilden had a right to protect hisself. But tyin' the man on that horse was cruel. Still, the judge says there ain't no laws to cover that."

"How's Ed taking it?"

"Harder than he'll let on. Monte said the man was cryin' last night after leavin' the Doc's office. He's tore up pretty bad. And . . . he's talkin' about goin' out there and seein' Tilden."

"That wouldn't be smart on his part."

"He's a growed-up man, Smoke. I sure can't stop him if that's what he wants to do."

"And he thought Tilden hung the stars and the moon."

"Lots of folks seein' the light about that crazy bastard. Monte told me to tell you something else too."

Smoke lifted his eyes.

"Tilden's replaced all them gunhawks that was shot in town. But he's scrapin' the bottom of the slime pit doin' it. He's hirin' the real hardcases. Cold-blooded killers. Range-war types. He's hiring some of them that was vigilantes down on the Oklahoma-Texas border. He's hirin' thugs, punks, cattle thieves, horse thieves . . . anybody who can pack a gun and even just brag about usin' one. Them dandies in town, The Silver Dollar Kid and Sundance and them other punks? Tilden hired them too."

"I guess we'd all better get ready for the balloon to bust, Charlie. I don't see any other way out of it."

Sally entered the kitchen and poured coffee. She set a plate of doughnuts on the table between the two men. Charlie grinned and helped himself.

"You heard?" Smoke asked his wife.

"I heard. I feel sorry for Paul. He wasn't quite right in the head."

Speaking around a mouthful of bearsign, Charlie said, "Out here, ma'am, man straps on a six-shooter, that gun makes him ten feet tall. Out here, they's a sayin'. God didn't make man equal. Colonel Colt did."

Paul Jackson died mid-morning, the day after he was shot. And once more, the undertaker's hack rumbled through the streets of Fontana. The streets were far less busy than they had been just a week before. The one remaining hotel had already announced plans to close.

Several TF riders had come to town, and the story of what had happened at the TF ranch was beginning to spread throughout the rapidly shrinking town. The TF gunhawks were drinking and laughing in the Blue Dog Saloon, telling the story of how Paul Jackson braced Tilden Franklin and how Paul had flopped around on the ground like a headless chicken after Tilden started putting lead into the man.

Stonewall stepped into the saloon just in time to hear the

234

story being told for the umpteenth time. Each time it had been told with a bit more embellishment. Stonewall had not really cared much for Paul Jackson, but Jackson had been a decent sort of fellow . . . if a bit off in the head. But he had been no thief or footpad, just a hardworking guy who deserved a better death than the one he'd received.

The deputy said as much to the gunhands.

The saloon suddenly became very quiet as the TF gunslicks set their shot glasses and beer mugs on the bar and turned to face Stonewall.

"You makin' light of Mister Franklin, Deputy?" a gunslinger asked.

Stonewall thought about that for a few seconds. "Yeah," he said. "I reckon I am. A fair shootin' is one thing. Torturin' a man for sport is another thing."

"Well, Mister Franklin ain't here to defend hisself."

"You here," Stonewall said softly.

Monte took that time to step onto the boardwalk.

The TF gunhawks jerked iron and Stonewall matched their draw. The Blue Dog started yelping and barking with gunfire. Monte stepped through the batwing doors, his hands full of Colts. Stonewall was leaning against the bar, hard hit, but he had managed to drop two of the TF gunslingers. The front of Stonewall's shirt was stained with blood.

Monte's Colts started belching smoke and fire and lead. Two more TF riders went down, but not before Monte was hit twice, in the side and upper chest.

Stonewall died on his feet, his gun still clutched in his fingers. Monte was knocked back against a wall, losing one Colt on the way. He lifted his second Colt and got lead into the last remaining TF gunslick before he slid into darkness.

The wounded TF rider stumbled outside and made it to his horse, galloping out of town, holding onto the saddle horn with bloody fingers. Joel ran out of the sheriff's office and lifted his rifle. The TF rider twisted in the saddle and shot the deputy through the head before he could get off a shot.

Dave jumped into the saddle and took off after the TF

gunslick. He ran slap into a dozen TF riders, on their way into town, the wounded TF rider in the middle of the pack. Dave was literally shot out of the saddle, a dozen holes in him.

Slim turned in his saddle and said, "Singer, take him back to the ranch with you." He indicated the wounded gunhawk. "And tell Mister Franklin that Fontana is ours!"

Dave was left where he had fallen, the deputy's horse standing over its master, nudging at Dave with its nose.

Bob Colby reined up in Smoke's yard in a cloud of dust. "Mister Smoke!" he hollered.

Smoke and Sally both ran from the cabin. "What's the matter, Bob?"

"Mister Luke tole me to tell you to come quick. Tilden Franklin's men done took over Fontana and this time they done 'er good. Sheriff Carson is hard hit, and all his deputies is dead!"

"Where's Johnny?"

"He took Ma over to a neighbor's house, then said he would meet you at Big Rock."

"I'm on my way, Bob."

Smoke instructed some of the old gunfighters to stay at the ranch in case any TF riders might choose to attack either the ranch or Ralph's new cabin, and told Ralph to keep his butt close by, and to carry his rifle wherever he went.

Smoke and the old gunslingers lit out for Big Rock.

" 'Bout time," Pistol Le Roux muttered. "I was beginnin' to think we wasn't never gonna see no action."

In the town of Fontana, the bully-boys who made up Tilden Franklin's army were having a fine ol' time exercising their muscle on the citizens.

The Silver Dollar Kid and the punk who called himself Sundance were strutting up and down the boardwalk, shooting at signs and anything else they took a mind to fire at.

Big Mamma lay on the floor of her pleasure palace, her

head split open from a rifle butt. A few of the TF riders were busying themselves with her stable of red-light girls. Free of charge.

At Beeker's store, the shopkeeper and his wife had barricaded themselves in a sturdy storeroom. They huddled together, listening to the rampaging TF gunslicks loot their store.

Billy lay in the loft of the stable, watching it all, his .22 rifle at the ready, in case any of the TF riders tried to hurt him.

Louis Longmont sat in his gaming room, rifling a deck of cards. His Colts were belted around his lean waist. A rifle and double-barreled shotgun lay on a table. Mike sat across the room, armed with two pistols and a rifle. Louis was not worried about any TF riders attempting to storm his place. They knew better.

Colton and Mona Spalding and Haywood and Dana Arden sat in the newspaper office, listening to the occasional bursts of gunfire from the town.

All had made up their mind they were leaving Fontana at the first chance. Perhaps to Big Rock, perhaps clear out of the state.

And at his general store, Ed Jackson and his wife were being terrorized.

13

"How in the hell did they manage to tree the town?" Smoke asked.

"I reckon the townspeople—them that's left—was in shock over the sheriff and his deputies bein' gunned down the way they was," Luke said. "And Tilden's bunch just overpowered them that stood to fight."

"How many men are we looking at?" Silver Jim asked.

"I'd say over a hundred," Charlie replied. "But Beaconfield sent word in about two hours ago that Tilden left a good-sized bunch at the ranch. I'd say he's got a good hundred and twenty-five to a hundred and fifty men under his command."

"You got any ideas, Smoke?

"Where is Monte?"

"At the Doc's clinic. He's hanging on, so I was told."

"Judge Proctor?"

"Out of town. Denver, I think," Luke said.

Smoke paced the street in front of the large general store of Big Rock. "It would be foolish for us to try to retake the town. If we leave here, Tilden would probably send his men from the ranch to take this place, burn it probably. And any ranch or farm up here he could find."

"You're right," Hunt Brook said.

"Damn!" Charlie said. "I hate to just sit here and do nothing, but I don't know what else we can do."

"I just wish I knew what was going on down at Fontana," Wilbur said.

Smoke grimaced. "I got a pretty good idea."

Smoke was silent for a moment. "I hope Billy is all right. I should have got that kid out of there before this."

The men fell silent, all looking in the direction of Fontana.

A group of TF riders had stripped Peg Jackson naked and were raping her, enjoying her screaming. Ed Jackson had been trussed up like a hog and tossed to the floor, forced to watch his wife being violated.

"You don't understand," Ed kept saying. "I like and respect Mister Franklin. We're friends."

One TF rider named Belton got tired of listening to Ed and kicked him in the mouth, then in the stomach. Ed lay on the floor, vomiting up blood and bits of teeth and the ham and eggs he'd had for breakfast.

Peg continued screaming as yet another TF gunhand took her.

In Louis's gaming tent, the gambler looked at his bouncer. "Mike, go get our horses and bring them around to the back. And if you find that boy, Billy, bring him along. I'm thinking that at full dark, when those rowdies get enough booze in them, they'll rush us. I'd like to get that boy out of this place."

"Yes, sir, Mister Longmont," Mike said, and was gone into the night.

Louis looked at the roulette wheels, the faro cue boxes, the card presses, the keno gooses . . . all the other paraphernalia of gambling.

"I shall not be needing any of it," Louis muttered. "When I again gamble, it will be in the company of ladies and gentlemen . . . with champagne and manners and breeding."

He rose from his chair, picked up his weapons, and walked into the back of the tent.

Mike returned in less than fifteen minutes, with saddled horses and Billy in tow.

"Any trouble?" Louis asked.

"One TF rowdy braced me," the huge bouncer replied. "I broke his neck."

The men and the boy mounted up. Andre said, "I will not miss this miserable place."

"Nor will I, Andre," Louis said. He pointed his horse's nose toward the high lonesome. "Quiet now," he cautioned. "Ride light until we're clear of the town."

"Boss?" Mike said. "Them thugs is rapin' the shopkeeper's woman. I could hear her screamin'."

Louis' face was tight as he said, "If she's lucky, that's all they'll do."

They cleared the town and then rode hard for the town of Big Rock.

"Grim," was Louis's one-word reply to Smoke's asking about Fontana.

"Can't we ride for the Army?" Hunt asked.

"Nearest Army post is four days away," Smoke explained. "And the next stage isn't due for twenty-four hours. If then." He looked at the old gunfighter called Buttermilk. "Think you boys could handle those gunhawks left at the TF ranch?"

Buttermilk smiled his reply.

"All right. Leave Dad Weaver and three others at the Sugarloaf. One in the barn with a rifle and lots of shells. Let me have Crooked John and Bull, and the rest of you take off to the TF. Pin 'em down and wear 'em down with rifle fire, then cut 'em down when they get enough and try to pull out."

Buttermilk nodded and turned to his compadres. "Let's ride, boys!"

Louis smiled. "Those old boys will lay up on the ridges around the TF spread and put so much lead in that house those gunhawks will be crying to get out."

"Those old men will allow their adversaries to surrender, won't they?" Hunt asked.

Louis cut his eyes to the lawyer. "You just have to be joking!"

Crooked John and Bull rode with Louis, Smoke, and Johnny North. Pearlie stayed behind with Luke and Charlie. The men rode slowly, sparing their horses, and making plans as they rode.

"I think we should let them get good and drunk," Louis remarked. "A full twenty-five percent of them will be passed out by night. That will make our work easier."

"Good idea," Johnny said. "And we need to get Monte outta there. Come night, I'll slip in from the blind side, through all them shacks that was left behind, and get to the Doc's place. We can hitch up the horses, put some hay in the back to keep Monte comfortable, and point the pilgrims on the way to Big Rock."

Smoke nodded his approval. "All right. While you're doing that, I'll ease in and see about Ed and his wife. Johnny, let's make it a mite easier for us. Bull, you and Crooked John create a diversion on this end of town. At full dark. You can leave your horses in that dry run behind the stable. Louis, how about you?"

Louis smiled. "I'll be doing some head-hunting on my own."

What they were going to do firmly implanted in their mind, the men urged their horses into a trot and began putting the miles behind them.

It was full dark when they pulled up, the lights of Fontana below them. They could hear an occasional gunshot and a faint, drunken whoop.

"I wonder where Tilden is," Smoke said expressing his

thought aloud. "If I could get lead in him, this would be over."

"Well protected, wherever he is," Louis said. "But what puzzles me this: why is he letting his men do this?"

"He's gone over the edge," Smoke said. "He's a crazy man, drunk with power. He's made no telling how many thousand of dollars on gold shares with the miners and doesn't care how much of it he spends. And he hates me," Smoke added.

None of the men needed to add that Tilden Franklin also wanted Sally Jensen.

"Let's go, boys," Smoke said. "And good luck."

The men separated, Smoke turning his horse's head toward the right, Johnny moving out to the left. Bull and Crooked John headed straight in toward the lights of Fontana, and Louis Longmont moved out alone into the night.

Each man stashed his horse in the safest place he could find and slipped into the town to perform his assigned job.

The diversion that Crooked John and Bull made was a simple one. They set several buildings blazing, lighting up one end of the town.

Smoke slipped to the rear of Jackson's general store and eased up onto the loading dock. His spurs were left hanging on his saddle horn and he made no noise as he pushed open the back door and entered the storeroom area of the building. Listening, he could hear the faint sobbing of Peg Jackson and the drunken grunting of men.

He wondered what had happened to Ed.

Smoke heard the excited shouting out in the street and wondered what kind of diversion the gunslingers had set. He glanced behind him, out the open back door of the store, and saw the reflection of the dancing, leaping flames reddening the night sky.

Grinning, he slipped closer to the cracked-open door that would lead into the store. He peeked through the crack and silently cursed under his breath.

He could see Ed, trussed up like a hog, on the floor of the store. The man's face appeared to be badly swollen. There was blood and puke on his shirt front.

Lifting his eyes, searching, he saw Peg. The woman had been badly used and appeared to be just conscious enough to sob. A TF gunhawk, his pants down around his boots, his back to Smoke, was having his way with the woman. Several TF riders were sprawled on the floor and on the counters. They seemed to be dead drunk and out of it.

Two TF gunslicks were leaning against a counter, drinking whiskey straight out of the bottle, an amused look on their faces as they watched the rape of Peg Jackson.

Those men seemed to be the only ones still conscious enough to give Smoke any cause for worry.

The sounds of gunfire came hard through the night air. It was followed by a choking scream. The two TF men looked at each other.

"Let's check that out," one said.

The other man nodded and they both walked out onto the boardwalk in front of the general store.

Smoke slipped into the large area of the store. Looking down, he saw that Ed was awake and staring at him through wide and very frightened eyes. Smoke nodded his head at the man and put a finger to his lips, urging Ed to keep silent. Ed nodded his head.

Picking up an axe handle, Smoke slipped up behind the rapist, busy at his ugly work. Smoke hit him on the side of the head with the axe handle. The man's skull popped under the impact and he fell to one side, dying as he was falling. Smoke glanced at him for a second. The man's head was split open, his brains exposed.

Smoke jerked Peg to her unsteady feet and handed her a blanket. She looked at the blanket through dull and uncomprehending eyes. Glancing toward the open front door, Smoke could not see the two TF gunnies who had stepped outside. Walking swiftly to the counter, he picked up one half-empty bottle of whisky and returned to Peg. He tilted her head back and poured the raw booze down her throat. She coughed and gagged and gasped as her eyes cleared a

243

bit.

She pulled the blanket over her nakedness and slowly nodded her head in understanding.

"Get to the back of the store," Smoke whispered. "And wait there for us."

She walked slowly, painfully, toward the rear of the store.

Smoke didn't bother cutting Ed's bonds. He just picked the man up and slung him over his shoulder. He walked swiftly out of the show and business area of the store, joining Peg on the loading dock. There, he dumped Ed on the dock and cut his bonds.

"Hitch up your team, Ed," he spoke softly. "And do it very quietly and very quickly. Take the old road that circles the town and head for Big Rock. A couple of miles out of town, pull up and wait for Spalding and Arden."

"My store!" the man protested.

Smoke almost hit the man. He controlled his temper at the last second and said, "Get your goddamned ass moving, Ed. Or I'll turn you back over to those TF riders. How do you want it?"

Shocked at the cold threat in Smoke's voice, Ed moved quickly to his barn, Peg walking slowly behind him, the blanket clutched tightly around her.

Smoke walked back into the store just as more gunfire erupted throughout the town. Smoke entered the store just as the two TF gunslicks walked back in through the front door.

They all saw each other and jerked iron at the same time. Smoke's Colts roared and bucked in his hands. The TF men were thrown to the floor as the .44 slugs from Smoke's guns hit big bones and vital organs. Smoke's draw was so fast, his aim so true, the men were unable to get off a single shot before death took them into its cold arms.

Smoke quickly reloaded and holstered his .44's. He walked to the gun rack and took down a sawed-off shotgun, breaking it down and loading it with buckshot, then stuffing his pockets full of shells. He took two new .44 pistols from the arms showcase, checked the action, and loaded them full, tucking them behind his gunbelt. Shotgun in hand, Smoke stepped out onto the boardwalk and prepared to lessen the odds just a tad.

The passed-out gunslicks in the store snored on, probably saving their lives . . . for the time being.

A TF gunslick made the mistake of riding up just at that moment. Lifting the Greener, Smoke literally blew the man out of the saddle, dumping him, now a bloody mass, onto the dusty ground.

He looked around him, his eyes picking up the black-dressed figure of Louis Longmont, standing on the board-walk across the street. Louis had a Colt in each hand, the hammers back.

"Where's Johnny?" Smoke called.

"Right up there," Louis said returning the call, pointing with a Colt.

Smoke looked through the smoky night air and spotted Johnny North, about a half a block away.

"I got the pilgrims on the way!" Johnny called. "Looks like Monte's gonna make it if he can stand the trip."

Reloading the Greener, Smoke called, "Let's do some damage and then get the hell out of here!"

One of the duded-up dandies who had been strutting about picked that time to brace Johnny North. "Draw, North!" he called, standing in the dusty street.

Johnny put two holes in the punk before the would-be gunhand could blink. The dandy died on his back in the dirt, his guns still in leather.

Two gunhawks came running up the street, on Louis's side. The gambler dropped them both, his guns roaring and belching gray smoke and fire.

Smoke heard a noise to his left and spun around, dropped to one knee and lifting the shotgun. As he dropped, lead whistled over his head. He pulled both triggers on the Greener, the buckshot spreading a TF rider all over a storefront and the boardwalk.

At the far end of town, Bull Flager was holding his own and then some, the old gunfighter Crooked John Simmons by his side, both gnarled hands full of Colts. Bull's shotgun roared and Crooked John's pistols belched death with each cocking and firing.

"Let's go!" Smoke shouted, and began falling back. He stepped into Ed's store just as one of the drunken TF riders reared up, a pistol in his hand.

Smoke shot him in the chest with the sawed-off and the gunnie died amid the corsets and the bloomers.

Running out the back, Smoke got his horse and swung into the saddle. He cut into an alley and came out just on the far edge of Fontana. With the reins in his teeth, both hands full of guns, Smoke galloped straight up the last few blocks of the boom town now going bust. Johnny North was right behind him and Louis Longmont just behind Johnny. Bull and Crooked John were waiting at the end of town, rifles in their hands, and their aim was deadly.

The five gunfighters took a fearful toll on Tilden Franklin's gunhands those last few blocks.

Most of the gunnies were busy with a bucket-line, trying to keep the raging fires contained at one end of town. Smoke, Johnny, and Louis rode right through the bucket-brigade, guns sparking the fiery night, adding death and confusion to the already chaotic scene.

Louis, Johnny, and Smoke sent the gunhands-turned-firemen running and diving and sprawling for their lives. Most made it; a few did not.

Louis knocked a leg from under a TF gunnie and the man fell backward, into the raging inferno. His screams were hideous in the fiery, smoky, gunshot-filled night.

Tilden Franklin stood in the best suite of the hotel and watched it all, his hate-filled eyes as hot as the flames that threatened to consume the town. He turned to the small woman who had been the sole property of Big Mamma and, in his rage, broke the woman's neck with his powerful hands.

He screamed his hate and rage and picked up the naked, ravaged woman and threw her body out the second floor window.

The young woman lay dead on the street.

Then, with slobber wetting his lips and chin, Tilden Franklin emptied his guns into the battered body.

"I'll kill you, Jensen!" the man howled. "I'm gonna burn your goddamned town to the ground and have your woman . . . right in front of your eyes!"

14

The old gunfighters who had ridden to the TF ranch house lay on the ridges that surrounded the huge home and made life miserable for those TF gunhawks who had survived the initial attack.

The moon was full and golden in the starry night skies, the illumination highlighting the bodies of those gunnies who now lay sprawled in death on the grounds surrounding the bunkhouse and the main ranch house.

Those trapped in the bunkhouse and in the main house were not at all happy about their situation. Several had thought the night would cover them as they tried to escape. Those with that thought now lay dead.

"What are we gonna do?" a TF gunslick, who felt more sick than slick, asked.

"Hold out 'til the boss gets back," was the reply. "There ain't that many of 'em up there on the ridges."

"Yeah, but I got me a peek at who they is," another paid gunhand said. "That's them old gunfighters. And I think I seen The Apache Kid 'mong 'em."

Nobody said anything for a long time. Nobody had to. They were all thinking the same thing. Toot Tooner and Red Shingletown had already been spotted, briefly. Now the Apache Kid. They all knew what that meant: these hard ol' boys didn't take prisoners. Never had. They expected no quarter, and they gave none.

"I ain't goin' out there, boys," a gunman said. "No way."

"I wish to hell someone had told me this Jensen feller was

raised up by Preacher. I'd have kept my butt up in Montana."

"He ain't so good," another said.

Nobody paid any attention to him. The man was speaking without any knowledge of the subject. He was too young to have any real awareness of the legendary Mountain Man known as Preacher. If he had, he'd have kept his mouth shut.

"So we wait, is that it?" The question was thrown out of the darkened room.

"You got any better ideas?"

Silence, and more silence.

Even with only the sounds of their breathing to be heard, none of the TF gunhands could hear the moccasined feet of The Apache Kid as he slipped through the kitchen and into the large dining area. Sutter Cordova was right behind him. There had been a guard at the back door. He now lay on the porch, his throat cut, his blood staining the ground.

Both men had their hands full of pistols, the hammers jacked back.

"Something is wrong!" a TF gunslick suddenly said, his voice sharp in the darkened house.

"What?"

"I don't know. But there ain't a shot fired in more 'un fifteen, twenty minutes.

"Maybe they pulled out?"

"Sure they did, and a hog is gonna fly any day now."

Apache and Sutter stepped into the room and started letting the lead fly. They were grateful to Smoke Jensen for giving them this opportunity to go out as gunfighters should. They had all outlived their time, and they all knew it. They had no one to live for, and no one to grieve for them when they died.

They were a part of the West's rapidly vanishing past. So they would go out as they lived.

The room filled with gray smoke, the booming of Colts and Remingtons deafening.

The Apache Kid died with his back to a wall, his hands full of guns. But the old man had taken a dreadful toll while he had lived this night.

Sutter Cordova went into that long sleep with a faint smile on his lips. His guns empty, the gunfighter buried his knife into the chest of a TF gunhawk and rode him down to the floor.

When the booming of the gunfire had faded away into the night, the other aging gunfighters walked slowly down to the big house. They checked out the bunkhouse and found no life there.

Carefully, they went into the house and lighted a lamp. They found one TF rider alive, but not for long.

"You old . . . bastards played . . . hell!" he managed to gasp.

"You got a name, boy?" Dan Greentree asked, squatting down beside the young man.

"It . . . don't matter." He closed his eyes and died.

"Funny goddamn name," Red Shingletown said.

"We'll bury them in the morning," Smoke said. "I'll come back into town and bring the minister with me."

"What'd y'all do with the dead TF gunnies?" Luke asked.

"Left 'em where they lay," Red replied. "Let somebody else worry with them."

" 'Pache and Sutter both tole me they was a-goin' out this run," Luke Nations said. " 'Pache had a bad ticker and Sutter was havin' a hard time passin' his water. It's good they went out this way. I'm right happy for 'em."

"You're happy your friends died?" Hunt asked, his robe pulled tightly around him against the night chill.

"Shore. That's the way they wanted it."

The lawyer walked away, back to his cabin. He was thinking that he would never understand the Western way of doing things.

"Peg Jackson?" Louis asked.

"Physically, not hurt too badly," Belle Colby said. "But like my Velvet, she's not good in the head. She said they did terrible things to her."

Belle walked back into the store where they had set up a

250

hospital.

"Monte?" Bull asked.

"He's in rough shape, but the Doc says he thinks he's gonna pull through."

"How about Ed?" somebody finally asked, although few if any among them really gave a damn how Ed was.

"He's all right," Haywood said, joining the group. "He's bitching about losing his store. It's just his way, gentlemen. And he'll never change. He's already talking of pulling out."

"He don't belong here," Charlie Starr said, lighting a tightly rolled cigarette. "This country's still got some rough and woolly years ahead of it. And it's gonna take some tough-minded men and women to see it through."

"What's the plan, Smoke?" Louis asked. "I know you've got one. You've been thinking hard for about an hour now."

"I'm gonna get a few hours sleep and then get the preacher. After the services, I'm riding into Fontana and get this matter settled, one way or the other. Anybody who wants to come along is welcome to ride."

They left the graveyard at nine o'clock the next morning. They had said their goodbyes to The Apache Kid and Sutter Cordova, and then those that had family to worry about them said their goodbyes to womenfolk and kids and swung into the saddle.

They left behind them some heavily armed hands who worked for Beaconfield and Mike Garrett, but who were hands, not gunhands, and half a dozen teenagers who were excellent shots with a rifle. In addition, Hunt, Colton, and Haywood were armed with rifles and shotguns. All the Western women could shoot rifles and shotguns as well as, and sometimes better than, the men. Mike, the big bouncer, was there, and well as Wilbur Mason, Dad Weaver, and Billy. The general store had been turned into a fort in case of attack.

Twenty-eight men rode toward the town of Fontana. They had guns in leather, guns tucked behind gunbelts, guns stashed in their saddlebags, and rifles and shotguns in saddleboots.

Smoke had warned them all that even though the previous night's raid into Fontana had taken some TF riders out, they were probably facing four or five to one odds, and anyone who wanted out had damn well better speak up now.

His words had been met with a stony silence.

Smoke had nodded his head and pulled his hat brim down low, securing the chin strap. "Let's ride."

There had been no stopping Ralph Morrow. He had stuck out his chin, picked up his Henry rifle, and stuffed his pockets full of cartridges. "I'm going," he had said. "And that's final."

The men trotted their horses for a time, and then walked them, alternating back and forth, eating up the miles.

Then they looked down on the town of Fontana . . . and stared at the long line of wagons that were pulling out.

Smoke looked at Silver Jim. "Find out about that, will you, Jim?"

Silver Jim rode down to the lead wagon, talked for a moment, then rode back to where Smoke sat his horse with the others.

"Big Mamma's dead," Silver Jim said. "She stormed into a saloon last night, after she learned that Tilden Franklin had raped and killed her . . . wife. Tilden ordered her hanged. They hung her slow. That feller I talked to said it took a long time for her to die. One of Big Mamma's girls tried to run away last night. Tilden's gunslicks caught her and . . . well, done some per-verted things to her, then they dragged her and set her on far. Tilden personal kilt Beeker at the store. Then his boys had they way with his wife. She set up such a squall, they shot her."

"Dear Jesus Christ!" Ralph muttered.

"Them people down there," Silver Jim said, pointing to the line of wagons, "is near-bouts all that's left of any decent folks, and some of them would steal the pennies off a dead man's eyes. That's how bad it's got down in town."

"So Tilden and his men are waiting for us?" Smoke asked.
"Dug in tight."

"Proctor didn't come back, did he?"

"They didn't say and I didn't think to ask."

Smoke stepped down from the saddle and said, "Let's talk about this some."

Dismounted, the men sipped water from canteens and ate a few biscuits and some beef packed for them before they pulled out.

"If we go in there," Smoke said, "we're going to have to take the place building by building, and like Silver Jim said, they're dug in and waiting. The cost, for us, will be too high."

"What choice do we have?" Luke said.

"Well, let's talk about that," Mike Garrett said. "We could wait them out while someone rides for the Army."

"No!" Ralph said, considerable heat in his voice.

"You want to explain that, Ralph?" Johnny said.

"Maybe I wasn't cut out to be a minister," the man said. "There is violence and hate in my heart. Anyway, it is my belief that people like Tilden Franklin should not be allowed to live. Back East—and I know, that's where I'm from— lawyers are already using the insanity pleas to get killers off scot free. And it's going to get worse. Let's not start a precedent out here."

"A what?" Johnny asked.

"Let's not let Tilden Franklin go free," Ralph said.

All present loudly and profanely agreed with that.

"There is another way," Smoke said.

"And that is?" Louis asked, knowing full well what was coming.

"I challenge Tilden Franklin. Best man with a gun wins."

"No," Louis said. "No. Tilden Franklin is a man totally without honor. Basically, he is a coward, a backshooter. He'd set you up, Smoke. No to your plan."

And all agreed with Louis on that.

"Well," Moody said. "We could burn the bastards out."

"How many days since we've had rain?" Smoke asked. "Too long. That's why Tilden ordered his men to put out the fire last night instead of concentrating on us. We can't risk a grass fire. Feel this hot wind? It would spread faster than anyone could contain it."

Charlie Starr grinned. "Besides, ol' tight-fisted Ed Jackson would probably sue us all for destroying his goods."

All the men enjoyed a tension-relieving laugh at that.

"Well, boys," Pistol Le Roux said, "that don't leave us with too gawddamned many options, do it?"

The men turned to tightening saddle cinches. They knew the discussion was over.

Hardrock swung into the saddle and looked at his friends. "You know what my momma wanted me to be?" he asked.

They stared at him.

"An apothecary, that's what."

Toot Tooner climbed into the saddle. "Shit, I wouldn't let you fix up nuttin' for me. You'd probably mix up something so's I couldn't get a boner up."

Sunset laughed. "Hell, you ain't had one in so long it'd probably scare you to death!"

The men swung their horses toward Fontana, lying hot under the sun and wind.

15

Hardrock, Moody, and Sunset were sent around to the far end of town, stationed there with rifles to pick off any TF gunhand who might try to slip out, either to run off or try and angle around behind Smoke and his party for a box-in.

The others split up into groups of twos and threes and rode hunched over, low in the saddle, to present a smaller target for the riflemen they had spotted lying in wait on the rooftops in Fontana. And they rode in a zig-zagging fashion, making themselves or their horses even harder to hit. But even with that precaution, two men were hit before they reached the town limits. Beaconfield was knocked from the saddle by rifle fire. The one-time Tilden Franklin supporter wrapped a bandana around a bloody arm, climbed back in the saddle, and, cursing, continued onward. Hurt, but a hell of a long way from being out.

The old gunfighter Linch was hit just as he reached the town. A rifle bullet hit him in the stomach and slapped him out of the saddle. The aging gunhand, pistols in his hands, crawled to the edge of a building and began laying down a withering line of fire, directed at the rooftops. He managed to knock out three snipers before a second bullet ended his life.

Leo Wood, seeing his long-time buddy die, screamed his outrage and stepped into what had once been a dress shop, pulled out both Remington Frontier .44's, and let 'em bang.

Leo cleared the dress shop of all TF riders before a single shot from a Peacemaker .45 ended his long and violent life.

Pearlie settled down by the corner of a building and with his Winchester .44-40 began picking his shots. At ranges up to two hundred yards, the .44-40 could punch right through the walls of the deserted buildings of Fontana. Pearlie killed half a dozen TF gunhawks without even seeing his targets.

A few of Tilden's hired guns, less hardy than they thought, tried to slip out the rear of the town. They went down under the rifle fire of Moody, Hardrock, and Sunset.

Bill Foley, throwing caution to the wind, like most of his friends having absolutely no desire to spend his twilight years in any old folks' home, stepped into an alley where he knew half a dozen TF gunnies were waiting and opened fire. Laughing, the old gunfighter took his time and picked his shots while his body was soaking up lead from the badly shaken TF men. Foley's old body had soaked up a lot of lead in its time, and he knew he could take three or four shots and still stay upright in his boots. Bill Foley, who had helped tame more towns than most people had ever been in, died with his boots on, his back to a wall, and his guns spitting out death. He killed all six of the TF gunslicks.

Toot Tooner, his hands full of Colts, calmly walked into what was left of the Blue Dog Saloon, through the back door, and said, "I declare this here game of poker open. Call or fold, boys."

Then he opened fire.

His first shots ended the brief but bloody careers of two cattle rustlers from New Mexico who had signed on with the TF spread in search of what Tilden had promised would be easy money. They died without having the opportunity to fire a shot.

Toot took a .45 slug in the side and it spun him around. Lifting his pistol, he shot the man who had shot him between the eyes just as he felt a hammer-blow in his back, left side. The gunshot knocked him to his knees and he tasted blood in his mouth.

Toot dropped his empty Colts and pulled out two Remington .44's from behind his gunbelt. Hard hit, dying; Toot laughed at death and began cocking and firing as the light before his eyes began to fade.

"Somebody kill the old son of a bitch!" a TF gunhand shouted.

Toot laughed at the dim figure and swung his guns. A slug took him in the gut and set him back on his butt. But Toot's last shots cleared the Blue Dog of hired guns. He died with a very faint smile on his face.

Louis Longmont met several TF gunhands in an alley. The gambler never stopped walking as his Colts spat and sang a death song. Reloading, he stepped over the sprawled bloody bodies and walked on up the alley. A bullet tugged at the sleeve of his coat and the gambler dropped to one knee, raised both guns, and shot the rifleman off the roof of the bank building. A bullet knocked Louis to one side and his left arm grew numb. Hooking the thumb of his left hand behind his gunbelt, the gambler rose and triggered off a round, sending another one of Tilden Franklin's gunslicks to hell.

Louis then removed a white linen handkerchief from an inside breast pocket of his tailored jacket. He plugged the hole in his shoulder and continued on his hunt.

The Reverend Ralph Morrow stepped into what had been the saloon of Big Mama and the bidding place of her soiled doves and began working the lever on his Henry .44. The boxer-turned-preacher-turned-farmer-turned-gunfighter muttered a short prayer for God to forgive him and began blasting the hell out of any TF gunhand he could find.

His Henry empty, Ralph jerked out a pair of .45's and began smoking. A lousy pistol shot, and that is being kind, Ralph succeeded in filling the beery air with a lot of hot lead. He didn't hit a damn thing with the pistols, but he did manage to scare the hell out of those gunhands left standing after his good shooting with the rifle. They ran out the front of the saloon and directly into the guns of Pistol Le Roux and Dan Greentree.

Ralph reloaded his rifle and stepped to the front of the building. "Exhilarating!" he exclaimed. Then he hit the floor as a hard burst of gunfire from a rooftop across the street tore through the canvas and wood of the deserted whorehouse.

"Shithead!" Ralph muttered, lifting his rifle and sighting the gunman in. Ralph pulled the trigger and knocked the TF gunman off the roof.

Steve Matlock, Ray Johnson, Nolan, Mike Garrett, and Beaconfield were keeping a dozen or more TF gunslicks pinned down in Beeker's general store.

Charlie Starr had cleared a small saloon of half a dozen hired guns and now sat at a table, having a bottle of sweetened soda water. He would have much preferred a glass of beer, but the sweet water beat nothing. Seeing a flash of movement across the street, Charlie put down the bottle and picked up a cocked .45 from the table. He sighted the TF gunhand in and pulled the trigger. The slug struck the man in the shoulder and spun him around. Charlie shot him again in the belly and that ended it.

"Now leave me alone and let me finish my sodie water," Charlie muttered.

The Silver Dollar Kid came face to face with Silver Jim. The old gunfighter grinned at the punk. Both men had their guns in leather.

"All right, kid," Silver Jim said. "You been lookin' for a rep. Here's your chance."

The Silver Dollar Kid grabbed for his guns.

He never cleared leather. Silver Jim's guns roared and bucked in his callused hands. The Kid felt twin hammer blows in his stomach. He sat down in the alley and began hollering for his mother.

Silver Jim stepped around the punk and continued his prowling. The Kid's hollering faded as life ebbed from him.

Smoke met Luis Chamba behind the stable. The Mexican gunfighter grinned at him. "Now, Smoke, we see just how good you really are."

Smoke lifted his sawed-off shotgun and almost blew the gunfighter in two. "I already know how good I am," Smoke said. "I don't give a damn how good you . . . were."

Smoke reloaded the 10-gauge sawed-off and stepped into the stable. He heard a rustling above him and lifted the twin muzzles. Pulling the triggers, blowing a hole the size of a bucket in the boards, Smoke watched as a man, or what was left of a man, hurled out the loft door to come splatting onto the shit-littered ground.

Smoke let the shotgun fall to the straw as the gunfighter Valentine faced him.

"I'm better," Valentine said, his hands over the butts of his guns.

"I doubt it," Smoke said, then shot the famed gunfighter twice in the belly and chest.

With blood streaking his mouth, Valentine looked up from the floor at Smoke. "I . . . didn't even clear leather."

"You sure didn't," the young man said. "We all got to meet him, Valentine, and you just did."

"I reckon." Then he died.

Listening, Smoke cocked his head. Something was very wrong. Then it came to him. No gunfire.

Cautiously, Smoke stepped to the stable door and looked out. Gunsmoke lay over the town like a shroud. The dusty streets were littered with bodies, not all of them TF gun-hands.

Smoke was conscious of his friends looking at him, standing silently.

Louis pointed with the muzzle of his pistol.

Smoke looked far up the street. He could make out the shape of Tilden Franklin. Smoke stepped out into the street and faced the man.

Tilden began walking toward him. As the man came closer, Smoke said, "It's over, Tilden."

"Not yet," the big man said. "I gotta kill you, then it's over."

"Make your play," Smoke said.

Tilden grabbed for his guns. Both men fired at almost the same time. Smoke felt a shock in his left side. He kept earing back the hammers and pulling the triggers. Dust flew from Tilden's chest as the slugs slammed into his body. The big man took another step, staggered, and then slumped to his knees in the center of the street.

Blood leaking from his wounded side, Smoke walked up to the man who would be king.

"You had everything a man could ask for, Tilden. Why weren't you satisfied?

Tilden tried to reply. But blood filled his mouth. He looked at Smoke, and still the hate was in his eyes. He fell forward on his face, in the dust, his guns slipping from his dead fingers.

It was over.

Almost.

16

They all heard the single shot and whirled around. Luke Nations lay crumpled on the boardwalk, a large hole in the center of his back.

Lester Morgan, a.k.a. Sundance, stepped out of a building, a pistol in his hand. He looked up and grinned.

"I did it!" he hollered. "Me. Sundance. I kilt Luke Nations!"

"You goddamned backshootin' punk!" Charlie Starr said, lifting his pistol.

"No!" Smoke's voice stopped him. "Don't, Charlie." Smoke walked over to Lester, one hand holding his bleeding side. He backhanded the dandy, knocking him sprawling. Lester-Sundance landed on his butt in the street. His mouth was busted, blood leaking from one corner. He looked up at Smoke, raw fear in his wide eyes.

"You gonna kill me, ain't you?" he hissed.

The smile on Smoke's lips was not pleasant. "What's your name, punk?"

"Les . . . Sundance. That's me, Sundance!"

"Well, *Sundance.*" Smoke put enough dirt on the name to make it very ugly. "You wanna live, do you?"

"Yeah!"

"And you wanna be known as a top gunhand, right, Sundance?"

"Yeah!"

Smoke kicked Lester in the mouth. The punk rolled on the ground, moaning.

261

"What's your last name, craphead?"

"M . . . Morgan!"

"All right Les Sundance Morgan. I'll let you live. And Les, I'm going to have your name spread all over the West. Les Sundance Morgan. The man with one ear. He's the man who killed the famed gunfighter Luke Nations."

"I got both ears!"

Before his words could fade from sound, Smoke had drawn and fired, the bullet clipping off Lester's left ear. The action forever branded the dandy.

Lester rolled on the dirt, screaming and hollering.

"Top gun, huh, punk?" Smoke said. "Right, that's you, Sundance." He looked toward Johnny North. "Get some whiskey and fix his ear, will you, Johnny?"

Lester really started hollering when the raw booze hit where his ear had been. He passed out from the pain. Ralph took that time to bandage the ugly wound.

Then Smoke kicked him awake. Lester lay on the blood-and whiskey-soaked ground, looking up at Smoke.

"What for you do this to me?" he croaked.

"So everybody, no matter where you go, can know who you are, punk. The man who killed Luke Nations. Now, you listen to me, you son of a bitch! You want to know how it feels to be top gun? Well, just look around you, ask anybody."

Lester's eyes found Charlie Starr. "You're Charlie Starr. You're more famouser than Luke Nations. But I'm gonna be famous too, ain't I?"

Charlie rolled a cigarette and stuck it between Lester's lips. He held the match while Lester puffed. Charlie straightened up and smiled sadly at Lester.

"How is it, punk? Oh, well, it's a real grand time, punk. You can't sit with your back to no empty space, always to a wall. Lots of backshooters out there. You don't never make your fire, cook, and then sleep in the same spot. You always move before you bed down, 'cause somebody is always lookin' to gun you down . . . for a reputation.

"You ain't never gonna marry, punk. 'Cause if you do, it won't last. You got to stay on the move, all the time. 'Cause you're the man who kilt Luke Nations, punk. And there's gonna be a thousand punks just like you lookin' for you.

"You drift, boy. You drift all the time, and you might near always ride alone, lessen you can find a pard that you know you can trust not to shoot you when you're in your blankets.

"And a lot of towns won't want you, punk. The marshal and the townspeople will meet you with rifles and shotguns and point you the way out. 'Cause they don't want no gunfighter in their town.

"And after a time, if you live, you'll do damn near anything so's people won't know who you are. But they always seem to find out. Then you'll change your name agin. And agin. Just lookin' for a little peace and quiet.

"But you ain't never gonna find it.

"You might git good enough to live for a long time, punk. I hope you do. I hope you ride ten thousand lonely miles, you backshootin' bastard. Ten thousand miles of lookin' over your back. Ten thousand towns that you'll ride in and out of in the dead of night. Eatin' your meals just at closin' time . . . if you can find a eatin' place that'll serve you.

"A million hours that you'll wish you could somehow change your life . . . but you cain't, punk. You cain't change, 'cause *they* won't let you.

"Only job you'll be able to find is one with the gun, punk. 'Cause you're the man who kilt Luke Nations. You got your rep, punk. You wanted it so damned bad, you got 'er." He glanced at Johnny North.

Johnny said, "I had me a good woman one time. We married and I hung up my guns, sonny-boy. Some god-damned bounty-hunters shot into my cabin one night. Killed my wife. I'd never broke no law until then. But I tracked them so-called lawmen down and hung 'em, one by one. I was on the hoot-owl trail for years after that. I had both the law and the reputation-hunters after me. Sounds like a real fine life, don't it, punk? I hope you enjoy it."

Smoke kicked Lester Sundance Morgan to his boots. "Get your horse and ride, punk! 'Fore one of us here takes a notion to brace the man who killed Luke Nations."

Crying, Lester stumbled from the street and found his horse, back of the building that once housed a gun shop.

"It ain't like that!" the gunfighters, the gambler, the ranchers, and the minister heard Lester holler as he rode off. "It ain't none at all like what you say it was. I'll have wimmin a-throwin' themselves at me. I'll have money and I'll have . . ."

His horse's hooves drummed out the rest of what Lester Sundance Morgan thought his reputation would bring him.

"Poor, sad, silly son of a bitch," Ralph Morrow said.

Charlie Starr looked at the minister. "I couldn't have said 'er no better myself, preacher."

The bodies of the gunfighters and Tilden Franklin were dragged to a lone building just at the edge of what was left of the boom town named Fontana. The building was doused with kerosene and torched just as a very gentle rain began falling.

"Lots of folks comin', Smoke," Charlie said, pointing toward the road leading to the high lonesome.

It was Sally and Belle and Bountiful and nearly all of those the men had left behind.

Sally embraced and kissed her man, getting blood all over her blouse as she did so. "How'd you folks know it was done with?" Smoke asked her.

"Hook Nose's people set up relay points with runners," she said. "They were watching from the hills over there." She pointed.

"What a story this will make," Haywood Arden said, his eyes wide as he looked at the bullet-pocked buildings and empty shell-casings on the ground.

"Yeah," Smoke said wearily. "You be sure and write it, Haywood. And be sure you spell one name right."

"Who is that?" the newspaperman asked.

"Lester Morgan, known as Sundance."

"What'd he do?" Haywood was writing on a tablet as fast as he could write.

Smoke described Lester, ending with, "And he ain't got

but one ear. That'll make him easy to spot."

"But what did this Lester Sundance Morgan *do*?"

"Why . . . he's the gunfighter who killed Luke Nations."

17

Ed Jackson and his wife went back East . . . anywhere east of the Mississippi River. They did not say goodbye to anybody, just loaded their wagon and pulled out early one morning.

Louis Longmont, Mike, and Andre left the town of Big Rock. Louis thought he'd retire for a time. But Smoke knew he would not . . . not for long. The raw and woolly West had not seen the last of Louis Longmont.

Word drifted back that Lester Sundance Morgan had been braced by a couple of young duded-up dandies looking for a reputation down in New Mexico Territory. Sundance had managed to drop them both and was now riding low, keeping out of sight. The report that Smoke received said that Lester was not a very happy young man.

Monte Carson recovered from his wounds and became the sheriff of Big Rock, Colorado. He married himself a grass widow and settled down.

The aging gunfighters pulled out of the area, riding out in small groups of twos and threes . . . or alone. Alone. As they had lived.

Charlie Starr shook hands with Smoke and swung into the saddle. With a smile and a small salute, he rode out of Big Rock and into the annals of Western history. Smoke would see the famed gunslinger again . . . but that's another story.

The *Fontana Sunburst* became the *Big Rock Guardian*. And it would remain so until the town changed its name just before the turn of the century.

Colton Spalding remained the town's doctor until his death in the 1920's.

Sally and Mona and Bountiful and Dana and Willow would live to "see the vote." But, there again, that's another story.

Judge Proctor returned and was named district judge. He lived in the area until his death in 1896.

The gold vein ran dry and all the miners left as peace finally settled over the High Lonesome.

The gold still lies in the ground on Smoke and Sally's Sugarloaf. They never touched it.

The last store in Fontana closed its doors in 1880. The lonely winds hummed and sang their quiet Western songs throughout the empty buildings and ragged bits of tent canvas for many years; the songs sang of love and hate and violence and bloody gunfights until the last building collapsed in the 1940's. Now, nothing is left.

Danner and Signal Hill died out near the turn of the century, but the town that was once called Big Rock remains, and the descendants of Smoke and Sally Jensen, Johnny and Belle North, Pearlie, and all the others still live there . . . finally in peace.

But peace was a long time coming to that part of Colorado, for not all the gunslicks were killed that bloody day in Fontana. Those few that managed to escape swore they'd come back and have their revenge.

They would try.

It would be many more years before Smoke Jensen could hang up his guns for good. Many years before Smoke and Sally Jensen's sons and daughters could live in peace. For Smoke Jensen was the West's most famous gunfighter. And for years to come, there would be those who sought a reputation.

But before that, on a bright, sunny, warm, late-summer morning, Velvet Colby called out for her mother and for Johnny.

The newly wed man and woman ran to Velvet's bedroom. Johnny North, one of the West's most feared gunfighters, knelt and took the girl's hands in his hard and calloused hands.

"Yes, baby?" he said, his voice gentle.

Velvet smiled. Her voice, husky from lack of use, was a lovely thing to hear. She had not spoken in months. "Can I go outside?" she asked. "It looks like such a beautiful day."

And a gentle, peaceful breeze stirred the branches and the flowers and the tall lush grass of the High Lonesome . . .

. . . along the trail of the last Mountain Man.

POWELL'S ARMY
BY TERENCE DUNCAN

#1: UNCHAINED LIGHTNING   (1994, $2.50)

Thundering out of the past, a trio of deadly enforcers dispenses its own brand of frontier justice throughout the untamed American West! Two men and one woman, they are the U.S. Army's most lethal secret weapon—they are POWELL'S ARMY!

#2: APACHE RAIDERS   (2073, $2.50)

The disappearance of seventeen Apache maidens brings tribal unrest to the violent breaking point. To prevent an explosion of bloodshed, Powell's Army races through a nightmare world south of the border—and into the deadly clutches of a vicious band of Mexican flesh merchants!

#3: MUSTANG WARRIORS   (2171, $2.50)

Someone is selling cavalry guns and horses to the Comanche—and that spells trouble for the bluecoats' campaign against Chief Quanah Parker's bloodthirsty Kwahadi warriors. But Powell's Army are no strangers to trouble. When the showdown comes, they'll be ready—and someone is going to die!

#4: ROBBERS ROOST   (2285, $2.50)

After hijacking an army payroll wagon and killing the troopers riding guard, Three-Fingered Jack and his gang high-tail it into Virginia City to spend their ill-gotten gains. But Powell's Army plans to apprehend the murderous hardcases before the local vigilantes do—to make sure that Jack and his slimy band stretch hemp the legal way!

THRILLERS BY WILLIAM W. JOHNSTONE

THE DEVIL'S CAT (2091, $3.95)

The town was alive with all kinds of cats. Black, white, fat, scrawny. They lived in the streets, in backyards, in the swamps of Becancour. Sam, Nydia, and Little Sam had never seen so many cats. The cats' eyes were glowing slits as they watched the newcomers. The town was ripe with evil. It seemed to waft in from the swamps with the hot, fetid breeze and breed in the minds of Becancour's citizens. Soon Sam, Nydia, and Little Sam would battle the forces of darkness. Standing alone against the ultimate predator—The Devil's Cat.

THE DEVIL'S HEART (2110, $3.95)

Now it was summer again in Whitfield. The town was peaceful, quiet, and unprepared for the atrocities to come. Eternal life, everlasting youth, an orgy that would span time—that was what the Lord of Darkness was promising the coven members in return for their pledge of love. The few who had fought against his hideous powers before, believed it could never happen again. Then the hot wind began to blow—as black as evil as The Devil's Heart.

THE DEVIL'S TOUCH (2111, $3.95)

Once the carnage begins, there's no time for anything but terror. Hollow-eyed, hungry corpses rise from unearthly tombs to gorge themselves on living flesh and spawn a new generation of restless Undead. The demons of Hell cavort with Satan's unholy disciples in blood-soaked rituals and fevered orgies. The Balons have faced the red, glowing eyes of the Master before, and they know what must be done. But there can be no salvation for those marked by The Devil's Touch.